I0760544

SECRETS AND PROMISES

the story of an
ITALIAN AMERICAN FAMILY

Anna Wilcoxson

FROM THE TINY ACORN . . .
GROWS THE MIGHTY OAK

Secrets and Promises

Printed in the United States of America.

For information, address Acorn Publishing, LLC, 3943 Irvine Blvd. Ste. 218, Irvine, CA 92602
www.acornpublishingllc.com

Cover design by ebooklaunch.com

Interior design and digital formatting by Debra Cranfield Kennedy

ISBN—978-1-952112-64-5 (hardcover)
ISBN—978-1-952112-99-7 (paperback)
Library of Congress Control Number: 2021910110

Author's Note

The characters in this novel are fictitious. Historical references and depictions are strictly the author's interpretation of these events.

To Virginia,
my guiding light and inspiration

Urbino
Our Family Tree
Brandi Orsolini
servant
?
Teresa Pasqualini
Ettore Brandi Orsolini
Virginia Lorenzetti
Francesco
Pietro
Delia
Emilio Ricci
Assunta
Urbano
Francesca
ginerva
Teresina
Annie mary
Primo
Emilia
Amedio
Toni
Spirito
Marianna
Emma
Anna
Listina
Virginia
Walter
Tino
Anna
Terry

Chapter 1

Back to the Beginning

"HOW DID you like Rome?" I asked Mom as I swung the rented Cinque Cento onto the autostrada, barely missing the sideview mirror of the oncoming car.

"Incredible. I forgot I was old," she answered.

I could relate. Even though Mom had a few years on me—she was ninety-six and I was fifty-four—the five days we had just spent in Rome made me feel young again. The vitality of the Eternal City had captivated us both with its history, its people, and its food.

"Dinner last night in the Piazza Monte was fantastic, wasn't it?"

Mom nodded her head vigorously. "The bottle of wine you chose went perfectly with my spaghetti carbonara."

"Montefalco Rosso, and as I recall, you drank most of it."

The night had been balmy, summer's last gift to the city before the autumn rains swept in. We'd sat at a table right on the edge of the piazza, feeling like participants, not spectators, in the vibrancy around us. A group of boys were kicking soccer balls against the ancient stone walls of the Ukrainian convent, and women wearing stilettos paired up with men in muscle shirts around the fountain. Within minutes, bottles of beer emerged from their tote bags and were passed around. Restaurant owners put on smiles along with their aprons, preparing for the long evening ahead. It is the Italian way to make you feel like part of the family, and Italians do it better than anybody else in the world.

From the minute we stepped off the plane at the airport in Fiumicino, Mom was the star of the show. Everyone wanted to know her story, and many congratulated her for daring to travel so far at her age. Several even looked in my direction and noted my courage in taking her. The truth was, even at ninety-six, Mom was more than capable. She walked without a cane, took no medication, and had the stamina of someone half her age. Her doctor, an old school Russian immigrant, hadn't raised any objections either.

Dr. Gavriluk had eyeballed the two of us over his crescent-shaped spectacles. "Virginia, at your age, this trip will be a change from your usual routine."

"I know," Mom replied. "Eat more fiber."

"Too much fiber can be just as bad." The doctor looked at me. "Anna, have you considered this?"

I laid a reassuring hand on his arm. "I'll bring Metamucil *and* Kaopectate. That way, we're covered."

Glancing over at her as we roared down the autostrada toward Umbria, Mom looked more alive than I had ever seen her. I guess I had made the right decision after all.

It had been a spur of the moment trip. Mom wanted to reconnect with the Italian family she had not seen in decades, and I wanted to see where my grandfather, Spirito Urbino, had grown up. Time was running out, and Mom's memory was fading. Sharing this last great adventure with her while we were both still kicking was at the top of my bucket list. We had brought with us a hand-drawn family tree that captured the names, dates, and lineage of more than a century of the Italian side of our family. Maybe if we got lucky, we might meet some of them.

Now, it was time to revisit the place where it all began. We were headed to the tiny village of Scheggino where my grandfather was born.

"Are you ready for this?" With one hand on the steering wheel, I reached out and grasped her gnarled fingers.

Mom let out a deep breath. "Too late to turn back now. Besides, I'm ready for a big plate of pasta and a big glass of red wine. How about you?"

We stopped at a roadside osteria. It looked like someone's home with its ocher walls, shutters thrown wide open, and chickens fluttering around outside. A faded wooden sign advertising pizza and beer was the only indication that it was a place you could get a meal. In Umbria, these country restaurants that serve what they raise are a primary source of income for much of the population. This means the little lambs and chickens following you in the yard during the day will be on the dinner menu in the evening.

"Didn't Spirito's sister, Assunta, have a place like this?"

We were seated inside, packed shoulder to shoulder with the other diners. Every table was filled.

"Dad's sister fed the shepherds in her living room." Mom replied. "They came down from Castelluccio with their flocks of sheep on their way to Monteluco. They slept in her barn but paid good money to eat her veal stew and drink her homemade wine."

Our *pranzo* was delicious—*strangozzi* pasta with black truffles—but I made sure I had only one glass of wine. We still had another hour of driving before we reached Scheggino.

"*Delizioso!*" Mom wiped her chin and started to pour herself another glass.

I put my hand over the rim. "One glass minimum until we get there. I need you to help me stay awake. Why don't you tell me the story of how my grandfather came to America."

Mom grumbled something about cutting into her naptime and why wasn't I writing this stuff down. But when I got her into the car and buckled in, she was off and running down memory lane.

"Your grandfather, Spirito, was a character. Restaurant owner, winemaker, businessman . . . and a few other things best left unmentioned." Mom gave me a knowing look. "He was born in Scheggino, one of five children. Two girls and three boys. They grew up working the land and playing along the banks of the Nera river. Like many young men in small Italian villages, the brothers dreamed of making their way to America. Urbano, the youngest, left at seventeen, and Spirito joined him four years later.

"Remember, at the turn of the century, America was the promised land for the underprivileged in Europe. Many believed that a chance for a better life, regardless of class, was possible. When they first arrived in Trenton, New Jersey, the brothers worked as common laborers, washing dishes and cleaning toilets. They wrote their oldest brother, Antonio, that if he didn't mind working the jobs nobody wanted, he should come. Less than a year later, Antonio arrived and found work as a blacksmith in Philadelphia.

"The work was hard but there was plenty of it, and the pay was better than anything back home. There was only one thing missing: female companionship. Women fell into three categories in Trenton in the early 1900s: prostitutes, working-class girls, and ladies from good families. Prostitutes served a useful purpose, but you certainly didn't want to marry one. Working-class women were poor, uneducated, and often had even poorer relatives back home who had to be supported. The nice girls were out of reach. Ladies of good breeding wanted to marry gentlemen with property, not Italian immigrants fresh off the boat. Their idea of the American dream was hiding behind a fancy house and thumbing their noses at everyone.

"Spirito realized he needed a woman who would not only clean his house and raise his children but also support his vision of opening a restaurant. Long hours, no pay, and lots of patience. Only in Italy would he find that kind of woman."

"So, he came back to Scheggino to look for a wife?" I asked.

"Yes. In 1912. Your grandfather was a handsome man—piercing blue eyes, a strong jaw, and a great smile. Of course, in Italy, any single man who had established himself in America was considered a catch . . . handsome or otherwise."

"But Nonna Marianna didn't come from Scheggino. How did Spirito meet her?"

"Visso, Marianna's village, was thirty kilometers away. News travels fast in rural villages, and Marianna's mother, Teresa Brandi Orsolini, was a widow with four unmarried daughters. Spirito's return presented an opportunity to marry one of them off."

"Marianna's father was killed when she was very young, right?"

"Murdered. Someone knifed him over money. Ettore Brandi Orsolini came from a wealthy family, and he was taken advantage of. In those days, Italy was a vengeful country, and people often turned up dead before the law could intervene. If he loaned money that couldn't be paid back, he was a fool."

Mom's words were harsh. It must have been a sore subject growing up. I knew the Brandi Orsolini family suffered greatly after the murder. Marianna was nine when it happened, and her youngest sister was only a year old.

"How did the family survive?"

"With no husband, Teresa was forced to go to work as a seamstress to support her family," Mom continued. "The law didn't provide welfare for widows. Teresa worked her fingers raw and nearly lost her sight sewing fancy lingerie for young ladies."

"You mentioned Teresa saw an opportunity . . . so she arranged for Spirito to meet her daughters? Wasn't that a little obvious?"

"I imagine, with four unmarried girls crowding up the house, being obvious was the last thing on her mind."

Teresa sat back and looked at her daughters. "Spirito Urbino has returned from America, and he is looking for a bride. He is coming here tomorrow night. This is not a random social occasion. I am confident one of you will win his heart."

Delia spoke up first. "Will he be going back to America?"

Teresa nodded. "Yes. The Urbino brothers have established themselves in Trenton, New Jersey."

"Trenton," Delia said dreamily. It sounded so exotic. Come to think of it, *anywhere* sounded more exotic than her dreary little village.

Teresa looked at Francesca, her oldest. "You are twenty-nine, well past marrying age. This may be your last chance."

"But I love Rodolpho. We are pledged to each other."

"Where is the ring? I haven't seen one yet," Teresa reminded her.

"Who cares about a ring?" Emma snorted. She was the youngest at sixteen and had her sights set on living in Rome and finding a rich old fool who would keep her in jewels. The wedding ring was optional.

"Ninina?" Teresa's eyes were gentle as she turned to her middle daughter.

Marianna was silent. She couldn't care less if she got married. Next year, she would be on staff at the elementary school. America was not in her plans.

Teresa frowned. "This family cannot afford to be choosy. I am tired of working my fingers raw while you dream about your future. If one of you is chosen, consider it a gift to your mother."

The following evening, Spirito arrived at the house with arms full of flowers and homemade pastries for his hostess. If he felt like a prized cow at market, he hid it with a slight bow and a winning smile. He only hoped they wouldn't examine his teeth . . . or his assets. Delia wore her most provocative gown, low necked and tight through the waist to accentuate her hourglass figure. Marianna chose a simple gray dress with tiny diamond earrings as her single adornment. The other two barely made an effort, hoping to be overlooked.

Pietro, the lone boy in the household, stepped forward and shook hands. He had but one thought: If a favorable outcome could lead to one less mouth to feed and one more bedroom to fight over, he was all for it.

Introductions were made, and everyone sat down to dinner. The food was delicious: bruschetta with truffle paste, homemade spinach, mozzarella lasagna, and veal in lemon sauce. For dessert, there was the best tiramisu Spirito had ever tasted.

"*Squisito!*" Spirito said as he looked at the trio of ladies. "Who made the tiramisu?"

Marianna looked down at her plate and blushed.

"Ninina made it," Teresa said proudly. She had forgotten that food could win a man's heart as easily as a pretty face.

Spirito had already noticed the one in the gray dress. Quiet, demure, but with eyes that kept track of everything. She made sure her guest had enough to eat and that his glass of wine was always full. She was the only one who helped her mother serve and remove the plates after each course. The others seemed content to let Teresa and Marianna tend to their needs without even offering to help. It was obvious to Spirito that Marianna was the worker in the family, and that impressed him more than all the cleavage, the saucy eyes, or the clever banter displayed that evening. If Marianna would have him, his choice for a bride was made.

Spirito sensed that Marianna was a reluctant participant in Teresa's quest to marry off her brood. He knew he would have to win her affections with more than fancy gifts or compliments. What she needed was a man who could provide her with stability, loyalty, and strength. Spirito suspected Marianna would value these qualities more than any other because she grew up without a father.

Marianna was grappling with a dilemma that would resolve itself only with great sacrifice. She had a dream of being an elementary school teacher. Working with the little ones gave her so much joy, and she had already secured a place in the community's school system. On the other hand, she was nearly twenty-three years old and still living at home.

She knew she could not disappoint her mother and refuse an offer of marriage.

Mom paused before she spoke again. "Marianna seemed destined to live her life for others instead of for herself. She blamed the murder of her father for altering the future she so desperately wanted."

"So, Spirito and duty won out in the end."

"Yes. They were married in La Chiesa di San Francesco in Visso. Three weeks later, my parents sailed for America."

Mom had dozed off as I turned the Cinque Cento off the main highway heading for SS-209 and our destination. The little town of Scheggino lay nestled in a valley surrounded by mountains, the Nera River running straight through its middle. As we drew near, a castle-like fortress rose up against the hillside, dominating the town. It looked as though nothing had changed in a thousand years.

As I drove across the stone bridge toward the piazza, I saw a sign that read, "*Villa Urbino*" and an arrow pointing up the hill away from town. We had come a long way to reconnect with our relatives, so, without a moment's hesitation, I changed direction and followed the path. At the top, to the left of the road, I stopped before an impressive ten-foot iron gate with "*A. Urbino*" engraved across the front. As I idled there, the gates slowly opened to reveal a long driveway and a glimpse of a villa in the distance.

"Wake up, Mom" I nudged her excitedly. "I think we're about to meet our relatives!"

Chapter 2

The Other Urbinos

AS WE passed through the gates and down the long driveway to the villa, a panorama of verdant countryside unfolded. The resort was ideally located, built into the cliffs overlooking the valley and the mountains beyond. There was a large swimming pool and an outdoor dining area with seating for a several hundred. Well-appointed guest rooms lined the edge of the cliff. It all looked like something out of a tourist brochure, except for one thing: the place was empty. Not a soul in sight. Disappointed, we were about to leave when a man came running toward us from the fields above the villa. He looked to be about forty-five, with sandy, disheveled hair and a face covered with dust. Sweat dripped from an open shirt, and his pants, half unzipped, were filthy. Wiping his hand on his sleeve, he stepped up to the car and extended his hand.

"*Sono Agostino*," he said in Italian. "I am Agostino." His clear gray eyes took us both in with a swift glance.

"Are you an Urbino?" I asked bravely, returning his handshake.

"*Sì*," he answered, "Agostino Urbino. I own this place."

I turned to Mom, who was eyeing him appreciatively, and whispered, "Does he look like one of us?"

"Too good looking," she said, without missing a beat. "And too tall. Our men were on the short side." She said this in Italian, obviously for his benefit. Agostino cracked up.

Ninety-six-year-old ladies can get away with anything, I thought.

"We are the Urbinos from San Diego, California." I reached into the car and handed over a folder of old photos and the family tree we had been studying.

Agostino looked through everything with mounting interest. When he saw the photo of Spirito's father, Francesco, he pointed to the top of the hill. "He's there, in our cemetery."

I looked at Mom. I knew she and Dad had traveled to Italy to visit relatives many years ago, but either she no longer remembered that her great-grandfather was buried there or she was being cagey.

"So, how do you know my family?" She eyed him suspiciously. "Are we related?"

Agostino took in the rented car and our expectant faces and probably realized he was looking at a couple of ladies on a crazy adventure to recapture their roots. As he handed back the folder, I had a distinct feeling he knew whose bright idea this was.

"Come with me," he said getting into our car. "I have someone for you to meet."

If Mom had any qualms about sitting next to a sweaty, filthy stranger, she kept them to herself. Halfway down the old Roman road leading to town, we stopped in front of an ocher fortress with an equally impressive set of wrought iron gates.

Agostino called out to someone inside the grounds, and the gates swung open. We drove past rows of manicured box hedges and rose bushes before we stopped in front of a series of steps leading to the front entrance. As we got out, I noticed a man sitting cross-legged on a small patio chair. He looked me in the eye and nodded, his hand resting on a holster protruding from his gun belt.

Things were getting interesting.

Agostino's grandmother, Gabriella Albani Urbino, was a sharp-eyed slip of a woman sporting a collection of bangles on her wrist and salon perfect hair. She treated Mom with the respect Italians always extend to the elderly no matter how many years separate them. In this case, it could only be only a year or two. Gabriella didn't look any younger than ninety-five.

The interior of Gabriella's home was as impressive as her gates. Eighteenth-century oil paintings lined the foyer and in the living room, comfortable sofas mixed with elegant armchairs were grouped around an ancient stone fireplace. A huge tapestry depicting a pastoral scene from the seicento hung on the opposite wall. Within minutes, pastries and a silver pot of steaming espresso were set on the coffee table in front of us.

Agostino plopped down on one of the satin chairs, dirt from his trousers rising in a cloud around him. "My grandmother is the grand-niece of Pietro Urbino," he told us. "He is the man who started the Urbino Truffle Foundation."

I was thinking quickly. I had heard of this family. Fabulously wealthy, they were known worldwide as pioneers of truffle cultivation in Italy. *And we have the same last name!*

"What brings you here?" The old lady was eyeing us now with interest.

"We are here to find our relatives," I began. "My grandfather and his family were born here. My great-grandfather, Francesco, is buried in the cemetery."

"Francesco," Gabriella repeated. "Yes, I knew Assunta, his daughter. What was your grandfather's name?"

"Spirito. Spirito Urbino."

Gabriella shifted uncomfortably in her chair. She glanced at Agostino. Their eyes met and held.

"Lovely to have met you." The words were pleasant, but the atmosphere in the room had changed. Gabriella motioned to someone behind us, and Mom was being gently lifted to her feet. The party was over.

We were escorted out the door and into our car faster than you could say the word *arrivederci* . . . which no one did. Not even a *ciao*. Clearly, Spirito's name had ruffled the old lady's feathers, but I had no idea why.

"I guess we aren't related to that bunch," I said to Mom as we drove down the hill toward town. "On the other hand, I'm not completely convinced. Same name, small town, all that Italian passion floating around . . . maybe there is more to the story."

Mom spoke under her breath. "Tread softly, Sherlock. You saw the heat our friend at the entrance was packing? I want to get home in one piece, preferably still breathing."

There are two piazzas in Scheggino—the original one located next to the castle and a newer one across the river, created by the Urbino Foundation to commemorate their ancestor, Pietro Urbino. The old piazza is simple and unadorned, consisting of a few stone benches and an old Roman fountain. The new one is a gigantic modern saucer that spits choreographed water formations in synchrony with piped-in music during the warm summer months. These days, the music is almost always American. The new fountain is impressive but exists in sharp contrast to the ancient feel of the town. I suspected it was built not only to honor the memory of the Urbino patriarch but also to function as an effective marketing tool for the truffle foundation. Ingenious.

Mom and I opted to hang out at the old piazza and eat a picnic lunch of items I had bought at the grocery store nearby: a marinated salad of olives and pepperoncino and panini with prosciutto and mozzarella. For dessert, we shared a melt-in-your-mouth prune crostata.

As we ate, several people came over to meet Mom and make her acquaintance. Old ladies with their black dresses and sturdy shoes, young couples sporting tattoos and piercings, even the rotund village priest stopped by to visit. I was surprised. Normally, inhabitants from small, rural villages are wary of strangers, especially American ones. I wondered if word had spread about our earlier encounter with Agostino and his clan.

As we were finishing up and getting ready to leave, a well-dressed older gentleman came up and introduced himself.

"Beniamino Urbino. *Piacere.*" He kissed Mom's hand and looked at me. "Zia Gabriella told me about you and your mother. I understand you have family here. If you have time, please stop by the corporate offices along SS45. You probably passed it on the way here."

I remembered seeing the huge modern compound for the Urbino Truffle Foundation outside of town as we drove in. "*Sì, grazie*, we would be honored."

I glanced at Mom and she nodded.

"Shall we see you in an hour or so?" he asked. I could tell this was not just a casual invitation. This was an *appointment*.

"We will be there," I assured him.

We did not have enough time before meeting Beniamino to go back to our rooms in Spoleto, so I let Mom nap in the car while I ventured out for a few minutes to explore the town.

Scheggino's castle was founded around A.D. 1000, probably as a fortress in defense of Saracen invaders. In the 1600s, Cardinal Graziani renovated the crumbling structure for his private use, with accommodations built within the walls for the rest of his entourage. Over time, the medieval rooms were bundled together and sold off to private citizens.

Today, the castle is a labyrinth of cobbled walkways leading up or down to various apartments. Pride of ownership is evident: porch steps swept clean, address numbers on hand-painted tiles, and pots of well-tended geraniums lining the stairwells. Nestled inside the labyrinth, the Church of San Nicola maintains its claim as the original owner's private chapel. The ancient frescoes remind current churchgoers of a time when devotion to God—and rich cardinals—guaranteed salvation.

The Nera River flows through the village in a serpentine curve, separating the ancient from the modern. Plain stucco houses have sprung up in recent years to accommodate the growing population of four hundred, but the town has carefully preserved its charm, another marketing tool by the savvy Urbinos, no doubt.

I looked at my watch. Time to wake Mom and head for the corporate headquarters. First, I needed to do a little homework on the history of the truffle in Umbria. Being informed never hurt, I figured, especially when dealing with experts. I googled the word "truffles" on my phone, and the name Urbino came up immediately. Beniamino didn't just work for the Urbino Truffle Foundation, he was CEO of all their operations in Italy.

Anyone familiar with the truffle knows that it is, essentially, a lumpy, brown ball of fungus that tastes like dirt and sells for two hundred dollars an ounce. The rich have claimed it, like caviar, as a necessity and will stop at nothing to get it. Truffles grow abundantly in Umbria, but locating, extracting, and transporting it to restaurants all over the world is the hard part.

Beniamino and his brother, Pietro, are the fourth-generation custodians of the Urbino Truffle Foundation that began with a small mom and pop operation in the mid-1800s. Beniamino's father, Claudio, had taken the business and turned it into a global entity, increasing production and distribution worldwide. By the 1940s, Claudio and his family had become rich beyond even *their* imagination. Today, his sons were continuing that legacy with increasing success. Their commitment to those little brown balls that taste like dirt would keep the Urbinos rich for generations.

Arriving at the entrance to the headquarters and identifying ourselves through the intercom, we watched the giant metal doors slowly open.

"The Urbinos sure have a thing about security," I said to Mom as we drove in, "I guess it comes with the territory of the rich and famous."

Stepping inside the stylish reception area, we saw glimpses of boardrooms on either side of the long, glass-paneled hallway. In another room, I could see a huge kitchen where demonstrations were probably held to educate the masses on how to cook with the expensive delicacy.

We were offered comfortable armchairs and asked to wait. I was praying Mom would stay awake long enough to get through the interview. "No dozing off until we get out of here," I whispered, squeezing her hand. "I have a feeling we are going to need our wits about us, and two wits are better than one." So far, even with the long day, her energy was holding up. I could tell she was having the time of her life.

"Right this way." The young receptionist pointed to a door on which the name "Beniamino Urbino" was engraved in gold.

As we walked in, Beniamino was standing behind his desk with a young man beside him. They both came forward. Beniamino introduced his son, Giovanni, and gestured for us to be seated. "Agostino told me that you brought records of your family. May I see them?"

I handed over the creased photos, crumpled notes, and my brother's famous handwritten family tree as we sat down. Beniamino looked at everything, conversing sotto voce with Giovanni. I could catch only one or two words in their rapid-fire Italian.

Beniamino looked up. "Your family tree appears to be incomplete."

"Incomplete?"

"There are some names that are not on here," Beniamino began. He paused when he saw my face. "You don't know, then . . ."

"Don't know what?" I said, confused.

Beniamino looked like he had just stepped in something he wished he hadn't. "Uh . . . what happened in 1906."

"All I know is that Spirito married my grandmother in Visso in

1912, and three weeks later they left for America. What are *you* talking about?"

Beniamino paused, picked up the phone, and made a quick call. He spoke to someone in an undecipherable dialect for a few minutes before hanging up and turning his attention back to us.

"There was some trouble concerning your grandfather before he left . . . the first time. So long ago, I doubt there are even people alive here who remember. Water under the bridge, as they say in your country."

Beniamino was backtracking now; there was more to this story than he cared to reveal. He regarded us coolly. "So, what are you hoping to find here?"

Mom, who had sat quietly until this point, stood up. "We are here to experience the hospitality and good will my father always said existed in Scheggino. So far, we have not seen a great deal of it."

The sarcasm was not wasted on either of the men. Beniamino reached behind him and took two bottles of Urbino truffle oil off the shelf. "I think we can remedy that." He handed one to each of us.

"I hope you enjoy yourselves in our little part of the world. *Buona fortuna*. Good luck." Beniamino gestured toward the door, and we soon found ourselves in the hallway and through the huge glass doors of the Urbino Headquarters.

As the security gates closed behind us and we drove toward Spoleto, I looked at Mom. She was already dozing off.

What a day it had been. I was so glad to have had her beside me. We would have time later to reflect on our brush with the powerful Urbino clan, but for now, it was time to rest and plan our next move.

The battle of reconciling the past with the present was just beginning.

Chapter 3

Betrayal

WE WERE having breakfast on the terrace of the Palazzo Leti, at a bed and breakfast that had once been the residence of a nobleman from the 1600s. There had been one of those brief but refreshing summer showers, and now the sun peeped out between rain-spent clouds. Like a beautiful woman stepping from her bath, the city of Spoleto emerged, wet and sparkling. Crumbling stone walls from her early days as a stronghold of the Holy Roman Empire still clung to the hillsides. To the north, ancient tile roofs mingled with mid-century storefronts reflecting a vibrant modern community. To the south, the thousand-year-old Rocca Albornoziana Castle towered in the distance. Pope Urban V had built it as a fortress in 1360, and Lucretia Borgia and her family had used it as a pleasure palace a century later.

"Do you know what Beniamino meant when he talked about 'Spirito's trouble'?" I asked Mom between bites of my crostata.

"Which trouble? He had a few." She sipped her cappuccino and stared out at the lush Umbrian landscape. "I always felt it started with the death of his mother."

I had heard the tragic story of my great-grandmother, Virginia, in snippets here and there as a child. I remembered thinking it was all a bit melodramatic, but being here in Umbria, with the remnants of Italy's past all around me, I felt differently.

Back in 1902, life *was* melodramatic.

Virginia Urbino looked up from her sewing and stared anxiously at the doorway. Her husband was not coming home tonight . . . again. She felt the familiar fear rising inside her, the fear that came over her when she was losing control.

"He hasn't been home for days. He's strayed before, Fiorella, but this is different."

The housekeeper wiped her hands on the towel and turned to face her mistress. "I will ask at the bar tomorrow."

"There is a woman, isn't there?" Virginia put her fists against her face and squeezed her eyes shut. "No, don't tell me."

Virginia tried to shut out the thoughts that taunted her. What did other people in town think of her husband's behavior? Were they laughing at her? Thinking about it made her crazy. Gossip could destroy a family, especially a family with five young children. Ginerva, her youngest, was only eight, but her boys must have known what was going on. *What a bad example Francesco is setting for them*, she thought.

"Maybe I shouldn't have moved out of our bedroom. That's when all the trouble started."

Fiorella stared at her. "And risk your life if you got pregnant again? Virginia, you are forty-eight years old. It could kill you to have another child. Five is enough!"

Fiorella walked into Andrea's Bar the next morning. "Francesco was here last night, wasn't he?"

Andrea stopped wiping down the counter and looked up. "Confidential information," he replied. "What business is it of yours anyway?"

Fiorella snorted. "Somebody's got to tell the wives what goes on in this town."

"Trying to put me out of business, are you? A little innocent flirting never hurt anyone. Including you." Andrea reached over and slipped his hand down her waist.

She flung his hand away. "Ugh. You're no better than the rest of them."

Angling to the other side of the bar, Fiorella tried again. "Francesco left with that homewrecker Lina, last night, didn't he?"

"Is that what the hired help calls me over at the Urbino house?" A handsome, dark-skinned woman stood in the doorway. She took a deep drag off her cigarette. "Give them an earful, Andrea. What do I care. Francesco is the randy one. You should see how hard his cock gets when I walk into the room." She took another drag and blew the smoke in Fiorella's face.

Homewrecker. Lina chewed on the words. She had been called worse. Half-breed, for one. The kinky hair from her Moroccan mother was a dead giveaway. Then there was the other word. Losing her virginity to her lecherous stepfather when she was fifteen gave her that title. She caught a glimpse of herself in the mirror behind the bar. Her face looked old, and her waistline . . . God, she barely remembered when she'd had one. The men had stood in line then. Now all she could attract were desperate old men tired of their wives. How could those women know what it was like for her? They took their comfortable little lives for granted. Sex was her only weapon against the cruelty of the world, and she had no qualms about using it. Lina remembered Francesco's voice, last night, as he reached for her naked body. "When will I see you again?" he had whined. He was obsessed with her, the old fool. Making love to her was probably nothing like being with his wife. Wild, free, no taboos. Well, pleasure had its consequences.

Lina took her eyes off the mirror and looked at Fiorella. "You should go back to your mistress and tell her to start looking for another place to live. I will be moving in soon."

Fiorella spit at her and walked out of the bar.

Lina took a seat at the counter and flashed a nicotine-stained smile at Andrea. "Men want sex like little boys want candy. They'll do anything to get it."

Virginia felt the fear spiraling. Fiorella had told her what Lina had said about moving in. The Moroccan woman was becoming more brazen.

"You are the one who should be kicking your no-good husband out."

Virginia looked at her housekeeper. It was always easy to give someone else advice. "Is it because I won't sleep with him anymore?"

"I doubt it. Most men in this town cheat on their wives."

Virginia knew this only too well. Italian men seemed to lack the genetic trait that kept them faithful. She had seen it in other marriages. Sometimes the signoras looked the other way . . . other times she'd seen the wayward husbands' belongings tossed out into the street. Virginia could not even imagine the humiliation of such a display . . . laid out for the whole town to laugh at.

"I don't have the courage to confront him." Virginia sighed bitterly. "Or explain his behavior to the rest of the town."

Fiorella tried to be kind. "You won't have to. Everyone already knows."

The following day started out like any other. Virginia had planned to go into the nearby village of San Felice to buy her weeks' worth of groceries, and Urbano had volunteered to accompany her. They would return by mid-afternoon. Little Ginerva was staying with her uncle Ferdinando, and Antonio and Spirito were harvesting crops in a neighboring field. Francesco was nowhere to be found.

Virginia and Urbano set out early. As they wound their way up the old Roman road, the valley opened up, revealing green farmland steaming in the morning chill. Summer was already yielding to autumn, and the Umbrian countryside was in full glory. On either side of the road, tiny shoots of wild fennel sprouted and bright blue primrose raised their heads to catch the first burst of sunlight over the mountains. Above them, the branches of the flowering locust trees formed a canopy as they passed by.

The beauty of the day was lost on Virginia. She was focused on the terrible turn her life seemed to be taking and her inability to control it.

Urbano took her hand. "We will get through this," he said.

Virginia turned toward her son, her eyes full of pain. "You will survive. For me, it may be too late."

It was late afternoon when they returned. Urbano dropped off the supplies inside the gate, promising to bring everything in after watering the horse. The boys had not returned, but as Virginia stepped inside the house, she heard a female voice and laughter coming from Francesco's bedroom.

A blinding fury overtook her as she reached the door of the bedroom and threw it open. They were in bed, Francesco and Lina, with their arms wrapped around each other.

Virginia's eyes met Lina's, and she saw a look of triumph. A look that said, *I have won.*

In that moment, Virginia's already fragile world collapsed, and her connection to reality cracked and shattered like glass. Only pieces remained . . . the pieces of her life. As she turned and ran, they scattered and dissolved into nothing.

In the eyes of the town, the circumstances did not absolve her of the crime of abandonment. *How could she leave her children?* the women in the village said afterward. For Virginia, running to the bridge to meet the rushing water, her children no longer existed.

Nothing existed except the overwhelming need for the agony to end.

Urbano was the first to find her. Sending the other two brothers to search the town, he ran toward the river. From the bridge, going southward, the Nera became a torrent of water that bottomed out at the village of Ceselli two miles away.

Halfway down, wedged between two rocks, he caught sight of her body.

"Mama!" he screamed, scrambling down the embankment to the water's edge. Even as he pulled her out of the raging river, he knew he was too late.

He was holding her in his arms when Antonio and Spirito found them. Urbano looked up at his brothers, his face ravaged with grief. "I couldn't get to her in time." He cradled her body, whispering over and over, "Mama, why didn't you let me help you? You didn't have to suffer alone."

Night was falling as the three brothers carried her back to the house.

Francesco did not return that night, and if he had, Urbano would have killed him. In the days that followed, Francesco refused to accept what Virginia had done. It was as if he blamed her for the disintegration of his family. He even refused to allow her to be buried in the town's cemetery up on the hill, forcing Antonio and Spirito to carve out a space for her in nearby Ceselli. An unmarked grave and their memories were all that remained of their beloved mother.

"Do you think Virginia's suicide was the reason the three brothers left Italy?" I asked Mom. We were on our second cappuccino. The sun had chased away the clouds and left the sky a brilliant blue. We were not in a hurry to go anywhere.

"I am sure of it. The family was torn apart. They would never again know the love and security they felt as children. The repercussions of being abandoned by a parent can last a lifetime."

Chapter 4

Sins of the Father

JUST BEFORE noon, we pulled into the parking lot off SS-209. On the west side of the river, where the new fountain had been built, were several restaurants, a bank, and a pharmacy. Beyond the glittering Nera, the old castle rose up, its rose-colored stone basking in the summer sun.

An old man was walking across the piazza with a middle-aged woman by his side. She was a lively little thing with eyes as big as saucers and a short crop of red hair. By the tender way she touched her companion's shoulder and adjusted the scarf around his neck, I guessed she was his daughter. The old man walked with a determination in his stride suggesting a refusal to surrender to the frailty of age.

As they approached the bench where we were sitting, I could see he had one glass eye that stared, unblinking, while the other darted back and forth watching everything around him.

"*Buon giorno*," I said to him and held out my hand. "*Sono* Anna, and . . . uh . . . *questo* . . ." I gave up and said the rest in English, "is my mother Virginia."

"I'm Enzo," he said, returning the handshake. "Enzo Verrocchio. This is my daughter, Leonia."

Mom whispered in my ear, "Do you know what *verrocchio* means in English?"

I did, and I hoped he hadn't heard.

"It means 'true eye,' if I'm not mistaken." The old man's one eye twinkled.

I winced. "I'm sorry. My mother meant no disrespect."

Enzo waved his hand. "None taken. It was a few years ago, an infection. If anything, losing an eye has given me a better perspective on life. I don't take my sight for granted anymore. Each day, when I can wake up and still see the beauty of the world around me, I feel blessed."

"Please, sit down." I gestured to the bench next to us. Leonia helped her father settle in, and she took the bench opposite us. "Your English is impeccable," I said to Enzo. "Where did you learn it?"

"In Rome. I am a retired history professor from the University in Assisi. We saw you yesterday, talking to Beniamino Urbino. Are you from the United States?"

"From California. We are visiting the village where my grandfather, Spirito Urbino, was born."

"Francesco's son" Enzo nodded. "My father knew your grandfather before he left for America. They were close friends." He turned to Mom. "You must be named after Spirito's mother, Virginia. Lorenzetti was her maiden name. A great tragedy the way she died."

My jaw dropped. This was too good. I glanced at Mom. I could tell she still had her guard up.

Mom was studying our new friend. "Did you ever meet my father?"

"I did. When I was a boy. When your father came back for the reading of his uncle's will."

"What year was that?" Mom asked him.

"It was 1923. I remember him telling me to hold on to my dreams. I was seven at the time."

"That sounds like him, all right. He used to tell me the same thing."

I flashed Mom a quick look that said, *Can we get on with it? If this guy gets away, we are back to square one.*

Mom settled back and gave me the thumbs up.

"There is much we don't know about our family after Virginia's suicide," I explained. "Spirito rarely talked about it."

"It was a difficult time," Enzo began. "There were many debts, and after the scandal, Francesco could not get work. You know about the scandal?"

"We know my grandfather had difficulty keeping his hands off the help," Mom spoke up. "Fidelity was not a strong point in the Urbino household."

Enzo wisely decided not to comment. "After Urbano left for America, Francesco's brother, Ferdinando, stepped in and offered to buy the property. His concern was for the youngest daughter, Ginerva, who was only nine when her mother died. He and his wife offered to raise the girl and provide a home for Spirito and Antonio."

"What happened to their father?"

"Francesco moved out and took up residence closer to town. The woman, Lina, left him soon after. Looking for better prospects, no doubt."

Hoping my luck had not run out, I asked, "Beniamino mentioned that Spirito was involved in some 'trouble.' Would you know anything about that?"

Enzo's eye was on me. "Yes, I know what happened. What did Beniamino say?"

"He didn't. He seemed damn uncomfortable if you ask me."

Enzo was silent as he studied Mom. "After so many years, some stones are better left unturned. Are you sure you want to hear this?"

Mom stared back at him. "What do you think we came for?"

"My father, who was also named Enzo, worked with Spirito as a field hand at the Villa Urbino in the summer of 1905," the old man began.

"You mean the villa, up on the hill, owned by Agostino?" I asked. "We were there yesterday."

Enzo nodded. "In those days, just after the turn of the century, it was owned by Agostino's great-grandfather, Angelo. Angelo was the brother of Pietro Sr., the truffle king. Although they were brothers, Pietro and Angelo were not close. Angelo was a farmer, choosing to grow vegetables and raise livestock on his twenty hectares rather than get involved in the truffle business, no matter how lucrative it was. Angelo and his wife, Mariella, had two sons. Agosto, at fifteen, was destined to be a farmer like his father. But Armando, the oldest, hated working the land and preferred hanging around the local bar with his friends. He was arrogant and disrespectful and spoiled rotten.

"Mariella didn't hide the fact that Armando was her favorite. Tall and broad shouldered, with the bearing of an aristocrat, he looked every inch the young *patrone*. He was a fastidious dresser, favoring the tight pants and tailored jackets that all the wealthy young men in Rome and Florence were wearing, and he kept the servant girls busy laundering his linen shirts and underwear. Everything Armando did was designed to attract the opposite sex, and, among a certain class of women, he was successful. The barmaids in town knew that flattery and attention were often rewarded with a generous tip or a free meal, and even a rough grope in a back alley could be mistaken for affection if a girl was lonely enough."

"How do you know so much about the Villa Urbino?" I asked, when the old man paused for a breath.

"I was fascinated with the wealthy Urbinos when I was a child, always begging my father to tell me what went on there. As field hands, my father and Spirito had access to the grounds and service areas, and little escaped their notice. The way Armando behaved with the servants was common knowledge. He would swagger into the laundry room and grab the buttocks of the girls bent over the hot suds. No one ever complained. They knew they could all lose their jobs if word got back to Angelo or Mariella."

Enzo paused, letting the next words sink in. "Agatha was different."

"Agatha? Who was she?"

"Agatha Altarocca. Her family came from Norcia, a village fifty kilometers to the east. She had come from a good family, but with employers all over Italy cutting back on jobs, her father had been laid off. Agatha and her older brothers and sisters had been forced to find work where they could. At sixteen, she was hired by Mariella to help with the housework in exchange for room and board and a small stipend."

Armando noticed her right away. Small-boned and fair, with blue, almond-shaped eyes, she had the classic features of a Botticelli Madonna. The first time Armando pinched her behind, she turned around and slapped him across the face.

"So, you are too good for me." He looked surprised. Obviously, she was not afraid of what could happen to her if his mother found out.

"I don't like being treated with disrespect," she answered, backing away from him and returning to her work.

Armando laughed, but he was immediately intrigued. *This one will be a handful*, he thought. He couldn't wait to get her into bed and teach her how to show some respect.

There was another young man who had noticed the blonde beauty as he worked in the fields of the Villa Urbino. Both Enzo and Spirito, as employees, ate their *pranzo* with the other servants in the cavern below the villa.

The cantina was sweltering and noisy that day. Servants' voices and the tinkling sounds of silverware and glasses could be heard throughout the underground cavern. The girls had untied the tops of their aprons, letting the breeze from the open door cool the sweat on their half-buttoned blouses. Agatha sat on the opposite side of the long wooden table eating an orange. Spirito's mouth watered as she popped a segment into her mouth.

"Gotta get the faro harvested by day's end," Enzo said. "Gonna be hot."

"Uh huh." Spirito was only half listening. He focused on a drop of sweat rolling down Agatha's neck.

"Real hot." Enzo watched Spirito.

"Hot, all right." The drop traveled lower, heading for the open collar of her blouse.

"We're going to be sweatin' like pigs." Enzo grinned.

It stopped, glistening, right between the cleft of her—"Sweatin' pigs," Spirito repeated.

"Hot enough to strip down and dive in the Nera naked." Enzo's voice was louder now.

The drop had disappeared into the lace bodice. "Dive in naked," Spirito yelled back.

The cantina was suddenly quiet. Everyone was listening. Agatha put down her orange.

Enzo dragged his friend outside and fell on the ground howling with laughter. Spirito wanted to punch him. "Very funny. I hope she didn't hear that last part."

"You got it bad, man." Enzo sat up and wiped his eyes. "*Fulmine.* The Thunderbolt."

"The Thunderbolt? What do you mean?"

"Old Italian curse," Enzo explained. "When you want a woman so bad you can't see straight. You can't rest until you make love to her . . . and then you can never get enough."

"You're crazy." Spirito pushed Enzo away. He was thinking of his father and Lina. *That will never happen to me.*

Agatha had noticed Spirito too. She had seen the way he helped the girls carry the heavy baskets of wet laundry to the clotheslines at the back of the villa.

Considerate. Respectful. Very different than the boss's son.

"May I carry that for you?" Spirito pointed to the basket Agatha was holding. He had been watching her from the fields as she struggled with the wet load and sprinted down to offer his services.

Agatha turned and smiled. "If it isn't too much trouble."

Spirito felt his throat tighten when she looked at him, and he knew his cheeks were burning. When her shoulder brushed against him, a jolt like an electric current ran through his body. "No trouble," he answered, his voice hoarse.

The next day, Spirito was feeding Pietro Urbino's pigs. The pen, housing only the best truffle hunting porkers, was on Angelo's property. The animals. were treated like royalty, but they were never overfed. They did their job better when they were hungry. "Tito, you are a glutton. Leave some for the others." Spirito reached out and stroked the tiny pink ears.

"You know what happens to them when they get too old to hunt."

At the sound of Agatha's voice, Spirito rose quickly and wiped his hands on his trousers. She was standing a few feet away.

"I know," he answered. "They end up on the dinner table."

"Maybe you shouldn't get so attached. You have names for all of them?" Her eyes were dancing.

Spirito nodded. "Tito, here, will be the first to go. He's so fat."

Agatha laughed. She reached out her hand to him and, without thinking, Spirito brought it to his lips. Agatha did not draw her hand away.

The sheer force of their attraction drew them together like

magnets. Soon Spirito and Agatha were meeting—away from prying eyes—at the cemetery. The tiny burial ground was up the hill from the villa, along the old Roman road that led to the neighboring villages. Almost always empty, it was the perfect place to experiment with feelings they could not ignore and to explore their shared passion where only the dead could judge them. In that sanctuary, far from a world that could not care less if they lived or died, the two young people discovered love.

"You'd better be careful," Enzo warned Spirito privately. "If I know the two of you are meeting at the cemetery, then others will find out . . . including Armando. He has his eye on her too."

Spirito's fists clenched. Absorbed in his passion, he had not noticed Armando's eyes watching Agatha. The thought of his hands on her enraged him. "I will kill him if he touches her."

"And that will be the end of you, my friend." Enzo put his hand on Spirito's arm. "Armando's family will put you away in a jail cell for the rest of your life—if you are lucky. A bullet to the head is the kind of justice you're more likely to get in these parts."

The frail old man seated next to us paused for breath.

"Papa, you are tired. I think that is enough for today." Leonia bent over her father and gave us a concerned look. "He is ninety-four and tires easily."

Mom and I had been so involved in Enzo's story, we had forgotten the time. The sun was heading west toward the top of the mountains, and when it sank below them, evening would not be far behind.

Enzo patted his daughter's hand and turned to Mom. "When you are my age, today is all you can be sure of. Would the two of you join us for dinner at our home this evening? Then I can tell you the rest of the story."

Thinking Mom needed to rest, I was about to decline when a

chirpy voice chimed in. "We would be delighted! And about that age thing, Enzo, I've got two years on you, and I'm not planning to kick the bucket any time soon."

Chapter 5

Retribution

ENZO AND Leonia had one of the apartments within the castle near the top. The narrow cobblestone stairs made our climb difficult, but stamina had never been a problem for Mom, and I wasn't about to let her make me look bad.

"Any chance our family is related to the famous truffle Urbinos?" I asked Enzo after we were made comfortable and two glasses of Prosecco were placed in front of us.

"What I am about to tell you may help answer that question." The old man paused and turned to Mom. "The next part of the story will be difficult for you to hear."

"I've lived a long time, Enzo, and I've always found that knowing more of the truth is better than knowing less of it."

Enzo looked at us both, his one eye wary and compassionate at the same time. He nodded and began speaking.

"Armando had never gotten over his obsession with Agatha, the young servant girl Spirito had fallen in love with. That became apparent in the summer of 1905 . . ."

Armando was returning from town, just as the sun had set, when he saw two figures leaving the cemetery. Not wanting to be seen, he stepped quickly behind the shadow of a tree and waited. Spirito and Agatha were in their own world, laughing and whispering in the half darkness. They exchanged a long passionate kiss and tender words of love before Spirito turned away toward home. Agatha walked through the iron gates and down the dirt road toward the villa.

"Why would you choose that farm boy when you could have me . . . or maybe you would like us both?"

Agatha whirled around to see Armando's tall frame silhouetted against the darkening sky.

"That farm boy knows how to treat a woman with gentility and respect—something you, even with all your breeding, could *never* understand."

Armando's face reddened. "*Puttana*. Slut." He spat at her. "You will regret those words." Turning on his heel, he strode ahead and disappeared into the grounds of the villa.

As Agatha lay in her bed that night, she realized her outburst could get her lover into trouble—not to mention cause her to lose her job and reputation if her boss found out. She had just drifted off to sleep when she felt a hand cover her mouth and her nightclothes shoved up around her waist. A hand reached between her legs and fingers shoved roughly inside her. She fought back and bit down on flesh. With a cry, Armando slapped her brutally across the face and clamped down harder on her mouth.

As Armando saw a thin line of blood trickle through his fingers, he became aroused. This bitch would find out about the privileges a man could claim on a servant in his household if he so chose. He hit her again. The violence and his desire escalated out of control, and the more she resisted, the more brutal he became. He left her at dawn only when her bruised and bloody body stopped fighting and lay still. Like an animal pinned by its prey, Agatha played dead to save her life.

When Agatha did not show up for work the next morning, Mariella went looking for her. *La Patrona* was aware of her son's tendencies where the servant girls were concerned, and one glimpse of Armando's bloody hand told her something had happened. What she wasn't prepared for was the severity of Agatha's injuries when she opened the door to her room. Without a word, she set about tending to the wounds, cleansing her body and dressing her in fresh clothing. The cuts on her face and bruising on her arms and thighs were not life threatening. The girl would heal, at least physically, Mariella decided. She tended Agatha herself, allowing no one to see her until the skin was healing and her bruises were less noticeable. The last thing she needed were questions involving the servants and her son.

Spirito was beside himself with worry. He knew Agatha was in some kind of trouble, but no one was talking. He hadn't seen her at the midday meal, and she had not appeared at the cemetery for days.

"Leave it alone," Enzo said. "Stay away from her, or you could make things worse for the both of you."

About a week after her disappearance, Spirito couldn't stand it any longer and stole into the servants' end of the villa. When he opened the door to her room, Agatha covered her face and huddled beneath the blankets.

"Don't," she cried. "Don't look at me."

Pulling aside the bedclothes, he gazed at her bruised body with horror. "Who did this to you?" he hissed. "Was it Armando?"

Tears were streaming down Agatha's battered face. When she didn't answer, he knew.

"He will die for this," Spirito spoke with chilling certainty.

As much as his rage threatened to consume him, Spirito knew he had to plan his actions carefully. His family's honor and Agatha's life depended on it.

Spirito told Enzo of his plan to extract revenge. "I will advise Armando to arm himself, considering the rumors and all—"

Enzo interrupted. "Bad idea, far too risky. And you might accidentally reveal yourself. No, I have to do it."

"Enzo, I don't want you involved in this."

"I'm already involved. I am your friend. Besides, that bastard has it coming."

Spirito sighed. He didn't like it, but Enzo was not backing down. "Just tell Armando to buy a gun. One that can't be traced back to him, should he need to use it."

"I know where he can get one. The last house on the western edge of town. Mario sells untraceable merchandise."

Spirito nodded. "The road leading to Mario's house passes the outside walls of the castle."

"Your wall," Enzo broke in.

"Right. Our storage areas share the same wall. You've seen the holes, where soldiers in medieval times put their guns during an attack. The openings are designed so no one can see in, but a clear view is visible from the opposite side. When Armando passes by to go to Mario's, I will avenge myself."

Enzo said, "You should wait until he comes back, when he has the gun. If the authorities find a weapon on Armando afterward, they will assume it was a duel."

Spirito clapped Enzo on the back. "Brilliant, my friend." Spirito hesitated. "Are you sure you want to do this?"

"I'm sure. I will wait by the stairwell and cue you when he approaches."

Hairbrained schemes are only attempted by those desperate enough to try them. Spirito knew Agatha would never get justice for what had been done to her. Armando would always be protected from any wrongdoing. Truffle money would make sure of that. There was only one way for a woman of Agatha's class to receive justice. If he had to assume the roles of judge, jury, and executioner to avenge his beloved, he was willing to take the risk.

The plan was working. Armando, already looking over his shoulder, needed no persuading by Enzo to arm himself. The appointment with the arms dealer was made for the following week.

On the evening of the transaction, Spirito made sure he was alone, and his gun was aimed at the road. He would have only one chance.

When Enzo saw Armando walking down the road, he gave the signal. Shortly after sunset, when the light was still good, a series of shots rang out. If anyone heard or saw anything amiss that evening, they didn't report it. It was as if an entire village chose to accept the fact that Armando Urbino, a no-good arrogant fop, got what he deserved.

One month after Armando's death, Spirito was summoned to the Villa Urbino. There had been no work in the fields as the villa was in mourning. The iron gates were closed, and there was a man standing guard. He had a gun strapped to his chest.

"Name?" The man had his hands on the gun and was looking at him.

"Spirito Urbino."

The man's eyes narrowed, but he stepped aside. Walking down the dirt path to the villa, Spirito knew there was a chance he might not come out alive or that handcuffs would shackle him for the rest of his life.

Entering the reception area, he saw Angelo, Pietro Sr., and a third man he did not know standing next to someone sitting in a chair. Two other men who looked like bodyguards were stationed at each entrance. Taking a closer look at the person seated, Spirito realized it was Agatha.

Her injuries had mostly healed except for the look in her eyes—

the look of a wounded animal. Spirito fought back the urge to run to her and hold her in his arms. If any harm should come to her because of his actions, it would be unbearable.

"This is my brother, Pietro, whom you know. And this is Doctor Sabatini, the family physician." Angelo gestured at both men, but he did not attempt to shake Spirito's hand. This sign of disrespect was not lost on anyone present.

Pietro Sr. stepped forward and took charge. "I will make this brief and to the point. This young woman here has given us some news that we think you should know about." He continued, "Doctor Sabatini, can you elaborate?"

Dr. Sabatini cleared his throat. "Agatha Altarocca has told us she is with child. About six or seven weeks along. I have examined her and can verify that this is correct."

Shaken, Spirito's eyes searched Agatha's face for the truth. But all he saw there was pain—the pain of someone who could not be comforted.

Pietro continued, "It has been brought to our attention that you and she have been intimate for many months although she admits you are not the only one. It appears she also had relations with Armando, Angelo's slain son."

"He raped me. Against my will," Agatha said defiantly. A sudden fire lit up her face as she looked at the three men. "There is a difference."

"So you say," Angelo cried out, pushing past his brother. "Maybe Armando would tell a different tale if he were here to defend himself."

Spirito started forward with fists clenched, but one look from Agatha stopped him. "The fact remains that either Spirito or Armando could have fathered the child." Pietro looked at Spirito. "On the evening of 'the assault,' you also had relations with her, isn't that correct?"

Spirito couldn't think fast enough. What was he supposed to say?

"Yes, he did." Agatha's reply was addressed to the three men, but her eyes were on Spirito.

Pietro walked over to a desk and picked up a sheet of paper. "I have a proposition for you. This document states that you acknowledge paternity of Agatha's unborn child, but that you relinquish all future claim to her or her offspring. It appears this girl wants her child to have your name regardless of who the father is." Pietro shrugged and turned his palms up. "These are her wishes. In exchange, you will agree to board a ship sailing for America as soon as it can be arranged. Agatha will remain, here, in Italy, and be supported and cared for by this family."

There was silence in the room, everyone waiting for Spirito's reply. He looked at Agatha for support, but she kept her eyes averted. He walked to the desk and picked up the paper. The document was already signed and witnessed by all four parties present. In one flourish, he added his name to the rest of the signatures.

"You are not as big a fool as I thought," Pietro said.

Without another glance at the seated figure, Spirito turned and left the room.

Chapter 6

Coming Home

"MANGA," Leonia ordered as she put plates of pasta marinara in front of us. Enzo was drained from all the talking but, apparently, not suffering from a lack of appetite. He began attacking the pasta with gusto, and Mom and I immediately followed suit. A succulent lamb stew came next, and everyone left the past behind to enjoy the present. There are some pleasures that need one's full attention, and good homemade Italian cooking is one of them.

Over caffè and limoncello, I had a few questions for Enzo.

"Why do you think Angelo's side of the family even cared what happened to Agatha? She was just a servant, after all."

"Mariella, Armando's mother, was the one who couldn't let go," Enzo replied. "If there was a chance her son fathered that child, there was no way she was going to let Agatha walk away. The child would be the last thing she would ever have of her son. Also, Mariella had seen the extent of the damage Armando had inflicted and knew she needed to keep Agatha under lock and key to preserve her family's reputation."

"And Agatha," Mom piped up. "Why did she want Spirito's name on the child's birth certificate if he was leaving for America?"

I volunteered a theory. "Maybe she couldn't stand the thought of her assailant being named as the father of her child. Agatha took advantage of her situation and demanded it. Mariella would have to agree or lose access to the child."

"My theory is she was thinking about her future," Mom countered. "Spirito's name on the birth certificate was a power play. As soon as the identity of the baby's father was known, she would lose that power, so why not ask for it while she still had some leverage? Spirito was dead meat no matter what if he stayed, so she got them to ship him off to America. Agatha had decided to take her chances and stick with the Urbinos. If she made herself useful, became an asset, they would not throw her out even when if they found out the baby was not Armando's. Staying put, she insured her survival and a future for her child."

Mind like a steel trap. I pointed to Mom's head and raised my eyebrows. Enzo and Leonia chuckled.

"And another thing," Enzo suggested. "Maybe Agatha knew something no one else did."

"Like what?"

"Armando might have raped Agatha, but that doesn't mean he successfully impregnated her."

"So, you're saying . . . it's possible she knew all along that the child could not be Armando's?"

"I'm buying that theory," Mom said.

"*Basta!* Enough!" Leonia interrupted. "I need some rest even if you all do not. We can discuss this tomorrow. Are you coming for *pranzo?*"

Never one to turn down a free meal, Mom accepted Leonia's offer of lunch, and the next day we found ourselves seated around Enzo's dining room table again.

"*Zuppa di faro* with homemade focaccia. This is what the peasants eat," Leonia said as she ladled the steaming liquid into bowls. "Protein for the long hours in the fields."

I looked at Enzo. "Your father was a farmer, uneducated, but you wanted something different. When did you know you wanted to go into academics?"

"It started when I was a boy. I was drawn to history . . . and the poets. My father had only a primary school education, but he enjoyed learning. He taught himself to read all these books you see here. He was my inspiration to go to university."

Mom was thumbing through the titles. "Marcus Aurelius, Virgil, Dante . . . *The Inferno* is here! One of my favorites."

Enzo nodded. "A good read. Still relevant today with its themes of betrayal and treachery."

"Shortcomings my family was not altogether unfamiliar with, it turns out," Mom said wryly.

"The other Urbinos weren't exactly saints," I pointed out.

Enzo shook his head. "Human nature hasn't changed much in a few thousand years, has it?"

Enzo was quiet a moment before he spoke again. "When Spirito came for the reading of the will, he made a great impression on me. He said he had a daughter who dreamed of being an interpreter one day."

"That was one of my dreams," Mom said. "I had quite a few."

"And did you get around to all of them?"

"I did . . . and one of them is sitting right here right beside me." Mom was speaking to Enzo, but she was looking at me.

"Would you like to meet the descendants of Spirito's uncle Ferdinando?" Enzo asked. "They still live in the same compound where your grandfather grew up."

"You're kidding."

"We do things differently in Italy. Families don't move often. Sons and daughters take over the property when parents get old, and the roles are reversed. Children care for parents just as their parents took care of them. A circle of life, you might say. To have a grandparent around to guide and influence you is a wonderful thing for a child."

I understood completely. My grandmother, Marianna, took care of me when I was young, allowing Mom to go to work every day. I can still remember those carefree days playing dress-up and eating dried figs fresh from the oven. My grandparents' house in San Diego held some of the best memories of my childhood.

"Who lives in the Urbino family compound now?" I asked.

"Ferdinando's great-grandchild Giorgio and an unmarried daughter. I would be happy to introduce you to them."

Enzo was clearly relishing his role as historian. Bringing generations together from different continents was right up his alley.

As we walked the short distance between the two residences, Enzo gave us some background on our current relatives. Giorgio, eighty, had been a contractor in his day and worked on government projects in Europe. He made some money and came back to Scheggino to live. His wife's family was from Ceselli, the next town over.

"I know of it," I interrupted. "Where the river bottoms out. That is where Urbano found Virginia's body."

Enzo nodded. "There is a wonderful Roman road that links the two towns. It passes through the fields at the west end of Scheggino."

"Wait," I said, realizing something. "The storage building where Spirito fired the shot . . . it's in the compound where we are headed, right?"

"It is," Enzo confirmed, "but I don't know if you want to bring that up until you are better acquainted. It might be a touchy subject."

We arrived at the gate and rang the intercom outside the entrance to the courtyard. After a few minutes, a woman came out of the house and walked toward us. She was in her early forties, slender and attractive, with a face Leonardo Da Vinci would have loved to paint.

The gate opened, and the Italian beauty flashed us a smile. *Move over, La Gioconda*, I thought to myself.

"*Buon giorno*, Renata," Enzo began. "These ladies are your relatives from America. Spirito's daughter, Virginia, and his granddaughter, Anna."

Eyes widened and sculpted eyebrows shot up.

"*Piacere*, a pleasure." Renata kissed us on both cheeks before giving us the once over. "*Entrare*," she said, motioning us inside. "I call my father."

A few minutes later, we heard high octane screaming coming from inside the house. "Papa! *Vieni!*" followed by a loud stream of Italian words I couldn't understand. There was no doubt Renata had inherited some serious vocal cords along with her looks.

As we waited, I took a look around. It was a beautiful property, enclosed on all sides by stone walls, with a spacious courtyard in the middle. On the west side was a two-story stone dwelling, and attached to it were three storage buildings running the length of the property line.

"*Saluti*." A male voice greeted us. We turned to see a little bald man with lively blue eyes and a happy grin. "I am Giorgio."

Introductions were made, biscotti and caffè brought out, and soon everyone was catching up on family history that had been buried for more than a century.

"So," Giorgio began, after a lull in the conversation. "You want to see where Spirito . . .?" he pantomimed firing a rifle.

Enzo, Mom, and I looked at each other. I guess it wasn't such a touchy subject after all.

Family secrets, even murderous ones, lose their intensity after a hundred years. From my ancestor's perspective, "Spirito's Revenge" was nothing but ancient history in an era that had far worse stories to tell. I just wasn't so sure the *other* Urbinos felt the same way. We walked over to the stone hovel where the infamous deed had taken place. Giorgio, with the dramatic flair of a tour guide, pointed out the exact hole where the weapon was fired.

"I have document Spirito sign when he come back for reading of will. When my great-grandfather, Ferdinando, die, Spirito only one to come from America."

"What about Spirito's father, Francesco?" I asked. "Couldn't he have signed it? He was still alive in 1923."

"Francesco, he already have de Alzheimer's. No one want him to sign *documenti*," Giorgio explained. "*Uno momento*, I go find it." Giorgio excused himself and trotted off in the direction of the house.

Spirito had suffered from dementia when he was around the same age. Shortly before his death, I remembered the once strong and vital man reduced to a vacant stare and a demented laugh. So far, Mom had escaped that fate. At ninety-six, her odds were pretty good.

When Giorgio returned with the document, we all gathered around the patio table and examined it. Essentially, it was a record of the distribution of Ferdinando's assets and a relinquishing of all claims of ownership by Francesco's family to any property belonging to Ferdinando and his heirs. It was signed by Assunta and Spirito, and dated July 8, 1923.

If there was an ulterior motive for showing us this document, Giorgio's smiling face offered no clues. I was beginning to appreciate the Italian talent for working a situation to advantage. Underneath that smiling face, I suspected Giorgio wanted Mom and me to know we had no claim to his property.

Well, two can play that game, I decided. If there was to be a future relationship between our two families, it was important to leave a good impression. I addressed myself to Renata. "I hope you will come visit us at our home in San Diego. We live ten minutes from the Pacific Ocean."

She lifted an eyebrow and favored us with another La Gioconda smile.

"*Meraviglioso!*"

It was time to say goodbye. As we stood outside the Verrocchio apartment with Enzo and Leonia, I couldn't help thinking this was probably the last time Mom would see them. Another trip across the Atlantic, for her, was unlikely.

"Your generosity and insight have been invaluable," I began awkwardly. "We wish to thank—"

Leonia grabbed me in a big hug and kissed Mom on both cheeks. One side of Enzo's face was wet with tears.

As we wound our way down the passageways of the castle and into town, I thought about the journey we had taken from the present to the past and back to the present again. We stopped on the bridge that divided the village. All around us, from the raging river beneath our feet to the Villa Urbino high on the hill, we saw the story of our family—a story still being written.

I looked at the two fountains squaring off on opposite sides of the glittering water. The old one, holding on to a thousand years of grit and endurance, and the new one, a testament to hard work and ingenuity. I knew the inhabitants of Scheggino would continue to benefit from both going forward.

Crossing the Piazza toward the parking lot and our car, I saw Beniamino Urbino. I waved, and he nodded his head and kept walking.

After a moment, as if reconsidering, he turned and headed toward us.

"*Buona sera, Signora,*" he said, kissing Mom on both cheeks. "It was a pleasure meeting you."

"The pleasure has been all mine," she assured him.

Fortified with a double diaper for Mom and a double martini for me, we settled down for the long flight home to San Diego.

We had breezed through customs. Yuri, the Ukrainian airport attendant, had taken charge of Mom's wheelchair, sprinting to the gate like it was a finish line. "She reminds me of my mama back home," he had confided with tears in his eyes.

I was exhausted. I glanced over at Mom in the seat next to me, bright-eyed and bushy-tailed.

I took a long pull of my drink and closed my eyes. I hoped she could be bright-eyed and bushy-tailed all by herself.

"That was one hell of a trip, wasn't it?"

I sighed. I guess the nap would have to wait.

"That Enzo sure tossed a big chunk of our family history at us. Did you happen to write any of it down?"

I smiled and pointed to my head. "It's all right here."

"That's what scares me. Your brain cells have already suffered substantially." She looked at my martini as confirmation. "We need to get this down on paper . . . for that book you're going to write."

"Wait, *I'm* not writing a book."

Virginia sat back and gave me that I-know-more-than-you-do look.

If I was going to get any sleep, I knew I'd better not argue. I retrieved a notebook and opened it to page one. "Do you have a title in mind for this masterpiece?"

"It depends."

"On what?"

"Who is the main character?"

I thought for a moment. "You."

Mom's eyes opened wider. "You didn't tell me this was going to be an *epic*."

PART II

Chapter 7

Growing Pains

WHEN MARIANNA stepped off the boat in Boston Harbor, the cold wintry landscape greeted her like a slap in the face. She scanned the crowd lining the dock looking for Urbano. He had promised to meet them when they got off the ship.

"Do you see him?"

Spirito was struggling with the luggage and waving away porters he couldn't afford to tip. "Keep looking. He's got to be here."

A young man came running up the gangplank holding a telegram. "Mr. Urbino? A message for you sir."

"*Stuck in Trenton. Take the train. See you there.*" Signed, "*Urbano.*"

Spirito scowled. It was already late afternoon. No more trains today. They would have to find lodging and get an early start tomorrow. Another broken promise by his unreliable brother.

Before Spirito left for Italy to find a wife, Urbano promised that his new restaurant would be a family affair. "Work for Everyone!" Urbano had assured him. Standing on the wharf with the freezing wind whipping around them, Spirito hoped it wasn't another exaggeration.

The following day, on the train headed for Trenton, Marianna got her first glimpse of this new country she was about to call home. Rain slashed at the windows of their compartment, threatening to turn to snow. Rows of grimy smokestacks billowed clouds of soot into steel-colored skies. Shanty towns and factories stood shoulder to shoulder along the tracks, and everywhere people were walking with determined strides as if to some important destination. What a far cry from her little town in Italy, she thought. She missed her family already.

Spirito was thinking his own thoughts. Six years had passed since he had walked out of the Villa Urbino and Agatha Altarocca's life. The passion and love they had felt for each other was over. It had been her choice, not his. He tried not to think about the child she had been carrying. Was it his? He would never know. He looked at the woman seated next to him and knew his future lay in another direction. Providing for his new wife and the children they hoped to have was his focus now. Marianna had given up her dream to share this journey with him, and he was not going to let her down. Her loyalty and willingness to work would be an asset in this country of unlimited opportunity.

The Ristorante Urbino in Trenton was little more than a glorified diner. *Urbano's Greasy Spoon* was more like it, Spirito thought. Glancing at his wife's face, he could tell she felt the same way.

"Fresh paint . . . a catchy sign . . ." Spirito began.

"New curtains and a good scrub." Marianna finished the sentence. They smiled at each other and rolled up their sleeves.

Urbano watched the two get to work and swallowed his proprietary pride. If Spirito and Marianna wanted to make the restaurant their own, he would not stand in their way. He had other plans.

Ever since Urbano had set foot in America, he had been nursing a dream to travel to the West Coast. Crossing the Atlantic, a passenger on the USS *Cretic* had told him about the great opportunities to be found there.

"A new era is beginning," the passenger had said. "The gold rush is over, but California is just getting started. Ever heard of San Diego? Perfect weather and right on the Pacific Ocean. It's going to be a goldmine someday, and I don't mean the sparkly stuff. Tuna fishing is big, and canneries are sprouting up like weeds. Lot of work there for fishermen."

"And restaurant owners," Urbano thought to himself.

Eight months after the newlyweds arrived, Urbano sat Spirito down at the counter after closing. "The restaurant is yours if you want it. I'm headed to California. You can buy me out cheap."

"Buy you out?" Spirito sputtered. "I've put more muscle into this place than you ever have."

"Okay." Urbano held up a hand. "Let's do this. I will keep my share of the business, but since you will be the one working it, you can keep the profits. That way, you don't have to pay me anything . . . until you sell."

"What happens then?"

"The selling price will reflect the value of both shares, whatever it is at that time."

"So, you will make money if the value has gone up." Spirito asked.

"It could also go down," Urbano reminded him, "but with Marianna involved, I doubt that will happen."

"Put it in writing," he told Urbano. "Before you leave for California."

Urbano scouted out San Francisco and Los Angeles first. The crowded streets, sky high rents, and competition for retail space was daunting. Diners, like the one he owned in Trenton, were a dime a dozen. He wanted to set up shop in a place where there was room to grow. Boarding the Santa Fe Railroad's West Coast Line, he headed south for San Diego.

Four hours later, Urbano stepped out of the station into cloudless skies and streets lined with palm trees. Walking south along the waterfront, he saw a frenzy of activity. The Pacific Canning Company was spitting out cans of tuna faster than trucks could load them. Fleets of fishing boats lined the wharf unloading nets brimming with their morning's catch. Nearby, crews were busy building another cannery. Business was booming.

Urbano liked what he saw. A town on the move but still small enough for an ambitious young man to make it big. All he needed was a partner who worked for free and kept the bed warm at night. He was twenty-seven years old. It was time to start looking for a wife.

Home, for the time being, was two rooms with a kitchen on the top floor of a run-down apartment building on C Street. Urbano was saving the bulk of his savings for the lease on his new restaurant space—when he found it. Each floor of the apartment building had two sets of tenants with a small landing space in between. The landlady, an elderly Irish battle-ax, lived downstairs on one side. Annie Mary, Bridget, and Nan lived on the other. They all worked for the Pacific Canning Company, a stepping-stone to the more important job of snagging a husband. Three ladies, one bedroom, and a hot plate.

Urbano lost no time in giving them the once-over. Bridget was Sicilian and would have been pretty if it weren't for the mustache on her upper lip. Nan had a set of teeth that could rip out a chain link fence. Annie Mary, on the other hand, was a knockout—with eager green eyes that looked at life like one big opportunity and breasts the size of Monteluco. If he wanted to get his hands around that tiny little waist, he needed to have a battle plan. Food was the only weapon in his arsenal.

"Homemade lasagna anyone?"

The three women who opened the door to their apartment lifted their noses in appreciation. Urbano walked in carrying the steaming platter of pasta and set it on the kitchen counter. "Good to meet you," he said, turning to face them. "My name is Urbano. I am a chef from

Italy who will soon have my own restaurant here. Would you like to sample one of my creations?"

They welcomed him with open arms. Even though all three viewed their talented neighbor as a catch, Annie Mary knew how to reel him in. The lure was darned socks and clean laundry. It wasn't long before Annie was spending more time in Urbano's apartment than her own, her clothes crowding up his closet, and her nylons drying in his bathroom.

"We have been seeing each other almost six months, when are you going to make an honest woman out of me?" Annie Mary had kicked off her work shoes and was spread out on Urbano's couch. She watched him as he put the final touches on the *osso buco* they were having for dinner.

Urbano had a big smile on his face. "I thought you'd never ask."

Annie looked up at him and waited. "Aren't you supposed to get on one knee?"

Urbano sat.

"You do love me, right?" Annie was getting worried now. "Or do you just want free housekeeping?"

"Both."

"How romantic. As long as you get what *you* want."

"And I suppose you want to spend the rest of your life sleeping with two other girls who smell like fish?"

Annie started to laugh and stopped. "Hey . . . are you saying I smell like fish?"

"Only certain parts of you." Urbano ducked as the flat of her hand came up.

Urbano caught it and jumped on the couch, pinning her beneath him. He reached in his pocket and pulled out a ring. "Am I forgiven?"

Annie looked at the tiny diamond like it was as big as the moon.

"Maybe." Her green eyes danced. "As soon as you make your first dime in that restaurant of yours, we're moving uptown."

"Uptown? Where's that?"

"South of Old Town. Uphill from the wharf." Annie was laughing now. "Away from the stink of fish."

Chapter 8

Baby Steps

URBANO'S former brainchild, the Ristorante Urbino, was undergoing a transformation. Spirito had changed the mostly Italian fare to include a few American staples. Steak and eggs. Bangers and mash. Rib-sticking dishes for the factory workers. Marianna had freshened things up with new curtains and bright colors on the walls.

"Wait until Urbano comes back," Marianna told Spirito. "He's going to hate it."

"He's not coming back. I got a letter from him yesterday. He found a space and has signed a lease. In fact, he has asked us to join him to help get the restaurant up and running."

"In San Diego? Oh, no. We have just gotten settled here in Trenton. Besides, you two can't work together. You have different ideas. He wants to cook regional Italian and you want to cook for the masses."

Spirito wasn't ready to give up the idea. "There's no reason why we can't do both. Urbano says San Diego is like a resort town. Sun every day and the Pacific Ocean to look at . . ."

"Who has time to look at the ocean when you're slaving in a hot kitchen all day? He will make you do all the work like he did here."

Spirito heard Marianna's words, but the dream of a life out West would not go away.

They could stay with Urbano and Annie Mary now that they had bought a house. Without telling his wife, Spirito approached the Franzeses about buying a third interest in the Ristorante Urbino. They were Sicilian immigrants who had savings and wanted to invest.

Spirito tried again a few days later. "*Cara*, let's take a trip to the West Coast and see what all the fuss is about."

"Who will run the restaurant? We can't just close up."

"The Franzeses. They want to be a third partner. It would free us up to travel."

Marianna sighed. "I have some news. I wanted to be sure before I told you."

"Told me what?"

"I'm going to have a baby."

Spirito reached out and took her in his arms. "Ninina, this is great news. When?"

"I am three months along. I will give birth in mid-April."

"We can still go. It's only October." Marianna could see that her husband had made up his mind. The pregnancy had made no difference. Why did he want to leave now when things were settling into a comfortable routine? For Spirito, there was always something better around the corner. She supposed she should be thankful it wasn't another woman. She could only hope that the partnership with Urbano soured so they could come home.

"Regional Italian dishes are fine for the occasional tourist or dago immigrant, but we need to cook for the regular customer," Spirito explained to his brother.

Urbano threw up his hands. "I'm sick of frying hamburger. My gnocchi are the best this town has ever seen. Whose restaurant is this anyway?"

"I thought it was ours."

It was a frequent argument between them. It had been only four months since Spirito and Marianna had arrived in San Diego, and already the brothers were at each other's throats.

She watched them from the sidelines. The partnership was doomed, but she was due next month. There would be no going back until the baby was born.

They named her Virginia, in memory of the mother Spirito had lost. She came out kicking and screaming, ready to meet the world head on. Her parents stared at her, astonished. Where had those genes come from?

"She's like my mother, Teresa," Marianna finally decided. "When my father was murdered, she didn't waste any time feeling sorry for herself. She went to work. Remember when you came to dinner in Visso to meet the family? That was no accident. Teresa engineered the whole thing. One of her three girls was going to America with you."

"I remember." Spirito chuckled. "Your mother was a real pistol, and beautiful. Heck, I would have married her if she'd given me half a chance!"

If Urbano's two-bedroom cottage on Ibis Street was small with four adults, the arrival of Virginia made it even more cramped. Annie Mary didn't complain. She loved helping take care of the new baby and quickly set about converting a downstairs closet into a nursery. More than once, Marianna saw a wistful look in her sister-in-law's eyes. It had been more than a year since Urbano and Annie had tied the knot, and they still had no little one of their own.

Marianna knew she was pregnant again before Virginia was a year old. Spirito was already making noises about returning to Trenton.

"The Franzeses want us back. They can't handle the restaurant by themselves."

Marianna doubted that. Just a ploy to get her to go back. "I'm not leaving until after the baby is born. You will have to get along with your brother until I can travel."

"When will that be?"

Marianna patted her stomach. "Whenever this one is good and ready."

If Virginia burst into the world like a tiger, Anna Urbino came in like a lamb. Docile and needy, she was the opposite of her sister. When Marianna laid her down at night, she would cry until someone picked her up, her little hands reaching out to be held. Anna was only quiet when she was resting in the curve of her mother's arms.

Despite all the chaos, Marianna enjoyed the challenges of motherhood. She had a role to fill. Two little lives depended on her, and it was her job to keep them safe. For the first time since leaving her native Italy, she felt content.

"We are going back to Trenton at the end of June," Spirito announced. "Urbano is driving me crazy."

Once again, Marianna felt duty push against her own happiness. Urbano held the purse strings, so she had no choice but to gather her family together and follow him.

Virginia and Anna had been looking forward all week to Leonora Franzese's seventh birthday party. It was to be held at the Community Park and all the children in the Italian neighborhood of Chambersburg were invited. There would be cake and ice cream, games, and party favors for all the guests.

The Urbino girls weren't often invited to parties because both their parents worked, but Leonora had gone to Marianna and insisted. Even though Leonora was a year older than Virginia, the two were best friends. They were fiercely competitive, always trying to beat each other in their studies and at play.

"Mrs. Urbino, it's my birthday, and I want Virginia to come." Leonora never took no for an answer.

"I have to work. I can't take her."

"She can come with me."

"And little Anna? She will feel left out if she isn't invited," Marianna added quickly.

Leonora made a face. This party was for girls her age, not babies. "Fine. Anna can come."

Virginia had never been to a birthday party as fancy as this one. Big black cars rolled up, and pink bowed girls with elegantly dressed mothers stepped out of them. The presents they carried were wrapped in beautiful paper, and cards with Leonora's name on them were taped to each one. She had no idea Leonora was so popular, but maybe it was her family that knew all these people. She knew the Franzeses were business partners with Papa, but they sure had a lot more money than her family did. Every time she saw Leonora's father and Papa in the back room, they were arguing. Papa never came out of that room looking happy.

At the party, Virginia found Anna's babyish behavior annoying. When Leonora opened her presents, Anna had to inspect each one and comment. She even played with them as if they belonged to her. The older girls kept giving Virginia dirty looks because she had brought along her little sister. She was so embarrassed.

By three o'clock, the party was winding down, and many of the families had left.

"Let's go check out Tomaso's house," Leonora said to Virginia. "I told him today is my birthday. He lives right there." She pointed to a red brick walk-up across a busy street.

Virginia looked at her friend, uncertainly. "I'm supposed to watch Anna. I promised Mama."

Leonora rolled her eyes. "Let someone else babysit the baby."

"I am not a baby," Anna replied. She looked hurt.

Come on, Leonora's eyes were taunting. *Can't you get away from her for a minute?*

Virginia turned on her sister. "Go find someone to play with. I'm sick of you always hanging around me."

Anna's eyes filled with tears, and she ran off in the direction of the park. Virginia felt bad. "Wait . . . I didn't mean it," she called after her.

Anna stopped and looked back, but Leonora grabbed her friend's hand and dragged her across the street.

As Virginia reached the other side, she heard a screech of tires behind her and a sickening thump like the sound of steel hitting something soft. She turned and saw a body underneath the car. There was no sound and no movement coming from the tiny, crumpled form in between the wheels . . . just a deathly silence.

"Anna's been hit by a car." The Franzese boy stood in the doorway of the restaurant, panting. His eyes were wide with fright.

Marianna dropped the stack of plates she was holding and started running. It was three blocks to the park, and already she could see a crowd forming and ambulance lights flickering. Spirito was right behind her.

Oh God . . . no . . . She sobbed, elbowing her way to the front. The small white form was being loaded onto a stretcher. Everything was quiet, and the attendants were no longer rushing. Marianna touched the unmarked face of her daughter. She could have been sleeping except for the trickle of blood running from the side of her mouth.

The attendant put his hand gently on Marianna's arm. "She died instantly, if it's any consolation."

She knew he meant to be kind, but Marianna flung his hand away and looked around frantically for Virginia. Her daughter was at the edge of the crowd. Her eyes were huge, and she looked terrified. Marianna grabbed her and shook her. "What happened? You promised me you would look after her."

"She's just a child," she heard someone in the crowd whisper.

Marianna whirled around in the direction of the voice, her eyes wild. "She's not old enough to obey her mother?"

"They're too young to be left alone. Why weren't you with them?"

Marianna looked at the woman who had spoken. Elisa Andolini. She knew who *her* husband was rumored to work for.

"Because I have to work. I don't have a rich husband."

Spirito put his hands on her shoulders. "Ninina, don't do this."

She turned and reached for him. "We have lost our child . . . our baby . . . our Anna . . ."

She felt herself falling as his arms went around her.

Virginia stood there, forgotten. Her sister was dead.

This was my fault. I killed her.

She backed away from the crowd and ran. She didn't even know where she was going. She just knew she had to get away from that horrible place. Running blindly, she didn't see the broken piece of cement. She tripped and fell. Something burned. She looked down at the blood on her knee as if she were in a dream. When she looked around, she didn't know where she was anymore. Her tummy was making her sick, and she threw up.

"Who do you belong to?"

Virginia looked up and saw a man and a woman staring down at her. Their faces were kind.

"No one."

"No one? That can't be. You are hurt. Let me see." The man knelt down and examined the knee. "Just a scrape. Let us fix you up."

The woman drew a handkerchief from her bag and cleaned up the wound. "Where are your parents? Do you live near here?"

Virginia wanted to trust them. She was cold, and she wanted her mommy. "My papa owns the Ristorante Urbino. We live close to it."

The couple glanced at each other. "We know where that is. We can take you." The man was strong and lifted her up like she was a feather.

"They must be so worried about you," the woman said to Virginia as they hurried along the darkening streets.

"They don't want me. I did something bad."

The man laughed. "Of course they want you. What could a little girl like you have done that was so bad?"

Virginia buried her face in his shoulder and sobbed.

The Ristorante Urbino was dark. Through the glass, the couple saw broken dishes on the floor. It looked like they had closed up in a hurry.

"Do you know how to get to your house?"

Virginia nodded. "It's not far . . . but . . . I'm afraid. They may not want me."

The man's face was grim. He didn't know what this little one had done, but no child should be afraid to go home. "Don't worry. I'll make sure you are safe."

The man carrying the shivering child saw a woman standing in the open doorway as he walked up the steps. "Mrs. Urbino?"

There was a heart-wrenching cry.

"*Figlia.*" Marianna grabbed Virginia from the man's arms and held her tightly. "Thank God, you are safe. Papa is out looking for you." She turned to the young couple standing in the doorway. "Thank you for finding her."

The man hesitated. "She was afraid to go home. She said you wouldn't want her."

Marianna put a hand to her mouth. "Not want her? *Dio mio*, she is all we have now!"

Chapter 9

Marianna

AFTER THE death of little Anna, a dark cloud seemed to descend upon Marianna.

She felt the loss of her youngest daughter physically, like a part of her body was gone. She had heard of people who still felt the pain of a limb that was no longer there. Then there were the mornings when she would wake up, before reality set in, before she remembered. What had been real was now nothing more than a memory, the memory of holding two babies in each arm and, later, two trusting little hands in her own.

Much of the joy she had recaptured after leaving Italy had been because of the births of her children. *Pupette*. That's what everyone called them. The Dolls. Dressed like twins, in outfits Marianna had sewn by hand, they looked too precious to be real. Marianna looked forward to sitting at the sewing machine in the evenings and creating beautiful clothes for her daughters to wear. Even their socks had lace edging embroidered with love.

They had been her one bright spot in the dull parade of customers and endless restaurant chores, her buffer against a country where she still felt like a stranger. When she was with her girls, guiding, instructing, and answering their questions, she had felt necessary.

After the initial shock of her loss, a sense of betrayal grew. Where had God been when Anna was crossing that street? Why wasn't the

Blessed Mother watching over her little girl that day? Her faith, always so strong, was shaken.

Spirito sensed the change in his wife when he came to her at night. She turned away, like she couldn't bear to be touched. Maybe if they had another child . . .

"Ninina, we could try again. You are still young."

How could she tell him that she was repulsed by the thought of making another baby? Like they were replacing the one they had lost. "Anna can never be replaced," she lashed out. "Another baby will not fix this. My grief will not magically disappear."

Spirito couldn't hold back his frustration. "You think you are the only one who is hurting? I have to go on. *We* have to go on. What choice do we have?"

Marianna didn't want to tell him that there was another choice. But it was too dark, even for her. Spirito's mother had made that choice, and she could not do that to him again.

Spirito wrote to Delia Brandi Orsolini, the sister in Visso who had dreamed of a life in America. Maybe if he could convince her to come, it would help Marianna's depression.

Playing matchmaker was not a role Spirito coveted, but he knew Delia would be more motivated if there was the possibility of a marriage proposal. He already had someone in mind.

Emilio Ricci was from Spirito's hometown of Scheggino. He had left Italy soon after Spirito, in 1909, and had done well for himself. He had worked his way up from factory worker to inspector, and now he made good money as an electrician. He was single and lived in the neighborhood.

"You know, Emilio, Marianna has a sister in Italy who is dying to come over. She's not bad looking either." Spirito held his cupped hands in front of his chest. "If you know what I mean . . ."

Emilio blushed. "How old is she?"

"She's thirty. A year younger than Ninina."

She could still bear me a child . . . or two . . . Emilio was thinking. "Can she cook?"

"Any woman can cook if you give her some lessons and are not too critical in the beginning. I will be happy to teach her."

"*Osso buco* and *stangozzi con funghi*. If she can make those, I will marry her."

"You haven't even seen a picture."

"If she looks anything like Marianna, she'll do fine."

Spirito beamed at the compliment, but Emilio's thoughts were more focused on three kids and a table laden with homemade Italian food.

Delia gazed out to sea at the tiny speck in the distance that would be her new home. Tomorrow she would meet the man who wanted to marry her, a man she had never met. He had sent a picture that only showed his face, and he wasn't smiling. What if he was short or fat or mean? Too late to turn back now, she told herself. She had to trust Spirito's judgment.

Marianna and Spirito were at the dock in Boston Harbor to meet her. The moment the two sisters embraced, it was like grasping a lifeline—twelve years and thousands of miles vanishing in an instant. The past was connecting to the present, and Marianna saw a glimmer of hope push through the dark clouds. She saw her mother in Delia's eyes, and she felt the warm sun of her native land in her sister's arms.

There was so much to catch up on during the train ride back to Trenton. Teresa, their mother, had died five years ago, Francesca was pregnant with her third, and Pietro, their brother, had finally gotten married.

"And Emma? Has she met her 'Papa Rica'?" Marianna's eyes glinted mischievously.

"She's in Rome, haunting the glitzy bars, wearing all her jewels. She'd better hurry and find that sugar daddy before the wrinkles set in."

Delia never was one to mince words. They both chuckled remembering their baby sister's obsession with wealth. Delia looked serious. "Is Emilio, my intended, very short? He sent me a picture. He seems good looking enough, but . . ."

Marianna spoke carefully. "Emilio has a good smile and all his teeth. He has a good heart, is eager to provide for you, and wants children. What more could you ask for?"

"He's short. I knew it. All his teeth? You make it sound like I'm buying a horse!" The sisters doubled over, shaking with laughter.

The winter of 1922, in Trenton, was one of the worst on record. New Jersey and most of the East Coast was slammed with heavy snowfall and freezing temperatures. Mounds of gray, shoveled snow piled up in front of stores, making deliveries and shopping for goods impossible. Businesses, especially restaurants, lost money when everyone stayed home.

Virginia, almost nine, came down with a bad case of pneumonia after walking home from school during a snowstorm. Children of working-class families did not have access to the bus and often traveled on foot to and from school. For Virginia, with her weak lungs, the walk proved life-threatening.

As her condition worsened, the fear that Virginia's life was in jeopardy grew. Marianna knew she could not survive the loss of another child.

"When Virginia is strong enough to travel, I want you to take her to San Diego to stay with Uncle Urbano," Marianna told Spirito. "If she stays here another winter, we could lose her."

Spirito couldn't believe what he was hearing. "Don't you want to go with her?"

"You go with her. Delia is here, and I can take care of the restaurant with the Franzeses. As soon as I can get them to buy us out, I will join you. Our daughter cannot wait that long. She needs sun. I will write Urbano's wife, Annie Mary. She loved taking care of our little ones when we were there."

"What about me?" Spirito asked.

"For the sake of your daughter, try to get along with your brother. Maybe some miracle will happen, and you can come up with a menu you both agree on."

Perhaps Marianna was right, Spirito thought. This was the second bout of pneumonia in two years, and with another child looking less and less likely, they couldn't take any chances. He was surprised his wife could abandon her child so easily, but he knew Marianna was going through a difficult time, more difficult than she let on. For the sake of her mental state and their future as a family, Spirito needed to give her the opportunity to resolve it.

It was mid-March before Virginia was well enough to make the trip to San Diego. The morning of their departure, Marianna stood on the platform and watched as the train pulled away from the station. Virginia looked out of the window with eyes that said, *Why aren't you coming too?* As soon as the train was out of sight, Marianna let the tears begin to fall.

What she had kept hidden from her family was that she needed time alone.

There were feelings she needed to work through before she could be a good wife and mother again. Spirito deserved a woman who could return his love, but how could she do that if she didn't even love herself?

Marianna's feelings toward Virginia were more complicated. At the time of Anna's death, Virginia had been six years old. Still a child. Marianna realized she had placed too much responsibility on one so young, always forcing her to sacrifice her desires in favor of her younger sister's. It was because Virginia was so capable that Marianna had given her the job of keeping Anna safe. If she could only take it back. Leave the restaurant earlier and spend more time with both of them. It was the knowledge that she could not change the past that haunted her the most.

There was another dark thought that lurked beneath the surface. Virginia seemed to have coped with the guilt that could have been so devastating, accepting the events of that terrible day as if she had played no part in its outcome. Marianna found herself questioning why her daughter was not grieving as much as she was, imagining that Virginia was glad she no longer had the burden of caring for her younger sister.

"I cannot have these thoughts," Marianna cried aloud. "They will destroy my love for my daughter. What kind of mother will I be if I do not come to terms with my loss and overcome the resentment I feel? It has been two years since the accident. Virginia accepted what happened and is moving forward with her life. I am the one who has not."

That was at the heart of it, Marianna realized. When her daughters were born, she had disappeared into their lives and never created one for herself. She had always bowed to the needs of others—her mother's wishes, her husband's whims—but what about her own needs? What was her future going to be like if she never did the things she wanted? Anna's death had exposed the void in her own life that had not been filled. She needed to find a way to fill it, or she would not survive.

When Marianna arrived at the cold, empty apartment that evening, the impact of what she had done hit her with full force. Her husband and daughter were heading to the other side of the country, and she had chosen to stay behind. She was face to face now with the dark clouds hovering on the edge of her sanity . . . but she was alone. There was no one to condemn, no one to blame, and no one to disappoint. Slowly, she took out pen and paper, and she wrote.

My Wish List.

Become an American citizen

Volunteer as a teacher's assistant at the elementary school

Marianna paused, remembering the little face in the window as the train pulled away. She knew the most important task that lay ahead was to find the courage to accept what was beyond her control and recapture her love for her husband and daughter.

Chapter 10

Finding the Way

"WHO IS the President of the United States?"

"Calvin Coal . . . edge," Marianna answered slowly.

"Cool . . . idge." Delia laughed. "The judge will want the name pronounced correctly."

Marianna sighed. "I'm never going to pass. The English language makes no sense."

"To an Italian," Delia reminded her. "Speaking English is a requirement if you want to be a US Citizen. Next question: What are the two branches of government?"

Marianna frowned. "Aren't there three branches? Legislative, Senate, and Representatives?"

"House of Representatives," Delia corrected her. "And you're right. There are three."

Marianna looked puzzled. "Why do the Representatives have a house and the Senates do not? Where do they live?"

Delia was laughing again. "It's just a term. It isn't a place to live. Political parties?"

"Republican and Democratic."

"Very good. You got that right."

"Now I have a question for *you*." Marianna smiled. "Why is the symbol for the Democratic party a jackass?"

Delia thought for a moment. "I don't have an answer to that one, but if I were you, I wouldn't ask that question in front of the judge."

When they stood in the courtroom a week later, the man in the black gown pushed his glasses up and looked Marianna in the eye. "Why do you want to get your citizenship? I see here, your husband has not petitioned."

Marianna stood up straight and took a deep breath. "This is my country now. I want to make it legal. And if I become a citizen, it will be an in-cen-tive"—she pronounced the words carefully—"for my husband to do it."

The judge nodded. "I have no doubt he will if *you* have anything to say about it. Congratulations, Mrs. Urbino. You are now an American."

That evening, Marianna, Delia and Emilio were seated at the Ricci's kitchen table. "You did it! You are an American citizen. The first one of our family." Delia poured liquid from an unmarked bottle into three glasses and handed one to her sister and one to Emilio. "This calls for a special dinner. Bootleg whiskey and Chinese takeout."

"Takeout?"

"It means a car delivers your meal to you at home, so you don't have to cook. Something new the restaurants are trying."

"Leave it to the Americans," Emilio grumbled. "I like my meals cooked at home."

"Well, maybe you should learn to cook so your wife gets a break once in a while."

Marianna laughed. "Now I know what I've been missing. Arguing with my husband. I need to tell you both something. I am planning to join my family in San Diego before Christmas. It has been seven months. Virginia is going to be ten in April, and I don't want to miss another minute of watching her grow up."

Delia squeezed her sister's hand. "I am so glad to hear you say that. And Spirito? Are you ready to be a wife again?"

"I am ready. The loss of Anna will always be a part of my life, but it is time to move forward. I realize, now, I am lucky to still have a child . . . and a husband to love."

Marianna's heart swelled when she thought about joining her family in San Diego. She took a sip from her glass. "Delia, you haven't touched yours."

Emilio turned to his wife. "Shall we tell her the good news?"

"What good news?"

"Delia is four months pregnant. She found out yesterday."

"Why didn't you tell me?"

Delia looked anxious. "I was afraid to tell you. I thought it would make you sad."

"*Sorella*, how can you say that? How could I not want happiness for you?" Marianna reached out and hugged her sister. "This is the best news. I am only sad I will not be here to see your child grow up."

"You will visit. You must." All three were silent. Finally, Delia spoke again. "When will you leave?"

"I have something to take care of first."

"The restaurant?"

"Yes. I am hoping to get the Franzeses to buy us out."

Delia and Emilio looked at each other. "When you say *us*, do you mean you and Spirito? Or Urbano?"

Marianna was confused. "I thought they both owned it. I think I need to talk to a lawyer."

Emilio smiled. "I know someone."

The offices of Benedetto, Salunto, and Prezzoli were up three stories in a brick building on Swan Street. Marianna's hand trembled slightly as she turned the knob on the opaque glass door and walked in. A bald, bespectacled man with an impressive set of eyebrows rose and extended his hand. "Marianna Urbino? I am Mr. Prezzoli. Emilio told me about you. Please, sit down."

Marianna reached inside her purse and slid a piece of paper over to him. "I found this among my husband's things. If I understand this, my brother-in-law, Urbano, still owns a portion of the Ristorante Urbino. Is that correct?"

Mr. Prezzoli looked at the paper. "According to this, yes. When you sell, provided there are no other investors, half of the proceeds will go to him. But this document is eleven years old and has not been signed by a notary. Plus, there are no witnesses. I'm afraid it would be worthless in a court of law. What other investors are there?"

"There are three investors. My brother-in-law, Urbano, Spirito and myself, and the Franzeses. Urbano and my husband are working in San Diego. I was hoping the Franzeses would buy us out so I could join them in California."

"Technically, then, the Franzeses own a third. If they choose not to honor this document, and I suspect that they will not, then all you can hope for is half of the value of the business." Mr. Prezzoli stood and held out his hand. "I'm sorry I couldn't be of more help."

"Thank you for your time." Marianna rose and walked toward the door.

"Wait a minute, Mrs. Urbino," the lawyer called out. "How long has your family owned that restaurant?"

"Eleven years. My brother-in-law bought it in 1912. The Franzeses joined in 1913. They manage it now."

"Does it do a good business? What kind of profit do you receive?"

"The tables are packed every night, but my margins are slim."

"So, you are paid your share of the profits each month from the Franzeses?"

Marianna nodded.

"How much?"

"Ten dollars a month, sometimes less."

"Who does the books?"

"Vito Franzese's cousin."

Mr. Prezzoli frowned. "Something doesn't seem right here. Come, sit down, and let's look at this a little closer. Do you have a phone number in San Diego? We might need to make a call."

"May I speak to you, Vito?"

Marianna stood in the doorway of the back office of the Ristorante Urbino. She was wearing her best gray wool suit and carrying a new handbag and gloves.

Vito Franzese was examining a sheet of blueprint paper on his desk. When he saw Marianna, he quickly rolled it up and pushed it to one side. "You look nice today, Marianna." There was a glint in his eye. "Something important?"

"May I sit?"

Vito nodded and gestured to the two swivel chairs in front of his desk. "Please."

Marianna took a deep breath. "As you know, Spirito and our daughter, Virginia, are in San Diego. Virginia's health is improving, and I have made a decision to join them. I would like to sell our share of the restaurant to you."

Vito nibbled on a pencil and leaned back, resting his legs on the desk. "I am glad your daughter is doing better. About your share, I hate to disappoint you, but the restaurant is losing money. I can barely afford to pay you anything each month."

Marianna hid her trembling hands in her lap and forced herself to look Vito in the eye. "I work here. The tables are full every night. How can you say business is bad?"

"Oh, Marianna." Vito shook his head condescendingly. "You have no idea. Rent increases, overhead . . ."

Without warning, Marianna grabbed the roll of paper off Vito's desk and swiveled her chair to face the other way. She unrolled the carbon. "Looks like plans for a new restaurant."

Vito tried to snatch them back, but Marianna held on.

"I was going to tell you about it . . ." Vito laughed nervously.

"*Pizzeria Franzese.*" Marianna read the name on the blueprint: "*Vito Franzese, owner. 120 South Warren Street*. That's at the end of the block." Marianna rolled up the blueprints. "I have a feeling I know where the profit money has been going. Architects and permits don't come cheap."

"You have no proof . . ." Vito said.

"We'll see what the courts have to say after a lawyer takes a look at the books."

"Marianna, come now. I think you have been reading too many novels." Sweat was beginning to bead on Vito's forehead.

"I have a way for you to save face." Marianna tried to keep the quaver out of her voice. "Read this." She pulled a document from her purse. "It was drawn up in 1913, ten years ago, before my brother-in-law left for the West Coast. You will see that Urbano relinquished only half of his interest in the restaurant to Spirito. The remaining interest is still in his name. He also states that, if the restaurant is sold, the buyer must buy out both brothers. Right now, the Urbinos own two-thirds of this restaurant."

Vito looked the document over carefully. "This will never hold up in a court of law. It is just an agreement between two brothers with no witnesses."

"How about the court of public opinion?"

"I'm sorry?"

"If you don't buy Urbano and my family out, I will personally tell everyone in this neighborhood what meat you *really* put in your beef stew and how the roaches run all over the counters at night. News travels fast, especially in Italian communities. This place will fold quicker than those rickety chairs you make the customers sit in. How will you buy pizza ovens if the money dries up?"

"The owners of the building have already approved the plans. Permits are pulled," Vito informed her.

Marianna pointed to the document. "With this and the bad publicity you're going to get, the owners won't want to go through with *Pizzeria Franzese*. Not to mention the months you will be in court trying to explain to the judge where our profits have gone."

Vito's feet were off the desk, and the pencil had somehow snapped in two. "You surprise me, Marianna. I didn't think you had the courage to confront a Franzese. I have many friends too."

Marianna stood. "Is this a threat?"

Vito was silent.

"I want a check made out to me with a memo stating the amount is for the sale of two-thirds of the value of the restaurant. My lawyer has worked out the current value based on the eleven years we have owned it, and an estimate of the profits we should have received. If you prefer to wait until we look at your books . . ."

Vito's lips were set in a thin line, and there were wet circles under the arms of his shirt.

Marianna withdrew a separate document from her purse. "Sign this. It is a record of what happened here today." She turned her head toward the door. "Leonora, Mina, will you please come in here?"

Vito's wife and daughter walked in as if they had been waiting outside the door. "These two are my witnesses. Leonora, tell your Papa what happened the day my Anna was killed."

Leonora hung her head and wiped away a tear. "I told Virginia to leave her sister and cross the street. She didn't want to do it, but I made her." Leonora broke free from her mother and ran into Marianna's arms.

Marianna stared at Vito as she held the sobbing child. Her eyes were as cold as ice.

Vito looked at the amount written on the paper. He took out his checkbook, signed the check and the document, and handed them over.

Chapter 11

Antonio

HE TORE out of the bushes before I could run for cover. Wild eyes stared at me from a black face streaked with dried sweat and blood. I could smell the fear on him.

I had not yet killed a man. But when he reached for his weapon, instinct and training kicked in, and I fired three shots aimed at his chest. He cried out before he went down. I stood over him with my gun to his head as he writhed in agony.

"The first one is the hardest. It gets easier." The voice came from the sergeant of my platoon who had witnessed the exchange from some distance away. He looked at me approvingly. "Congratulations. You are a real soldier now."

I looked down at the man I had shot. Blood was streaming out of his mouth, and his eyes had glazed over. As I felt the bile rise up in my throat, I sank to my knees and emptied the contents of my stomach.

Toni woke and sat up in bed. He was drenched with sweat. He had had that dream again, he realized, the one about the war. A stab of pain shot through him, and he gripped the edge of the bed until his body stopped shaking. Morning sun hit the glass of the half open window, and a shaft of it lit up the room like a spotlight. The promise of a new day brought him back to reality.

He made coffee and pulled himself together.

It had all started with a chance encounter with an army recruiter passing through his childhood village of Scheggino when Antonio was seventeen. The horse-drawn wagon had broken down on the highway, and Antonio walked over to see what the problem was.

"Probably a broken axle, he said. "I can fix it."

"Ever thought about getting paid to see the world?"

Antonio stopped and looked up. "You mean joining up?"

The recruiter nodded. "The government wants to maintain its presence in Ethiopia now that the Treaty of Wuchale has made it an Italian Protectorate. We are gaining a foothold in the New World Empire of Africa, and you could be a part of it."

"Would there be fighting?"

"You bet. Those people don't want us there. They still think it's their land."

Toni thought about it. The adventure sounded good—and the money—but fighting wars for a government that sacrificed its people to further their political ambitions did not.

"You would do well in the Italian Infantry," the recruiter continued. "They would put you to work fixing machine parts, weaponry, gear trains, anything broken. Great experience for your future as a mechanic."

It was tempting. Antonio, as the oldest boy in his family, wanted to be the first to strike out on his own and forge a path for his future. A military career could help him do that. After corresponding with the security office in Rome, Antonio made his decision to join the African campaign.

The day he left, the whole family stood in the courtyard of the Urbino compound to say goodbye.

Virginia, his mother, was heartbroken. She twisted her handkerchief into a tight ball, fighting the urge to hold her firstborn tightly in her arms. She wanted to tell him not to go, but she knew that was not what he needed. This was a chance for him to grow and develop as a man, and she must not stand in his way.

Francisco had the opposite reaction. No son of his had expressed an interest in a military career, and he welcomed the thought of it.

"Make us proud. Italy and your family are counting on you," he said, putting his arms around his son and holding him close. Seeing the horrors of war, or worse, dying from them, never entered his mind. The honor and accolades he would receive as the father of a war hero was all he thought about.

It was the first time Antonio could remember being touched by his father as an adult.

Urbano and Assunta looked at Spirito with admiration. Spirito reached out and clasped his brother's hand. "Just come home," he said.

For Antonio, like all the other starry-eyed recruits, the army proved to be a far cry from life in a country village. Barracks were crude, and the training was brutal, but the worst part by far were the skimpy rations masquerading as food. Antonio put up with all of it and was happy to finally be assigned to a garrison in Liguria, near Rome.

Almost immediately, his unit was shipped out to Eritrea, in Southern Ethiopia. He arrived at the fort of Mekele only to see it fall to Ethiopian troops. The atrocities he witnessed were nothing compared to the Battle of Adwa where he saw hordes of men on both sides slaughtered without mercy.

Defeat for the Italian army was inevitable, and in 1896, they surrendered to Ethiopian nationals. Their dream of a New World in Africa was over.

A few weeks after he returned home, the nightmares began—flashbacks of mangled bodies, the cries of dying soldiers on the battlefield, the stink of rotting flesh. But mostly he dreamed of the men he had killed. He knew it was either him or them, and a split-second decision determined who lived or died. But the pictures in his mind still haunted him. Instead of relishing the accomplishment of a duty fulfilled, Antonio felt he had been part of a killing machine that sacrificed young men for political gain. Those who survived were given medals and called war heroes; those who did not had their names engraved in stone on commemorative plaques. He cringed when his father and others in the village clapped him on the back and called him a tribute to his country. In his dreams, he knew who he really was—an assassin hired by a deluded government to prove to its people that the Roman Empire still existed.

The decision to follow his brothers to America had been an easy one. With his mother gone and his family torn apart, a fresh start seemed like a good idea.

Toni, as he liked to be called now, found a job as a mechanic at the Chadwick Engineering Works in Pottstown, Pennsylvania. His brothers were in Trenton, working in the restaurant business, but Toni had his sights on being part of the growing automotive industry. In addition to farm equipment and machinery, Chadwick produced high-end luxury cars like the Chadwick Six, a large, well-built machine that sold for six thousand five hundred dollars. Toni would be part of the team building it.

On Toni's second day on the job, a good-looking young man came into the warehouse where the engineers and assembly line employees were working.

"Antonio?" A voice reverberated through the huge building, and a dozen heads lifted. The voice tried again. "Antonio Urbino?"

"Over here," Toni answered. He was half buried under the hood of a Chad Six.

"Augustine Modesto." The young man held out his hand. "Call me Augie, please. I work in the showroom selling these babies." He patted the hood of the car Toni was working on. "Heard you needed a place to stay. I've got a walk-up on High Street with two bedrooms, and I sleep in only one of them. Six bucks a month—that's half of what I pay. You can walk to work."

Toni was in no position to refuse. The hotel he had been staying in for the last two days was six dollars a night.

"*Piacere* . . . uh . . . I mean, it's a pleasure. And please call me Toni. I'll take that deal and move in tonight. I'm Italian and need to learn English. Maybe you can help me."

"I know a place where you can learn it real quick. The pub down the street from our apartment. Immigrants from all over the world drink there."

The Velveteen Rabbit, like its name implied, suffered from delusions of grandeur. Its owners had originally envisioned a clientele of stockbrokers and businessmen gathering for lunch, but instead, it attracted the working-class Irish and Italians from the factories nearby. When customers started referring to it as The Rabbit Hole, then The Hole, the owners raised no objections.

It was a lively place, especially on Friday and Saturday nights when the long, wooden bar and a score of tables were packed with men drinking their paychecks away.

The Arsi sisters, who served the night crowd, had two rules that welcomed no exceptions: Affectionate gestures on the part of the customers were strictly forbidden, and no requests for private services in the upstairs rooms would be tolerated. Vina poured whiskey at the bar and listened to the poor slobs who told her of the hopes and dreams that had brought them halfway around the world. An immigrant herself, she could relate. At the ripe old age of twenty, she was everyone's mom, big sister, and Mother Superior rolled into one.

Her sister, Listina, was a year younger and worked the tables on the floor. She was short and sturdy with the olive skin and the soulful eyes of her Sicilian ancestors. If a rowdy customer got too friendly, her gentle manner could turn in an instant, and she would put him in his place with a quick jab to the ribs. Most of the men were too drunk to take offense, and complaints to the management were few.

The girls came from Syracuse, a seaside town on the island of Sicily. The sun and sea drew hordes of tourists in July and August, but the rest of the year, its inhabitants scrimped and sacrificed. As soon as they had saved enough for two tickets in steerage, the Arsi sisters headed for Boston Harbor. So far, the dream of a better life was turning into the reality of working at a bar for peanuts with not a single marriage proposal in sight.

The men who came into the showroom looking to buy a Chadwick Six had two things in common. Money and good taste in women. While discussing the finer points of horsepower and Corinthian leather seats with his male customers, Augie's eyes would follow their beautiful young companions as they slid manicured fingers along burnished steel and checked themselves out in the car's glass windows. He would breathe in the scent of rosewater and face powder and hear the sound of silk stockings rubbing up against elegant thighs as they passed him. He longed to touch their fresh youthful skin and grab a handful, but he was careful never to cross the line. His job depended on it.

"Pretty little thing, ain't she?" Augie stepped up to the florid-faced man eyeing the Chad Six. "Got more curves than my boss's mistress."

The man's mouth dropped open, and he stared at the young salesman for a second. Then he started laughing. His female companion didn't think it was funny.

Augie tried another one. "Did you know the Chad Six has one of the largest tanks of any car sold today? She holds more gas than my aunt Bessie."

The laughter was louder this time. "Say, young man, you're quite a salesman. I'm looking to add to my fleet. I'll take two of them."

Augie winked at the sweet young thing who was now cuddling up to her Sugar Daddy. She didn't even glance in his direction.

He had much better luck with the waitresses and barmaids at The Hole.

Augie started stepping out with Vina, the barmaid, not long after Toni moved in. Suddenly the apartment on High Street was no longer a bachelor pad, and on weekends the bedroom door to Augie's room was closed. Toni tried not to hear the laughter, and other noises coming from inside, but it was hard not to imagine what was going on in there. It made him realize how much he desired female companionship himself . . . if only he wasn't so afraid.

"I feel sorry for Toni, always coming home alone. Don't you?" Vina said to Augie one evening when they were alone in the apartment. "He needs a woman."

"He's too shy to even talk to one." Augie thought for a moment. "What about your sister, Listina? I've seen him looking at her at the pub. Does she like him?"

"He has legs, a job, and he isn't already married. What's not to like?" Vina responded. "I'll talk to her."

They all went out together the following week. There was a Vaudeville show playing a few blocks from The Hole, and the four of them splurged for a box seat so they could all be together. There was singing, dancing, and comedy, but the main draw was a performance by a young lady who called herself "The Pride of Pottstown."

Vina gave Toni a wink. "She's famous for leaving nothing to the imagination."

Listina blushed and Toni squirmed, but there was no way they could escape. As the performance progressed, the crowd roared its appreciation. Glancing over at his date, Toni realized she was just as embarrassed as he was.

"This smells like a set up," he whispered in Listina's ear and nodded toward the other couple. They both burst out laughing, and a moment later, he felt for her hand and held it.

The courtship began slowly. A stolen kiss in the alleyway behind the bar, strolling home hand in hand after Listina's shift, talking of the future. Toni could feel the fire begin to climb when he touched her. He wondered what it would be like to have her beside him, in his bed and in his life.

Toni bought a sapphire ring with tiny diamonds in a rosette setting. It took his entire paycheck, but an engagement was not something to be taken lightly. Shaking like a leaf, he got down on one knee.

"Yes," Listina said, before he uttered a word, sparing them both the ordeal of the proposal.

"Let's have a two-fer—a double ceremony," Augie suggested when Toni told him the news. Never one to miss a good line, he added, "Two heifers for the price of one!"

Everyone was on board, and three weeks later, the Arsi sisters were married women—proving once and for all that America was the land of opportunity. Sometimes it just needed a push in the right direction.

On the wedding night, Augie's bedroom was filled with the sounds usually associated with that time-honored tradition. But behind Toni's door, a different reality was taking place. Even in the loving arms of his bride, he could not control the direction of his thoughts or erase the images he had tried so hard to forget.

"You are just nervous, darling," Listina whispered. "When we get to know each other better, things will improve."

But they didn't, and then the nightmares returned. In the nights when Toni would wake up drenched and shaking, Listina rocked him like a baby until he relaxed. She cried only after he had fallen asleep in her comforting arms.

The marriage lasted barely a year. Listina wanted children, and it wasn't fair to her that Toni could not fulfill his part of the bargain. The marriage was annulled, and the two walked away without bitterness. Toni moved out of the apartment shortly afterward.

The coffee was cold, and the Pennsylvania skyline had clouded over again. Toni looked at his watch. He was due at Chadwick's Engineering Works in less than an hour.

At forty-three years old, he already felt that life had passed him by.

Chapter 12

An Unexpected Gift

THE LETTER was addressed to U. Urbino, General Delivery, San Diego, Calif. The black border around its edges announced at once the nature of its contents. Spirito hesitated before opening it, wondering which family member had died.

Saluti, Antonio, Urbano e Ginerva,

We have sad news. Ferdinando Urbino, your uncle, has died. Your presence is requested on 8 July 1923, at the family home in Scheggino, Italy.

It was signed, *"Giovanni Urbino,"* Ferdinando's oldest son and new head of the family.

Short and sweet, Spirito thought. No mention of his father, Francesco, or his sister, Assunta. No mention of why someone from America had to be represented, unless his father was too ill or incapacitated to be a viable male presence.

"Who died?" was all Urbano said when he saw the envelope.

"Uncle Ferdinando."

"Too bad. I was hoping it was someone else."

They both knew who that was. Their father, Francesco, had been enemy number one since the suicide of their mother. All three brothers held him accountable for her death and made no apologies for wanting him out of their lives.

Spirito continued. "They want one of us to represent the family when the will is read. The lawyers don't do that unless there are assets to be distributed. Maybe Ferdinando left us some money."

Urbano thought about it. "Toni's in Philly. I can't go, I have a restaurant to run, and the patent's almost complete on my U-Ban-O chili con carne product. I'm working on branding it."

"Branding?"

"Making a product so popular that people identify it by its name, like Jell-O."

"Jell-O? I thought you were making chili."

Urbano threw up his hands and raised his eyes to heaven. "Why do I even bother to explain."

Spirito chuckled. He loved getting a rise out of his brother. Urbano took everything so seriously, he never knew when someone was joking.

Urbano looked at his brother. "Why don't you go? You're the logical choice." Spirito knew what he meant. *You don't have a business to run . . . you're dispensable.*

Spirito resented the inference. He wanted to open a restaurant of his own here—working for his brother was no walk in the park—but he needed capital. A lot of it. Maybe Ferdinando had left them something. It was worth investigating. "I am happy to go, but a ship's passage across the Atlantic doesn't come cheap these days. If you want me to represent the family, my expenses need to be paid out of whatever assets we get."

"But we don't even know if there *are* any assets," Urbano answered.

"That's right, you don't. Those are my conditions. Take them or leave them."

Urbano shook his head. "What choice do I have?"

"What about Virginia?" Spirito said, "I can't take her with me."

"I can look after her. It will be a pleasure," a voice called out from the kitchen. Wiping her hands on her apron, Annie Mary walked into the living room. "Virginia and I can take the bus together to Washington Elementary in the mornings. She will be safe with me."

Urbano had gotten lucky with that one, Spirito couldn't help thinking. The joy of living was still there in those big green eyes. Even the fact that they hadn't had children of their own hadn't dampened her enthusiasm. Some people were content with what they were given and made the most of it. Annie was one of those. Ironic. The woman who couldn't have children was mothering someone else's child and grateful for the opportunity.

"Thank you, Annie. I will be back by August. With you taking care of her, Virginia won't even miss me."

Spirito booked passage on the SS *Cretic* on June fifteenth and arrived in Italy a few days before the reading of the will was to take place. It had been twelve years since he had seen his native country. One war had already been fought without him, and even though no one realized it, by 1923, the seeds of the next were being planted.

Things had changed, Spirito noted as he made his way from Rome to Scheggino.

Motor cars had replaced the horse and buggy, and the roads had been paved to accommodate modern travel. New housing and commercial buildings had sprung up around the base of the old walled villages. It was obvious that Italians now preferred to live in spacious ground floor residences rather than stone hovels at the top of a mountain.

Scheggino, on the other hand, was much the same as he remembered it. The residences of the Urbino truffle clan had grown a bit, annexing space up and out on their already over-sized villas, but that was all. The rich got richer, Spirito thought, and the poor . . . well, the poor just stayed poor.

It felt good to be home, he realized as he walked up the cobbled path inside the castle to Enzo Verrocchio's apartment. Glancing up at the Villa Urbino in the distant hills, he tried not to think of where Agatha was now.

A major change had occurred in the life of his childhood friend, Enzo, since Spirito's last visit. The young man who had aided in the plot for revenge all those years ago was married and had a seven-year-old son. Annika, a local Romanian girl, kept a clean house and wasn't stingy with her smile. The Verrocchio home was modest, with only a couch by the fire for guests, but the warmth of their hospitality made Spirito feel like a member of the family.

"For a farmer, you sure have a lot of books." Spirito eyed the shelves on either side of the *camino*. "*History of Rome*. *Roman Poets of the Augustan Age* . . . Have you read all these?"

Enzo laughed. "Most of them. I have to keep up with my son. He is already asking more questions than I have answers for." He brought out the young boy who had been standing shyly in the background. "Enzo Jr. is in his second year and at the top of his class."

Spirito studied the boy, thinking of his own daughter, Virginia, who was only a few years older.

"Do you want to be a farmer like your father?"

"No," Enzo Jr. answered immediately. "I want to be a teacher . . . of history." He looked down at his shoes as if embarrassed that a farmer's son dared to aim so high.

"My daughter, Virginia, is three years older than you, and she wants to learn languages and be an international interpreter. Hold on to your dreams, young man, and you may see them come true."

Later, sitting by the *camino's* roaring fire, with two glasses and a bottle of grappa between them, the two friends caught up on their lives.

"The Urbino Truffle Foundation is getting richer while everyone else is still recovering from the war. Winning has not helped the working class in Italy," Enzo lamented. "Truffles, on the other hand, seem to be a recession-proof commodity. The old man, Pietro Sr., has passed the reins of the business on to his son. Claudio is thirty-seven years old now. Can you believe it? He was only twenty when . . . when we were working at the villa. He is already taking the company to new heights. A worldwide marketing strategy is in the works."

The two friends sat staring into the fire.

"Where is she?" Spirito asked quietly.

Enzo didn't have to ask. He knew who *she* was. "Agatha lives in the Urbino Palazzo."

"The ancient villa of the old Urbino nobility? From the 1300s?"

"That's the one. I guess the new Urbino money bought it from the previous owners. It is a beautiful place."

"Is she alone?"

Enzo's eyes met Spirito's. "No, she lives with her son, Santo."

Another round of silence. There were so many questions Spirito wanted to ask, but the only way to know the truth was to go and see her.

Enzo tried to warn his friend. "Remember what happened the last time I told you to stay away from her? Let the past be. You are married now. What would you gain by seeing her again?"

I would know if her son was mine, Spirito wanted to say. But, if he was to go and find her, no one must know. Not even his best friend.

On the morning the will was to be read, Spirito rose early. The air was still cool and fresh, and the sun had not yet appeared over the eastern rim of the mountains. July was the hottest month in Scheggino, the countryside in hiatus waiting for autumn to begin its cycle of growth. The hillsides were still green, but the leaves of the trees bordering the river were beginning to crisp at the edges and turn yellow. Sunflowers were bowing, past their prime, and unpicked plums and apricots lay rotting in the dewy ground beneath the trees. He could smell the manure in the fields and hear the first crows of the roosters as they announced the start of a new day. Spirito breathed it all in, and his childhood came flooding back.

The memories were bittersweet. He remembered walking through the mountain passes with his father to Spoleto, gathering wild asparagus to serve at the mid-day meal. He remembered tending the vegetable gardens beyond the village walls with his two brothers. Looking back on it now, Spirito felt it was a time of youthful innocence, a time before he knew that bad things could happen. His mother's suicide had changed all that, and his father's infidelity had been the cause. Spirito hoped he would not have to see him today.

The gate swung open, and he entered the courtyard of the Urbino compound. There was a table set up outside, and two gentlemen in dark suits were conferring over a sheaf of papers. Ferdinando's oldest son, Giovanni, came over to greet him.

"Thank you for coming all this way. My father would have been so happy to see you here." Giovanni looked older, more mature, the burden of responsibility as the new patriarch resting firmly on his shoulders.

Spirito returned the greeting. As they walked to the others grouped around the table, there was a movement at the gate, and everyone turned to see a middle-aged woman guiding a frail old man into the courtyard.

The man's faded blue eyes stared vacantly ahead, the gnarled hands grasping a cane for balance. He shuffled with the disjointed uncertainty of a body whose muscles no longer remembered their proper function. The face caught Spirito's attention. Once so familiar, and now barely recognizable, it was the face of a man who had lost his place in the world and would never get it back. It was the face of his father.

Overcome with emotion, Spirito embraced his sister, Assunta, and kissed her on both cheeks. He had not seen either of them since he had left the first time, in 1906.

Seventeen years ago.

Assunta had tears in her eyes when she turned and addressed her father: "Papa, this is your son, Spirito."

The old man's eyes rested on the man standing before him. "I have no sons. I have only a daughter." He reached for Assunta's hand and grasped it firmly in his own.

Spirito couldn't tell if the insult was intentional or a symptom of the ravages of time. It didn't matter. In the eyes of his father, he had ceased to exist.

With all the parties present, the two suited gentlemen introduced themselves. "I am Dottore Fabio di Russo, and this is my associate, and notary, Signore Pizzuto. We are here to represent the interests of the deceased, Ferdinando Antonio Urbino, and to read his Last Will and Testament."

The notary acknowledged the group with a nod and began speaking: "All Real Property will be bequeathed to Ferdinando's sons, Giovanni and Gino, and their immediate families. This includes this residence and all its structures and the two hectares of land outside the walls. All furniture, jewelry, and valuables will be distributed among these same family members."

Signore Pizzuto paused and looked up from his papers. His eyes were now resting on Spirito and Assunta.

"As you know, Ferdinando cared deeply for his brother's family, taking responsibility for their care and treating them as if they were his own. Through the years, he set aside money for each one of Francesco's children. I am here today to distribute those funds." The notary pushed a piece of paper toward Spirito. "You will acknowledge that you represent your brothers, Urbano and Antonio, and your sister, Ginerva, all of whom remain in America. Please sign here."

Spirito looked at the written figure and was surprised at the enormity of the sum. Even when divided among four people, it was enough for a down payment on a restaurant of his own in San Diego.

Dottore Di Russo addressed Assunta. "You are here representing the interests of both you and your father, correct?"

Assunta nodded and glanced at Francesco. There was no sign of comprehension in his face nor any indication that he objected. The lawyer continued.

"Ferdinando has taken the liberty to provide the funds for Francesco, when it becomes necessary, to be placed in an *ospicio dei vecchi*, a hospice facility in Spoleto. This will take the burden off you and your family to care for him at the end of his life."

Everyone at the table understood what a gift this was. A loved one with dementia was a terrible strain emotionally and financially on a family in Italy. Having the money to place them in a home was not available to everyone. The glow in Assunta's eyes reflected the gratitude she felt. Her uncle's generosity would mean she could have her life back again.

The irony of the disparity between his uncle and his father was not lost on Spirito—two brothers sharing the same genes but polar opposites in every other respect.

As the lawyers finished up and got ready to take their leave, Spirito breathed a sigh of relief. Ferdinando had seen to it that those left behind would be taken care of, and the opportunity to take this gift and make it grow was an added bonus. Ferdinando's generosity would mean a chance for his own family to gain a foothold in San Diego. A restaurant of his own, where success or failure rested solely on his shoulders, was something to look forward to. The hatred that had consumed him for most of his adult life was gone. Spirito felt only pity for his father now. There was no escape from the prison of dementia, and it was a fate he would not wish on even the bitterest of enemies.

He walked down the passageway toward the river and stood on the bridge separating the town. Looking up at the stone façade of the Villa Urbino in the distance, he knew there was one more part of his past he still had to resolve.

Chapter 13

Love Among the Ruins

THE ANCIENT walled town of Spello was built in 1295, on the southern flank of Mount Subasio, fifty kilometers from Scheggino. Interspersed with charming arches and views of the Umbrian hills, it had drawn noblemen, their mistresses, and those mistresses' lovers for centuries. The Baglioni Chapel where Pinturicchio painted his fresco "Cycle" drew them, but the discreet inns and pleasure palaces tempted them to stay.

Spirito walked through the thirteenth-century Porta Consolare and into the walled fortress where the Palazzo Urbino was located. The open-air foyer of the palazzo was a stunning bit of architecture. Ornate wrought iron light fixtures in the shape of dragons hung from vaulted ceilings. Arched porticos welcomed guests into a courtyard decorated with mosaic floors and a marble fountain. Above, a wooden gallery extended beyond the walls of the palazzo forming a medieval balcony.

"This is where Agatha lives now," Spirito mused. She had done well for herself in the last seventeen years.

A moral tug of war had been raging inside Spirito ever since he had heard of Agatha's whereabouts. It was a battle between mind and heart, between duty and desire. He had seen the path of infidelity his father had chosen and the damage it had caused. He had also known a beautiful woman whose love for him had been snatched away by an act of violence. He wished he could let Agatha live her life without his interference, just as he wished his wife and daughter's love could be enough for him. As he climbed the staircase toward the entrance to the Palazzo Urbino, he wondered which side would win.

The bell sounded, and he heard footsteps approaching from inside. The door opened and a young man stood in the doorway. Spirito stared at him in disbelief. It was like looking in the mirror at a face that once belonged to him.

The young man stared back.

"Who is it, Santino?" a female voice called from somewhere inside the room.

"Please come in," the young man gestured.

When Agatha saw Spirito step into the room next to her son, her breath caught. She looked in wonder at the two identical strangers, unknown to each other but both so close to her heart. Recovering her composure, Agatha drew the young man toward her. "Santo, please welcome an old friend."

There was an awkward silence before the two men shook hands. "I must be going, Mother," Santo said quickly. "I am needed at the offices."

"Santo works at the new Urbino Truffle Foundation offices in Spello," Agatha said proudly. "He will be an executive there one day."

Santo smiled politely. "My mother's expectations sometimes exceed my own. It was a pleasure meeting you . . . *Signore?*"

The older man hesitated and glanced at Agatha. She gave a slight nod. "My name is Spirito. Spirito Urbino."

Santo's eyes widened slightly, and his face colored.

"A pleasure." He turned abruptly, gathered his things, and left the palazzo. When the door closed behind Santino, Spirito breathed a sigh of relief. Now he knew for sure.

The interior of the Palazzo Urbino was exquisitely furnished. White silk drapes hung from a series of French doors opening to the balcony beyond. Settees in ivory brocade, fine art, and a sprinkling of Italian Baroque antiques dominated the formal reception rooms. The walls were a deep coral red.

The elegance of the surroundings was exceeded only by the woman who stood among them. She wore a peach drop waist dress that clung to her slim frame, accentuating every curve. It was in the latest flapper style that came to just below the knees, revealing shapely legs and trim ankles. Spirito saw, at once, that the intervening years had only enhanced Agatha's beauty.

"Does Santo know about us?" Spirito asked. They had made themselves comfortable in the morning room overlooking the courtyard. Cappuccinos and biscotti were quietly placed on the marble table by a servant as soon as they sat down.

"So, you saw the resemblance?" Agatha looked at him intently.

Spirito nodded. "It is unmistakable. He is my son."

"I suspect Santo has heard the rumors. I do not keep him sheltered from the world."

"Does he know why I had to leave you? About the 'deal' I made with Pietro Urbino?"

"Santo knows his mother made a decision to protect the people she loved, and that is why his father had to go away," Agatha spoke without bitterness or regret. "Angelo and Mariella honored their part of the bargain. They have always treated me and my son with respect. The Urbinos gave us an opportunity for a better life, and I chose to accept their generosity. My son will become an important part of their work and the success of their company."

"An opportunity I could never give him." Spirito's eyes were hard.

Agatha placed a hand on his arm. "The past cannot be altered. Let us look to the future."

"And you? Why are you not married?" Spirito knew he was pushing.

"It has been my choice. I have everything I want."

He looked around the room. He risked overstepping, but he had to know. "And who pays for this?"

"Claudio, Pietro's son. As you remember, he was a young man of twenty when it all happened. As he got older, he assumed the responsibility of my care and that of my son."

"Does Claudio have a wife?"

Agatha answered calmly and without hesitation. "Yes. Olivia. We are good friends. Santo is engaged to their daughter, Lidia. They will be married next year when they both come of age. I don't have to tell you this, but it is better not to have secrets. Claudio and I are not lovers. There was a time when that might have been possible, but that is not the decision I made."

Agatha sat back and regarded Spirito. "Now, have I answered all your questions satisfactorily?" Her eyes sparkled.

Spirito smiled. "You disarm me. You always knew how to do that. You must know I tried to find you when I came back twelve years ago. I had the insane idea that I could take you back to America with me. I asked everywhere, but you had disappeared."

"I did not want to be found. I wanted to raise my child far away from Scheggino. The Urbinos helped me."

They both fell silent, thinking their own thoughts, lost in the past. In this fancy palazzo, those stolen moments in the cemetery twelve years ago seemed to belong to two different people—before the innocence of young love was replaced with a hard reality.

And yet, just being in her presence, Spirito could feel the heat of desire well up in him. The sexual connection was still there, a raging force coursing through his body, electrifying and uncontrollable. He ached to touch her, taste her, claim her once again as his. Was she feeling it too?

Agatha broke the silence. "I was lying when I said I have everything I want." She closed her eyes and sighed. When she opened them, there was another look in her eyes.

Suddenly, they were reaching for each other, the fire of their passion reignited. The heat of it flamed up, threatening the barriers of discretion. Without a word, Agatha took his hand and led him to her bedroom.

Trembling slightly, she faced him. "Touch me," she whispered, "and let me remember."

The half-light of the afternoon sun blazed through the arched windows. He slowly undid the buttons at her throat and slid the fabric gently over one shoulder. Her skin felt soft like the silk of her dress. As he bent down to kiss the pale, smooth flesh, she moaned. He uncovered the other shoulder and let the dress drop to the floor. He saw that her body had lost none of the suppleness of youth—her breasts still round and full but her hips and thighs more womanly than before. She had matured from a bud just beginning to open into a rose in full bloom. She had the sensuality of a woman now, a woman who knew the power she had over him. Agatha reached up and ran her fingers through his hair, breathing in his scent.

"How I have missed you," she said.

He drew her close, her body reaching for him like a moth to flame. He touched the curve of her breast with his hand, tentative at first, then stronger as he saw her nipples harden. His fingers traveled to her belly and down. Suddenly his mouth was there, his tongue finding her. She cried out, her voice full of surprise and wonder. Fistfuls of his hair were in her hands as she found his mouth and wrapped her legs around him. He lifted her up and carried her to the bed.

For an instant, the face of Marianna flashed before his eyes. "God help me," he whispered, "I cannot stop myself."

The fire between their bodies rose up, stronger now, and engulfed them. They did not think about tomorrow or what this moment would mean for the rest of their lives. They thought only of their pleasure, the memory of yesterday, and the love that had been denied them.

Later, lying beside her sleeping form, Spirito looked up and saw the blood red sky framed in the Moorish arches of the Palazzo. The day was almost over. Soon, Santo would be returning home.

They hadn't planned for it to happen. It was like being in a dream and trying to control its outcome. They felt powerless against the intensity of their passion even when they both knew it would be agony to be parted again. Spirito's tears mixed with her own as Agatha held him until it was time for him to go.

On the trip home, and in the years that followed, Spirito often thought of that afternoon of love high in the hills of Mount Subasio, in the fabled town of Spello. He felt the pain of separation and the longing for her touch, but there was no guilt, and there were no regrets. He could only hope that Agatha felt the same way.

Chapter 14

The American

SPIRITO stepped back to look at the new sign over the front door. In bold white letters, "*The American*" announced its presence in the neighborhood like a cocky new kid in town. There was an American flag painted on a panel next to the entrance and an awning shading the four tables along the sidewalk. Outdoor dining. In Italy, it was done all the time—cobblestone streets so full of tables you could barely walk through. Spirito hoped the idea would catch on in San Diego.

The American, at 426 West Broadway, was still a work in progress. Workers had been putting in long hours since November, outfitting the space from a retail clothing shop into a place that served food. After school, Virginia and Annie Mary walked the six blocks from Washington Elementary School to the restaurant, where the nine-year-old sometimes spent entire evenings bent over a table doing homework. Nothing could interfere with his daughter's studies, Spirito noted proudly. He had no doubt there would be a scholar in the family before long.

Soon after returning from Italy, Spirito had signed a lease and rented a small two-bedroom walk-up on C Street and Ninth Avenue. It was close to the restaurant, and he and Virginia could walk back and forth while the work was in progress.

Urbano had stuck his head in and offered suggestions once or twice. Even though his restaurant was only a few blocks away on Fifth Avenue, he did not come by that often.

Sibling rivalry, no doubt. Spirito wasn't buying into it this time. Harmony and a positive attitude were essential now that Marianna was finally coming home.

"Are the tablecloths going to be red, white, and blue too?"

Spirito looked up. *Speak of the devil,* he thought. *Urbano has decided to put in an appearance.* At forty, his brother had grown a little stouter, and his sideburns were streaked with gray, but the competitive edge was still there.

"Actually, the pattern on the fabric will be stars and stripes. And there is going to be a giant Statue of Liberty over there." Spirito kept a straight face and pointed to an empty spot in the corner.

Urbano laughed uncertainly.

"Hey, Frank," a voice called from the back room. "Where do you want these boxes?"

Urbano looked at his brother. "They call you Frank?"

"Well, Francesco *is* my middle name, and no one around here can pronounce Spirito."

"You're becoming a real American, aren't you?"

"Better for business." Spirito pointed to the sign overhead.

Urbano had a funny look in his eye. "Then I guess you won't mind if I call you *Francis*.

Spirito winced.

Urbano shaded his eyes and looked up at the sky. "Christmas Eve, and it's seventy degrees. Unbelievable. I'm sure the weather is not as good in the rest of the country. "When is Marianna coming?"

"On the six o'clock train, tonight."

"If you are too busy, Annie and I can meet her," Urbano volunteered.

So unlike him to be helpful, Spirito thought. *There must be a reason.*

"I could show her my restaurant. Then, we can see yours."

Spirito fumed silently. *Ah, so that is it. My wife, who I haven't seen in almost nine months is coming, and it's still all about you.* "Oh, no,

Virginia and I will meet the train. It's all been decided. Thank you anyway. But if you would like to wash out all the serving trays and give the stove a good cleaning while we're gone . . ."

Urbano's response was quick. "Would love to, but I've got to oversee the dinner prep at my place tonight. Give Marianna my best. If you want me to look over your menu, let me know. Glad to contribute." With a wave of his hand, he took off toward Fifth Avenue and disappeared into a crowd of pedestrians.

Virginia and her father were heading to the Santa Fe Rail Depot at five-thirty that evening. She had been waiting for this day for almost nine months, and now it was here.

"Are you happy your mother is coming home?" Spirito asked as he turned the corner onto Kettner Street and saw the train station just ahead.

"Happy and scared," Virginia responded. "I hope she will be glad to see me."

Spirito nodded. "I know. I feel the same way."

Virginia saw her first—a petite, dark haired woman waiting on the platform with a pile of suitcases around her. She wore a stylish suit and smart looking hat that could only have been made by those hands that had sewn baby clothes for two little girls. Something was different about her, Virginia noticed. This was not the timid and overworked person she had waved goodbye to from the window of a train all those months ago. This was a confident woman who had found her place in the world.

"Mama, *ti vedo!* I see you!" Everyone turned to look. A young girl was running down the crowded platform toward a well-dressed woman with outstretched arms.

"Look at you, so grown up." Marianna cried, holding her daughter at arms-length. A moment later, she crouched down and searched

Virginia's face. "*Cara figlia*, can you ever forgive me?"

Virginia looked surprised. "Me? Forgive *you?*"

"For not being here all these months. I don't know if you can understand this, but there was something I had to figure out."

"I think I know what it is, Mama."

Now it was Marianna's turn to be surprised. "You know?"

"You had to figure out how to come back to us."

Marianna's eyes filled. "Yes. That's it . . . exactly."

"I have learned something too," Virginia said.

"What have you learned?"

Virginia's answer came slowly. "That if someone tells you to do something you think is wrong, don't do it."

"And?"

"Sometimes you get only one chance to love a sister."

Marianna grabbed her and held on. "Or a daughter," she whispered.

"Welcome home." Spirito lifted his wife's chin and looked into her hopeful eyes. "We have missed you."

Marianna's voice was strong. "I am here . . . to stay."

Spirito sighed and wrapped his arms around both of them. They were a family again.

"I present to you . . . The American!" Spirito spread his arms wide and looked at his wife expectantly.

Marianna surveyed the disorganized mess before her. The kitchen still had unopened boxes of supplies piled in a corner, and discarded packing crates littered the dining room floor. The grimy stove looked like it had been bought secondhand and not cleaned since the last owner used it.

Not wanting to dampen her husband's enthusiasm, she put on a brave smile and rolled up her sleeves. "It's a good beginning," she said. "Now, let's get to work."

After the workers had gone home, the reunited Urbino family pulled up chairs in the darkened restaurant to discuss their finances. Marianna looked over the list of expenditures and bank statements.

"The money from Spirito's portion of the Ferdinando inheritance is almost gone, but it looks like most of the major expenses for the restaurant are over. In a couple of months, it will be making an income. With the money from the sale of the Trenton interests, we will buy a house."

"Some of the 'Trenton interests,' as you put it, belong to Urbano," Spirito reminded her.

"I will have a talk with him about that. I think I can convince him to split it with us. Even with half, we have enough for a down payment."

"I know a good area," Virginia piped up. "A few blocks east of the Catholic church is where you can find something cheap."

Spirito and Marianna looked at their daughter in amazement. "How do you know so much about real estate?"

"I see things walking to the restaurant from school. The Italians are moving away from the waterfront and spreading out."

Her parents glanced at each other. Virginia's comments showed an understanding of the housing market far beyond her years.

"Tomorrow is Christmas Day," Marianna announced. "After Mass, we will take a walk and see what's for sale.

The house on Albatross Street, between Hawthorn and Grape Street, was a three-bedroom, one-bath bungalow with a backyard and a distant view of the waterfront. It was listed for six thousand five hundred dollars. Two weeks after Christmas, the Urbino family contacted an agent and met him at the property. In addition to the 4,000-square-foot lot, there was a laundry room, a basement, and a shack out back that Spirito was already eyeing possessively.

"Three bedrooms is more than we need," Marianna said. "Maybe we should look for something smaller."

"There is room for Toni to live with us, or you could take in a boarder," Virginia suggested. "This is a good buy."

The agent raised his eyebrows and nodded. Spirito and Marianna looked at the agent, then at each other, and laughed. Their daughter seemed to have thought this through better than they had. Now all they had to do was convince Urbano.

Marianna told Urbano about the conversation she had had with the lawyer and Vito Franzese's response. What was clear now to the Urbino brothers was that they had lost control of their restaurant. Leaving town and expecting Marianna to keep track of what the Franzeses were up to had been unrealistic. The fact that she had gotten their money back was a testament to her ingenuity and courage.

"I can't believe you got him to give you the money," Urbano exclaimed. "If it weren't for you, Vito would have screwed us both. Keep all of it, you earned it."

If Marianna was surprised at her brother-in-law's generosity, she kept it to herself. "Thank you, Urbano. I hope this is the beginning of a new chapter for the Urbino brothers."

Marianna and Spirito put in a cash offer of six thousand dollars for the house on Albatross Street. It was accepted the following day.

With eight weeks to go before the April first Grand Opening, work began in earnest at The American. A new restaurant appliance called the deep fryer was brought in to make strips of potatoes called "French fries." The hamburger had a new accompaniment. An existing wooden bar, normally reserved for the beer crowd, was refurbished to accommodate extra seating. With Prohibition in full force, "near beer" was all that could legally be served, and it tasted so bad, most restaurant owners didn't even bother to put it on the menu. Two large industrial fans were installed in the dining area to keep the flies from resting too long on surfaces while customers were eating. Grimy walls were scrubbed and refreshed with bright white paint, and prints of the waterfront and downtown hung on all the walls. Marianna added potted plants and colorful stenciling around the doorways and windows, giving the atmosphere a much-needed feminine touch. It was finally coming together.

The Fourth and Broadway location was ideal for attracting shoppers, businessmen, and workers from the tuna canning factories down by the wharf. By 1924, San Diego had become a major center for the fishing industry with fisherman and their fleets supporting a handful of canneries. The Pacific Canning Company, Van Camp, and The San Diego Packing Company employed hundreds of workers at the foot of Twenty-Sixth Street. Fuel docks and ship-building warehouses lined the wharf going north. After work, the employees took the streetcar up from Market Street to the center of town. This was the clientele Spirito was counting on to fill his tables. He would serve thick steaks with French fries, sausage and scrambled eggs, and chicken pot pies. The one thing that would *not* be on the menu was tuna.

Spirito had written Toni to tell him of the house they had bought and offering him the use of the third bedroom should he decide to move to San Diego. Their correspondence had become spotty in recent years, and Spirito feared that he was losing touch with his oldest brother. Maybe the offer of a place to live near family would be a good move. Spirito had not heard back, and with the opening of the restaurant, he let the matter drop. When things settled down, he promised himself he would try again.

The day of the Grand Opening finally arrived. Bunting on the railings lining the street flapped gaily in the breeze, and the outside tables sported new tablecloths in a stars and stripes motif. The patriotic theme turned heads. People strolling up and down Broadway stopped to admire the festive decorations and peruse the menu posted outside. By noon, every table was filled. The American would stay open until late afternoon, but tonight, a celebration was planned for family, staff, and all the workers who had helped in the transformation.

By the time the last lunch customer had been served, it was four in the afternoon, and everyone was flagging. It was time to wind down and relax. Spirito was clearing the last of the empty beer mugs and totaling up the cash when he looked up and saw a short, balding man with sad eyes framing the doorway. It took a minute before a smile of recognition spread across his Spirito's face.

"Toni! *Sei venuto!* You have come! Marianna, Virginia, Urbano, look who's here!" Everyone came running, and soon Toni was surrounded. Even Urbano eyes filled up when he saw his brother walk in the door. Spirito noticed the dark circles under Toni's eyes and the wrinkles that had not been there before.

His brother did not look well.

Sunshine and fresh air might be just what he needed, Spirito thought. San Diego had helped Virginia; maybe it could help Toni too. He was glad he had agreed to buy the house with the extra bedroom.

Spirito looked around him. Marianna was bustling about setting a new place at the table, and Virginia had both arms around her uncle, her face pressed against his cheek. Toni looked embarrassed but happy, basking in the warmth of a reunited family. All the people Spirito loved, except one, were here with him tonight. He felt the longing for Agatha flare up and subside into a dull ache. He could live with that ache knowing the love and loyalty of his family would be there to sustain him.

Raising his glass, Spirito addressed the crowd. "*Saluti*, my friends. *Buon Appetito!*"

Chapter 15

The Venetian

FAUSTO Tasca didn't mind doing without a shave; he didn't even mind the odd hours or bad pay. An artist's life required many sacrifices. Skipping a good meal was not one of them.

On the day of the Grand Opening of the American, Fausto had sauntered by and asked what time they opened for breakfast. At seven the next morning, he walked in, sat down, and ordered the Hungry Man Special.

Spirito eyed the ragged clothes and stained jacket. "Meaning no disrespect," he began, "but how do you intend to pay for this breakfast?"

Fausto's stood up, his dignity obviously offended. "I may look like a beggar, but that doesn't mean I am one. See these hands?" He held up ten fingers stained with a variety of colors. "Paint. Not dirt. I am painting all the frescoes in La Madonna del Rosario church. You have heard of it, no?"

Spirito was immediately contrite. "My apologies. To make up for it, I will cook you breakfast myself."

In a few minutes, he returned with a large platter of fried potatoes, two sausage links, and scrambled eggs with tripe. Beef innards were a delicacy in Italy. He set the plate down with a flourish.

The painter held up a coffee cup to be filled. "You are forgiven."

Fausto had been hired by Father Rabagliati to paint two murals and the ceiling of the newly built Our Lady of the Rosary Catholic Church on Columbia Street. The Crucifixion fronting the apse and the Resurrection over the entrance were already creating a stir in the neighborhood. The scenes he painted were vivid: There was wonder in the eyes of the thief as he gazed at the man who hung alongside him, greed on the faces of soldiers drawing lots for the garments of the crucified, and grief in the prostrate body of Mary at the feet of her dying son. Redemption, avarice, and agony. All the drama found in the most famous churches in Italy, right here, in San Diego.

Despite their initial misunderstanding, Spirito got on well with the eccentric artist. In those quiet morning hours, there was time to talk about the country they had both left behind.

Originally from the Lombardo region of Italy, Fausto had moved to Venice in his early twenties, drawn to the captivating beauty of the ancient city. He saw palazzos from the sei cento lining the canals, their patinated walls clashing with the green-gold water. The sunsets, reflected in the murky depths of the Tiber, burned like liquid fire. He saw endless scenes waiting to be painted, but he also saw a city full of impassioned artists like himself. Not all of them could earn a living wage on the basis of their talent. When the offer came from Father Rabagliati to travel to America to paint an entire church, Fausto packed up his paint box and set sail for the sleepy little town of San Diego.

"When will you be done at the church?" Spirito asked as he poured more coffee into the artist's cup.

"I am almost finished painting the stain glass windows. Then I go home to Venice," Fausto replied. "There is only work for sign painters here. That kind of work may fill my belly, but it does not feed the soul."

This one, Spirito thought, would not sell out so easily. Creating art was essential to Fausto's existence, and without commissions, he would not be happy. Ever since the artist had first walked into the restaurant, Spirito had been formulating an idea in his head. Now seemed like a good time to test it out. "I have a proposition for you," he began.

The cup of coffee paused on its way to Fausto's lips, and one eyebrow lifted suspiciously.

"I would like to commission you to paint portraits of my mother and my wife's parents. From photographs, naturally, as they are all deceased."

"And what would be the payment for these portraits?" Fausto loved to paint, but he also valued his time and talent.

"We could work out a trade; payment will be in money and food." As an afterthought, Spirito added, "The weather in San Diego is much better than Italy in November."

Fausto thought it over. The winter months in Venice could be brutal. His studio had flooded more than once when the canal waters rose. "Fifty dollars a painting. I buy the canvases and paints, and you supply the food. I eat three meals a day. And I paint better with rib eye steaks in my belly than hamburger."

The price was steep but too tempting to refuse, and Spirito did not want to risk negotiating with the temperamental artist for fear of insulting him. "Deal," he said.

Both men shook hands.

Fausto sat back and lifted his coffee cup. "I will begin tomorrow. Now, I need sustenance. Bring me that piece of cheesecake I saw in your case . . . and more coffee!"

True to his word, Fausto began working from old photographs Spirito had of Marianna's parents. These were taken prior to 1897, before Ettore Brandi Orsolini was murdered. When the Venetian painter began to work with the oil color on canvas, the Urbino family was amazed at how the images came to life. Teresa's complexion became flushed with the beauty of youth and Ettore's elegant profile a faithful reminder of his family's noble heritage. Marianna was deeply grateful to have such an extraordinary memento of her past.

Virginia, in her first year of Roosevelt Junior High School, rushed to the restaurant every day after school to see the progress Fausto was making. She had developed a schoolgirl crush on the crusty artist and would sit at his table and pepper him with questions while he ate his dinner. Fausto was good at analyzing people; he could spot cunning or insincerity a mile away on a person's face. Virginia possessed neither. She was candid and spontaneous, and Fausto found her great company.

"I will be confirmed on May first at Our Lady of the Rosary," Virginia reminded Fausto. "You will be there, of course."

"I will be there, *cara*, even if I have to paint every one of your relatives." Fausto winked and touched her cheek. Virginia blushed and dropped her eyes, not wanting him to see how happy she was.

Early one morning in January, as the artist and Spirito were alone in the restaurant, the subject of future paintings came up.

"I am almost finished with your mother's portrait. We will begin, next, with your father, *sì?* I do not have a photo of him."

Spirito's face changed, and he looked away. "I was not planning to . . ." He paused and sighed. "Ah, my friend, family relations can sometimes be difficult. I did not get on well with my father. His actions contributed to my mother's suicide, and I have never forgiven him."

Fausto spoke quietly, "I was not given that choice, to not love my father. He died when I was very young. You may regret it one day." He looked at Spirito with a twinkle in his eye and added, "Especially when I become famous!"

Spirito thought about what Fausto had said. The chance to have portraits painted of both his parents by a master was an opportunity that didn't come around often. Pressing a photo of Francesco into the artist's hands, he said, "Paint him without the hat."

The murals were finished at Our Lady of the Rosary by December

1925, and in January, Father Rabagliati began raising funds to buy the lot next door and erect a Parish Hall.

Marianna joined the Arch Confraternity of the Holy Rosary, a group committed to social activities in the Italian community, and Virginia became a member of an auxiliary branch known as the Children of Mary. Their first big event would be a confirmation ceremony followed by a procession to the waterfront for the blessing of the vessels. The statue of Our Lady would be hoisted onto the shoulders of the strongest Portuguese and Italian fishermen and paraded down India Street. The way the fishermen saw it, paying homage to Our Lady of the Rosary never hurt when sailing out to sea hoping for a good catch.

Toni had moved into the extra bedroom at the Albatross house and found work at Lou's Garage on India Street. They specialized in servicing high end automobiles, and with all the wealthy "businessmen" owning nightspots downtown, there was no shortage of fancy cars needing upkeep and repair. Frank Boncompagni's Duesenberg and Jimmy Fratello's Packard could occasionally be spotted on the hydraulic lift getting a grease job. Toni enjoyed the work and found California less stressful than Philadelphia. Marianna mothered him too much, and Virginia was always begging for a ride in his Ford sedan, but San Diego, and the Albatross house, were beginning to feel like home.

"Do you have another portrait for me to do?" Fausto asked between mouthfuls of sausage and eggs.

Spirito could sense that, with the warmer months ahead, the artist was longing to return home. He knew he had to come up with an excuse to keep him here a little longer.

"My brother, Antonio. Could he sit for a portrait?"

"But of course. If he would consent to pose. It is not easy to stay still for many hours at a time."

"You can come to the house and do some sketches. We will see how it goes," Spirito said. "Marianna makes a delicious tiramisu."

Fausto's eyes lit up. "I am free tomorrow. Sketching and then dinner, *sì?*"

April fifteenth, 1926, was a day Virginia would remember as a special time for her family, a time when they were all still together. It was her twelfth birthday, and the Urbinos were celebrating with a dinner party in her honor. Preparations had been going on all day; the gum wood bookcases and fireplace mantel had been polished, windows on the enclosed porch washed, and the hardwood floors waxed until they shone.

Marianna's homemade tiramisu rested on the sideboard in the dining room underneath the large bay window. As Virginia looked toward downtown and its humble skyline, a feeling came over her that she was destined to live a long and satisfying life. Great things would come her way if she was brave enough to reach for the goals that she had set for herself. She felt a depth of gratitude for the loved ones who had gotten her here and the sacrifices they had made. Soon it would be her turn to contribute to the Urbino story. She couldn't wait to get started.

As the family took their places at the table, the portraits Fausto had painted looked down from their places of honor like invited guests.

Marianna passed the bowls of steaming pasta to Urbano on her right, then Annie Mary, and then Toni. Spirito produced two carafes of homemade wine and began filling everyone's glasses. It felt like a multi-generational family reunion.

"Where's Fausto?" Virginia asked as she sat down. "He promised to be here."

As if on cue, there was a loud knock, and the door swung open.

A ragged figure clutching a bouquet of roses strode into the room. "I am here, *Principessa!* For you, I make special appearance." Fausto Tasca's eyes took in the guests and the table laden with food. "And for Marianna's tiramisu, of course!"

Marianna handed him a full glass of red wine. "*Benvenuto*, welcome!"

"To the princess," he said, raising his glass and addressing Virginia. "May you live a long and happy life, and may all your dreams come true!"

"Hear, hear," everyone cried as all the glasses were raised. "*Saluti, Carissima* Virginia!"

The portrait of Antonio, newly completed, rested against the easel in the front bedroom where the light was best. The face on the canvas was worn, no longer young, but the eyes were intelligent and warm. A half smile played on the lips as if holding back a secret their owner was reluctant to tell. At Toni's request, the medal of the African Campaign was painted on the right front pocket of his jacket.

Toni studied the painting before turning to Fausto. "You have captured me without revealing too much of the turmoil that lies beneath the surface. I thank you for that."

Fausto accepted the observation as a compliment and nodded his head. "I saw the pain," he admitted, "but I chose not to let it overwhelm your goodness. I hope you understand when I tell you it was an honor to paint a man who has suffered much. I hope I have done you justice."

"I believe you have," Toni said.

What Fausto did not say was that he guessed the nature of the trauma he saw in Toni's eyes. He had painted men who had come back and women who had lost sons, and he knew the casualties of war were not always left on the battlefield. He knew there were some who wished they had died alongside their comrades.

The confirmation of twenty young ladies, including Virginia Urbino, and the procession to the waterfront was a celebration, not only of the completion of the church, but of the hard work of everyone in the community. With the vision of an Italian American priest and the talent of a young artist, Our Lady of the Rosary would become a gathering point for the neighborhood and a jewel in the crown of Little Italy.

Fausto stood in the balcony, looking down at the crowd filing in. The celestial panels that adorned the ceiling and the stained-glass windows he had painted filled the church with a kaleidoscope of light and color. Barring some unforeseen disaster, he figured they should still be around a hundred years from now. Fausto nodded at the figure of Virginia, so innocent in her white dress and veil. She looked up and waved.

This would be the last time he would see her and the people he had come to love in the quiet but endearing little town of San Diego. It was time to return to his native Italy where the glittering canals and the ancient palazzos of his favorite city were waiting for him.

Chapter 16

Antonio

"*PAISANO*, you got time to work on my little *putana?*"

Toni rolled himself out from underneath the truck and looked up. The man towering over him was swarthy and muscular with hands the size of ham hocks. The cold look in his eyes did not match his smile.

Toni scrambled to his feet and wiped his hands on dirty overalls. "Of course, Mr. Boncompagni. What seems to be the problem?"

"Call me Comp. Everyone else does." He caressed the curve of his Duesenberg's fender. "Like my mistress, she needs her parts lubricated regularly." He laughed and winked at Toni.

"I'll get right to it . . . uh . . . Comp." Toni smiled weakly. "She'll be ready by this afternoon."

"Good man. Come by the club sometime. I'll buy you a drink."

Toni shuddered as he watched the big man stroll toward Broadway. He knew where The Havana was and what went on there. Reputed to be the most exclusive nightclub in town, the club provided a variety of services. A man could get a drink and a woman and lose his shirt at the blackjack tables discreetly located in the rear of the building. Large sums of money were exchanged in those rooms, and no one was invited back until all debts were paid off—one way or another.

Frank Boncompagni owned a handful of nightclubs like The Havana in San Diego and had an interest in multiple bars, brothels, and gambling operations throughout the city. There were other businesses, too, that had no signs on their doors, but everyone knew they existed. Especially if you needed a loan. His connections to the Los Angeles underworld were common knowledge, and if you were smart, you stayed clear of him.

Downtown San Diego in the 1920s had developed a seamy underside, and many believed Prohibition was the cause. By attempting to eradicate the forces of evil, the Temperance Movement had only succeeded in allowing businessmen with questionable reputations to make the rules. Men like Comp and Jimmy Fratello capitalized on vice—a commodity that had been fueling an economy for decades. Men—and women—liked to drink, fornicate, and gamble. Comp and Jimmy were supplying a demand that polite society had tried to eliminate. They understood that just because it wasn't legal didn't mean people wouldn't find a way to get it. In their eyes, corruption existed not because men were evil, but because the law had created an environment that allowed evil to flourish.

On the corner of India and Ash Streets, Lou's Garage had the best repair shop in the downtown area. It was half a block long with a huge indoor garage and space outside to park as many as ten vehicles. Repairing high-end motor cars was Lou's specialty.

Lou Zamboni's area of expertise did not conflict with men like Comp and Jimmy, and he soon found himself maintaining their fleet of Duesenbergs and Packards on a regular basis. Customers with expensive cars paid the bills and kept food on the table for Mary, his wife, and their two kids.

Lou's family lived in a two-bedroom bungalow on Columbia Street, one block up from the Garage. His mother-in-law, Celia Lallo, lived next door. The arrangement had its advantages, like built-in babysitting, when Louie and Mary wanted time alone without the kids, but there were drawbacks as well. Celia loved to give advice on how the young couple should raise their two sons, Lou Jr. and Jack. Then there was the little part about the down payment on the bungalow, a gift from Celia on their wedding day. Even though he was grateful for the financial assistance, he knew there would be strings attached. In the end, Lou resigned himself to the fact that when you got married, the bargain includes the in-laws, so you might as well get used to it.

Celia had been a widow going on five years now. Her husband, Vincenzo, and his crew had gone out fishing one morning, headed for the Sea of Cortez in Mexico, and never returned. They found his boat a week later, smashed to bits on the rocks after an early winter storm hit the coast. The bodies were never found. Every morning since then, Celia went to seven-thirty Mass at Our Lady of the Rosary and lit a candle for his soul. She trusted that God had a reason for leaving her without a husband.

Toni got on well with the Lallo and Zamboni families and was often invited to share mid-day meal with them at Celia's house. Lou's son, Lou Jr., was five and already showed a talent for art, and two-year-old Jack's antics kept everyone on their toes.

"You've never married?" Celia asked Toni one Saturday afternoon. They were sitting on her front porch, digesting the *pasta con fagioli* she had cooked while the children played. Celia believed life was too short to be anything less than candid, and Toni respected that.

He fought to keep his eyes on hers and not look away. "I was, once. It didn't work out." Celia nodded, but kept silent, waiting for him to continue.

"There are things in my past, my experience in the war in Africa, that have affected my peace of mind." Toni hadn't intended to say even this much, but something in Celia's manner made him feel he could trust her. "I don't sleep well. I have nightmares."

Celia put her hand lightly over Toni's and kept it there.

"I know a young man, Dr. Bonaventura, who has just finished his residency and has opened up a practice nearby. His approach to medicine is different. He believes that we can prevent illness by lifestyle choices and holistic techniques. Some of his ideas are taken from eastern methods of healing."

Toni stared at her. "That's a bit far-fetched, isn't it? Mumbo jumbo for desperate people?"

"I see him regularly. He has helped my body and my mind recover from the loss of my husband. Have you ever heard of acupuncture, using needles to target stress? The Chinese were using it a thousand years ago. It might help you with your nightmares."

Toni made an appointment mainly to put an end to Celia's insistent prodding. He'd see what this Voodoo doc had to say and take home the bottle of wheat germ oil, but no way was he going to let anyone stick needles in him. It gave him nightmares just thinking about it.

Dr. Bonaventura's offices were located on Fourth Avenue, a few blocks west of Balboa Park. In 1930, many properties in that area were zoned for commercial and residential use. Doctors and lawyers could see clients in their offices downstairs and live on the top floors. Convenience and saving money often trumped privacy in the early days of a professional career.

"Good morning, Mr. Urbino. I am Dr. Bonaventura. A mouthful, I know. Call me Dr. B."

The young man holding out his hand looked to be about thirty-five years old, boyishly handsome, with masses of dark curls escaping from his surgical cap. He wore hospital scrubs and a stethoscope across his broad, athletic chest.

"Excuse my appearance, I have just come from Mercy Hospital. We are doing some new treatments for cancer with drugs recently developed overseas. Exciting stuff."

Toni stared at him in amazement. This was hardly a fanatic muttering incantations while pricking people with pins. This guy looked like a real medical doctor, even if he was a little on the young side.

"I'm Toni. A pleasure. I must confess, I have been lured here by a mutual friend, Celia Lallo. She raves about you."

"She is a fine woman. Ahead of her time in accepting treatments that are not yet mainstream. Come into my office. Let's talk."

Dr. Bonaventura listened as Toni talked about the atrocities he had seen and the havoc it had caused him both emotionally and physically.

The young physician had seen cases like Toni's, especially after the war. Men came home mere shells of their former selves, or worse, violent psychopaths unable to differentiate between the battlefield and civilian life.

When Dr. Bonaventura spoke again, it was both as a doctor and as a human being. "One of the most important things to accept is that what happened to you was not your fault, despite what you did or didn't do." He paused to let those words sink in. "I have seen people much worse off than you get better. But I will not delude you. The treatment is a process that requires a receptive attitude and an enormous amount of patience."

Toni was adamant. "No needles, Doc. Other than that, I'm all yours."

"Agreed. First, I'd like to have a few X-rays done. You mentioned your panic attacks often include stomach pains. We need to take a look inside."

Toni was scared, but there was something about this man that he trusted—a sense of his commitment to medicine and the well-being of his patients. The mark of a gifted doctor. Toni decided to put himself in Dr. B's care and give him the positive attitude he required.

Before leaving, they discussed methods of treatment Toni could practice outside the office: changing disturbing thought patterns to calming ones, massage and breathing techniques, and meditation.

"The only thing I meditate on, Doc, is whether the engine needs an overhaul or the burial ground."

Dr. B laughed. "Ask Celia to help you. Did you know she does massage? She has even worked on patients, here, from time to time. Great pair of hands."

Toni turned away quickly before Dr. B could see him blush, but not quick enough to miss the twinkle in the young doctor's eyes.

Under the treatment of Dr. Bonaventura—and Celia—Toni seemed to flourish. The breathing exercises were helpful, but it was the massages by Celia's capable hands that really worked the stress out of him. Relaxed, he could deal with things better, and he felt hope for a normal life beginning to grow again. At the Albatross house, Marianna watched as the relationship between Celia and Toni grew stronger.

"Do you think Celia and Toni are an item?" Marianna slid two homemade biscotti toward Spirito as he sipped his coffee. It was Sunday, the Urbinos' day off from the restaurant.

"Mmm, not sure." Spirito had his head in the pages of the *Union Tribune*.

"He didn't come home last night."

Spirito put down his paper and looked at his wife. He could tell the conversation was just beginning. "What I think doesn't matter; it's what *you* think that's important." He had that "happy wife, happy life" look on his face.

Marianna ignored the sarcasm. "Did Toni ever talk to you about his marriage with that barmaid in Philly?"

"A little. She was a good person, and I believe she loved him."

"What happened, then? The marriage lasted only a year before it was annulled. You know what that means."

Spirito sounded irritated. "No, but I'm sure you will tell me. What *does* that mean?"

"That it was not consummated."

"Marianna, is this any of our business? The man suffers from a mental illness because of what he saw in Africa. Maybe it affected his ability to . . ." Spirito's voice trailed off. He didn't need to finish the sentence.

"I've noticed a change in him since he's been seeing Dr. B," Marianna continued. "The treatments are helping, don't you think?"

"Whose treatments? The doc's or Celia's?" Spirito eyes were taunting her.

Marianna blushed. "So, his . . . uh . . . *problem* has been resolved?"

"Let's just say that Toni seems to have broken down a barrier with the help of a pair of talented hands."

Marianna blushed again. The conversation was over.

In the fall of 1931, Dr. Bonaventura asked for a second set of X-rays, looking for a reason why Toni's stomach pains persisted. This time he noticed something that wasn't there before.

"Toni, can we talk for a moment?" Celia had walked down to the Garage from her house and was standing next to him.

Toni had his head under the hood of Frank Boncompagni's latest treasure and didn't even look up. It was a 1914 Knox Runabout, pretty and flashy on the outside but a disaster underneath. The previous owner had not taken care of it, and now it was Toni's problem. Comp would not be happy unless the newest member of his harem was in perfect shape.

"Celia, what is it? I'm on a deadline with this car."

"It's important, Toni."

Finally, he tore himself away from the tangle of tubes and steel and looked at her. She was pale, and her eyes looked frightened.

"You have to see the doctor right away."

He didn't need to ask from the look on her face. It was something serious. Whatever it was, Toni reasoned, it could wait until tomorrow. Comp's latest treasure came first.

When Toni walked in to the office, Dr. Bonaventura came around from behind his desk and clasped his patient's hand. "Thank you for coming."

A shaky sigh escaped Toni's lips as he saw the X-ray image lit up on the far wall. "Good news travels fast, right, Doc? Celia said you wanted to see me."

Dr. B decided Toni would appreciate the more direct approach.

"The X-rays we took last week show a mass on the inner lining of your stomach." Dr. B walked over to the X-ray image and pointed. "Unfortunately, we see more masses in the liver and kidneys. It looks like cancer, and it has spread." The physician persona took over, and he continued almost impersonally. "There are encouraging clinical trials being done with hydrogen mustard gas that can atrophy the cancer with radiation—"

Toni held up a hand. "Enough. No needles, remember? And I'm not a lab rat." He paused. "Ironic, isn't it? I am the most content I have ever been in my life . . . and now this. I guess some happiness is better than none." Toni's head came up, and he looked directly into the doctor's eyes. "Don't think I'm not grateful for the help you have given me. It has made the last few years worth all the pain."

Dr. Bonaventura's young face looked worn. "I am not without hope. Tomorrow we will do a biopsy . . ."

The physician's voice trailed off when he saw Toni's face. More quietly, he said, "Go home and hug your loved ones. Make each day count."

Toni worked at the Garage for as long as he could. The pleasure he took in working on the cars and the distraction from thinking about his illness were important to him. Celia kept up her muscle relaxation treatments, and when he got too weak, she worked on him at the Albatross house. Having her there always made him feel better. The Urbino family took turns caring for his needs, Virginia spending all her free time reading stories, chatting about her last year at San Diego High School—anything to keep his spirits up.

"I won't be able to see you graduate," Toni smiled sadly. "I have great hopes for you. I know you will go far."

Virginia laid her head on his chest and wept.

Celia lit two candles now as she knelt before the statue of Our Lady after morning Mass.

Spirito had the hardest time of everyone accepting the cruel hand fate had dealt his older brother. He had received word this past February that their father, Francesco, had passed at the age of eighty-seven.

"I forgave him long ago," Toni told Spirito. "You must also. Be grateful for your health and your wife and daughter. Make peace with your past, or it will shorten your life."

Antonio Urbino died quietly on the morning of June second, 1932, with the Urbino family and Celia by his side. He seemed calm at the end, as if the events that had caused him so much pain had been put into proper perspective, and he had forgiven himself. He seemed to accept that there had been some meaning to his life, that he had given joy to others despite, or maybe because of, his struggles. Those present knew that even though they would be denied the pleasure of his company in the years ahead, Antonio Urbino was finally at peace.

The funeral was held at Our Lady of the Rosary with Father Rabagliati presiding. Dr. Bonaventura, the Zambonis, and friends

Toni had made in the community came to pay their last respects.

After the service, as the Urbino family turned to leave the church, they saw the last two rows filled with men in dark suits, their hats in their hands. Frank Boncompagni reached out and shook Spirito's hand as he passed. "He was a good man," he whispered. The men behind him nodded.

The procession bearing Toni's casket passed under the church entrance and down the stairs to the street. A flash of sunlight on steel greeted the congregation as they stepped out into the warm summer day.

Double-parked in front of the church and lined up halfway down Columbia Street was every car Toni had worked on belonging to Comp and Jimmy. The hoods sparkled, and the line of polished chrome bumpers gleamed in the morning sun.

It was the only way they knew how to pay tribute to the quiet mechanic who treated their cars like members of his family. Silently, the men in dark suits filed out of the church and drove them away.

Chapter 17

Taking Flight

SPIRITO WAS getting restless. His restaurant, The American, had been the realization of a dream, but the pride of ownership he had felt at the beginning was already fading. The regulars were fickle; if their day-to-day routine changed—a new job, a different apartment—they stopped coming. New customers complained if a dish wasn't hot enough or something on the menu wasn't available. And Fausto Tasca had gone back to Italy.

Toni's absence at the Albatross house was felt more deeply than anyone imagined. His portrait hung in a bedroom that was now empty and silent, the sad eyes and half smile a constant reminder of the gentle presence they had lost. Marianna and Virginia walked through the rooms like ghosts with faces drawn and eyes filled with sorrow. When Spirito couldn't stand it anymore, he retreated to his little shack in the backyard and tinkered with his latest project.

A while ago, the patch of ground to the right of the shed and the two side yards that flanked the house had been planted with concord grapes. When he was rewarded with a sizable crop, he crushed the grapes with the skins on to create the natural formation of yeast, added honey for sweetness and let it all sit in a vat for three days.

Back in his native Scheggino, he had watched the proprietors of the osterias make wine in a similar fashion. Homemade wine was commonplace in the countryside of Umbria, and every year, large glass containers were brought out of storerooms to be filled.

During the Prohibition years, Spirito had amassed a store of five-gallon jugs and fashioned tops for them designed to release gas but no oxygen. The liquid was siphoned into these containers to ferment, and a month later, the wine would be poured into bottles, ready to drink. When Prohibition was finally over, Spirito planned to serve the strong, hearty wine in his restaurant.

In July of 1932, however, a young couple approached Spirito with an offer to buy The American. They reminded him so much of his own family eight years ago—so hopeful, so anxious to be a success that the endless hours of work seemed like nothing. Without talking it over with his wife and daughter, he accepted the offer.

Three weeks after selling The American, Spirito noticed an empty space on the corner of First Avenue and Broadway. It was a prime location, and all the restaurant equipment was negotiable. The fact that the previous restaurant had failed did not enter Spirito's mind as he stood across the street and contemplated its future. It stood directly across from The Pickwick Hotel, a popular tourist destination, and the streetcar stopped right in front. At the very least, Spirito reasoned, he could do a good breakfast business.

The creative juices that had dried up under the weight of too many burdens began to flow, and he felt the familiar flicker of excitement take hold. Perhaps an Italian theme this time, where guests at the Pickwick could cross the street and imagine themselves transported to Italy. This was the opportunity his family needed to shake off the darkness that had descended upon them. He couldn't wait to break the news to Marianna and Virginia when he got home.

Virginia, at eighteen, had begun making her own plans. The joy of graduating from San Diego High School was overshadowed by her uncle's death, and the desire to extend her boundaries grew stronger. She wanted to be part of the great world she read about in books and magazines, not just watch it from the sidelines like her parents did.

The future she had envisioned for herself was taking shape.

After the dinner dishes had been cleared, Spirito asked Marianna and Virginia to join him at the table to discuss something important.

"I have found a great location for a new restaurant project," he began. Instead of murmurs of approval and a volley of questions, Spirito was met with silence. Marianna's face was a mask, and Virginia looked bored. Ignoring the lack of enthusiasm, he forged ahead.

"Picture this—a *Buon Appetito* sign across the front; red, white, and green awnings; bottles of Chianti lining the walls . . ." Spirito stood and opened his arms wide. "Italy in San Diego!" As an afterthought, he added quietly, "I will need your help, of course."

Now it was Marianna's turn. "You did not ask for our opinion when you sold The American even though Virginia and I worked just as hard as you to make it a success. How much profit did you make after adding up all the costs of ownership in eight years? And now you want to start all over again a few blocks away. Haven't you noticed on India Street the Italian restaurants starting to pop up? The Solunto and DePhilippis families have already started a trend, and your location is too far east to join the party."

Spirito was irritated. This was not the response he was hoping for. "It is directly opposite the Pickwick Hotel. We will make it on customers coming for breakfast alone."

Marianna sighed. "Italians don't eat breakfast, just coffee and pastry. The theme is wrong, then. The American was a better idea, but now you have given it to someone else."

A long pause followed Marianna's assessment.

Virginia decided now was the time to break the news.

"Mama, Papa, I have applied and been accepted as a student at the San Diego State Teacher's College. It is a training facility for teachers. The fall semester begins September fifteenth."

Both her parents were stunned. *College?* No one in the Urbino family had even *considered* going to college.

"How will you afford the tuition?" Spirito asked.

"I have been promised a job working in the college library, which will allow me to stay on campus during the day. They are willing to work with my schedule of classes, and the job will pay for my tuition."

"How will you get there? Where is this college?"

"It is a brand-new campus at the east end of Mission Valley. I can take the bus. Route 71 goes up Fifth Avenue to University Street and from there to the college."

Spirito and Marianna glanced at each other. They should have seen this coming. At eighteen, their daughter was poised to spread her wings, and they both knew they could not stand in her way.

"I will be happy to help at the restaurant on weekends and school breaks, and I will be home every night." Virginia's voice was gentle, but in her eyes, there was a steely resolve. Her future was hers to make, and no one was going to stop her.

Later that evening, after Spirito had retreated into his shed, Marianna sat alone in the darkness of her bedroom. Silently, she gave in to the tears that had been waiting to fall. A feeling of utter loneliness enveloped her, a loneliness she had not felt since the death of her daughter, Anna.

"Mama?" Virginia stood in the doorway. "What's wrong?"

Marianna looked up and saw a strong, confident woman standing there. When had that happened? The little girl who had met her at the train station was gone. Virginia had grown up. "I am afraid you will abandon us. Your new world will make us look uncouth and provincial." The tears began again, and she made no effort to stop them.

Virginia sat down next to her mother and put her arms around her. "I will not abandon you, Mama, and I will never be ashamed of being your daughter. Do you think I would leave you alone to pick up the pieces of Papa's broken dreams?"

Marianna looked hopeful. "You promise?"

Virginia nodded. "Cross my heart."

The new campus of San Diego State College had been relocated the year before from downtown to Montezuma Mesa. Overlooking the vast fields of Mission Valley, its new whitewashed buildings reflected San Diego's Spanish past, and the new state-of-the-art gymnasium was a confirmation of its future. The school was initially developed as a training facility for teachers with a curriculum focused on English, Arithmetic, and History. When it broadened to include certificates and degrees and then courses in French and Spanish, Virginia had taken notice.

At the end of her senior year of high school, Virginia had filled out an application and written an essay on immigrant families struggling to give their children a better life. In addition to the Romance languages, Virginia listed interests in literature, European history, and opera. Within a month, she'd received a letter from President Edward Hardy inviting her to join the college's fledgling language program in the fall. He personally promised to find her a job on campus to help with tuition.

As Virginia walked through the arcades to the main quad on her first day of classes, she knew she belonged there. The corridors of academia—the Library Tower and the classroom buildings—beckoned. She thought of what her mother had said about a whole new world opening up, a world where her parents could not follow or guide her. The iron resolve weakened for a fraction of a second, and she wondered if she could handle the challenges that lay ahead. Then she thought about the alternative—a life of cooking, cleaning, and diapering babies. All that would come later, but now was her chance to take a bite out of the apple and see how it tasted.

The French classes with Madame Browning were her favorite.

She had been placed in the beginning level at the start of the term, but after the first week, Madame moved her up to intermediate. In Virginia's opinion, even the more advanced students were sadly lacking basic grammar and vocabulary skills.

Toward the end of the fall semester, Madame Browning approached Virginia as she gathered her books together at the end of class.

"Mademoiselle Urbino, may I have a word with you?"

Virginia's heart leaped into her throat. She was still intimidated by the woman who not only headed the language department and taught all the French classes but also organized the Alpha Mu Gamma Sorority and Le Circle French Club on campus.

Despite being total academic snobs, Dr. Eliza Browning and her husband, Lee, who taught Spanish, were worshiped by students and faculty alike. A reference from either one could guarantee a job in any school on the West Coast after graduation. The couple, walking through the quad at lunchtime, could not have been more different. Eliza's tall, athletic body contrasted sharply with her bookish-looking husband. In spirit and vision, however, they were equally matched. The goal they shared—building a strong language department in a growing institution—solidified the partnership. Only later, when she got to know them better, did Virginia notice the cracks.

"I have been watching you," Madame Browning began. "You have a wonderful proficiency in both French and Spanish. Señor Browning thinks so too. Would you consider tutoring the less gifted students outside of class? The pay is good."

Virginia appreciated the compliment, but she needed to be honest about her situation. "I am honored to be considered, but my hours at the library take up all my free time, and I need the job to pay for my tuition."

"If you were free of that obligation, would you enjoy tutoring?"

"Oh, yes. I'd much prefer it to checking out people's books and pretending to be busy."

Madame laughed. "I will see what I can do."

The Brownings conferred with President Hardy, and it was decided that Virginia would better serve the school in a tutoring role. There were plenty of students who could be library clerks. For Virginia, the increased pay was incidental. She would gladly have done it for free.

In her new role, Virginia demonstrated an enthusiasm for her subject even if the students she tutored did not. It amazed her how many of the jocks expected to get a pass on proficiency simply because they could throw a ball or run fast.

"Are you Miss Urbino?"

Virginia looked up from her desk. Chip Reardon's huge frame was blocking the doorway. She recognized him right away. You had to be from another planet not to know who *he* was: San Diego State's star quarterback and the language department's worst student.

"Mrs. Browning sent me. I guess we're going to be study buddies." The athlete grinned conspiratorially at Virginia as he lumbered into the room and squeezed his body into a desk chair in the front row. His knees bumped the top of the desk, and his shoulders hung out a foot from either side of the backrest.

Study buddies? You've got to be kidding, Virginia thought. Based on his grade point average, "studying" was probably the last thing on his mind.

Virginia pulled herself up and tried to look professional. "I think buddies is the wrong word, Chip. As your *tutor*, I am here to improve your study habits—especially where French is concerned."

Chip looked appropriately chastised. "Yeah, sorry. I guess it's no secret I'd rather get tackled by a linebacker than take a French vocabulary test."

"Funny you should mention the word vocabulary because that is exactly what I have here. This test will help me determine where your strengths and weaknesses are."

Chip shifted uncomfortably in his tiny seat. He set his baby blue eyes on his tutor's face and gave her a seductive smile. "Why don't we talk about you instead, Miss Urbino. I'm sure you are much more interesting than some silly old test."

Virginia whipped out a sheet of paper and found a pencil. "This shouldn't take you more than thirty minutes, but if it takes longer, I will be happy to wait here until you are finished."

Chip's face fell when he looked at the test. There were at least twenty questions, all of them in French. His smile was gone, and beads of sweat formed at the edges of his short blonde hair. "Uh . . . one thing, Miss Urbino . . . Does spelling count?"

Virginia wasn't sure if she had heard correctly. "Does spelling count on a vocabulary test? Chip, what do you think?"

Despite the Chip Reardons of the world, Virginia reveled in campus life. The clubs were a real treat and a departure from the life Virginia had known growing up. There were lectures by professors from other universities and coffee and dainty pastries to enjoy, but the best part was getting the chance to practice her language skills on esteemed professionals. She was fearless in engaging them in conversation, and even the most pretentious of intellectuals was charmed by her.

Madame Browning had just finished giving Virginia the tutoring schedule for the coming week. She put down her pencil and smiled. "Virginia, are you free this Saturday? Lee and I want you to come to our home for lunch."

Virginia had to think. She always worked at her father's restaurant on weekends, and with the Depression showing no signs of letting up, her parents needed all the help they could get. On the other hand, how often did an undergrad receive an invitation to lunch at the home of her superiors? Refusing such an invitation, Virginia knew, would be rude. "I would be delighted . . . and honored. When shall I be there?"

The Brownings lived in a two-story Spanish Revival on Ampudia Street in Mission Hills. Taking the streetcar up First Avenue and down Washington Street to Fort Stockton Drive, Virginia was impressed by the charm and eclecticism of the neighborhood. She caught glimpses of Point Loma through tree-lined streets on one side and gaping canyons giving way to Mission Valley on the other. On the riviera above Old Town, fresh breezes from the Pacific cooled tiny bungalows and mansions alike.

Walking through the foyer and into the dining room of the Browning home, Virginia saw a table laid out with exquisite china and stemware, and a centerpiece of bird of paradise stems.

"It is all so lovely. Thank you for inviting me."

Lee came forward and led her to the table. As Virginia reached for the chair, he stopped her. "A lady of breeding will always wait for a gentleman to pull out the chair for her, and as she sits, he will adjust it. You must allow him to do that. Here, I will demonstrate."

Once seated, Eliza explained to Virginia that a knowledge of proper etiquette would help her move in certain circles with ease. "The Alliance Française, for example, is giving a buffet luncheon at the Casa del Prado in Balboa Park next Saturday. We would like you to come as our guest."

"Eliza is the keynote speaker," Lee added. "Today, we will be instructing you on the manners necessary for such an occasion."

Virginia flushed with embarrassment. They must think her a

person of low breeding to go to all this trouble. Did she appear so ignorant that lessons had to be given? Provincial. Uncouth. Those were the words her mother has used. Is that what these people thought of her family? Eliza and Lee were looking at her so kindly, thinking they were doing their protégé a tremendous favor. How could she show anything but gratitude even if what she felt was humiliation?

Virginia sensed this was a pivotal moment in her life. She could take offence at the inference, or she could embrace it in the spirit in which it was given.

Smiling coyly, Virginia looked down at the ornate table setting. "What an array of cutlery I see here. I certainly could use your guidance. At my father's restaurant, the customers are lucky to get a knife and fork!"

Chapter 18

Changing of the Guard

SHE KNEW there was something wrong the minute she stepped into the house. Virginia had been dropped off by a classmate after a late lecture and had set her books down in the darkened living room. The sound came again—a cry of pain and a string of curses in Italian. *Papa.* She rushed through the hallway toward the back bedroom.

Spirito lay sprawled on the floor, a gaping wound running down the length of his leg.

There was blood everywhere. Marianna was trying to stop the flow with cotton strips soaked with hydrogen peroxide.

"*Sale! Porta me sale!*" Spirito kept repeating, his gaze fixated on the deep cut and the blood oozing out of it.

"He keeps asking for salt. He wants to pour it into the wound to stop the bleeding." Marianna's voice was shaky.

"Salt? That's crazy."

"We do it in the country back home all the time. Salt prevents infection."

"What about the pain?"

"You need to have plenty of grappa handy."

Spirito was becoming hysterical and trying to get up.

"*Sale!*" He was screaming now.

Virginia went to the kitchen and found the box labeled "iodized salt" and headed back to the bedroom. As she knelt beside him, Spirito sat up and grabbed the box with his free hand and flipped open the lid with the other. In the next instant, he tossed away the bandages and began pouring the salt directly into the wound. The cut sizzled like sausage frying in a pan, and the box slid from his hand, scattering white granules all over the floor. The sound that came out of his mouth was one of pure agony, like the cry from a dying soldier on a battlefield.

"Get the whiskey," Marianna told Virginia through clenched teeth.

Half a bottle was poured down Spirito's throat before the screaming and the bleeding stopped.

"He needs to go to the hospital," Virginia whispered. "This could get infected."

"No hospitals!" Spirito thundered.

"Dr. B will come by tomorrow and take a look at you." Virginia's voice was firm. "There will be no argument."

Spirito grumbled but offered no resistance. Dr. B was family.

"What happened?" Virginia demanded after they had cleaned the wound and put Spirito in bed.

Marianna bowed her head. Virginia led her to the living room where they could speak privately.

"He slipped coming out of the shed and fell over an upright saw. He had left it in the path and forgotten about it."

"Was he drunk?"

Marianna was silent. Virginia knew the answer. She had smelled the alcohol on him when she first entered the room.

"I know I haven't been home as much lately. You need to tell me . . . is his drinking out of control?"

One look from Marianna was enough.

Virginia was shocked. "Has he ever laid a hand on you?"

Marianna's response was immediate. "Never. He bears his burdens alone. That's why he drinks—to forget them."

"What burdens? Is the restaurant losing money?"

"Yes. Every day. The night crowd isn't there because we're too far away from Little Italy, and we're losing the regulars for breakfast because they all know he drinks. His hangover is obvious, and his mood unpredictable."

"Why didn't you tell me, Mama?"

"What can you do? Besides, your reputation at the college is at stake. You do not need us to bring you down."

"You are my family. Don't hide things from me. I need to know so I can help."

Marianna nodded and closed her eyes. "He needs to sell the *Buon Appetito* before it loses all its value. But then, what do we live on?"

"I was going to tell you this weekend. I am graduating this June and have been offered a fellowship at State for a year. One hundred eighty dollars a month. I can support us."

Marianna's eyes shone with a mixture of pride and relief as if a great load had been lifted from her. "*Figlia mia*. What a daughter you are."

When Dr. B came to look at the wound the next morning, his response surprised Virginia. "Spirito's treatment was better and quicker than what the ER could have done. Salt cauterizes and disinfects at the same time—if you can stand the pain." Dr. B smiled down on his patient. "You're a tough son of a bitch, aren't you?"

Spirito chuckled, then winced as if it even hurt to laugh.

Spirito's wound healed, but it left a permanent scar on both his leg and his psyche. He seemed to have become an old man overnight, and his frustration over his waning strength made him difficult to live with. He showed up for work less and less, letting his staff take over the mechanics of running the restaurant. Even from the start, everyone knew the *Buon Appetito* was going to fail. It was like the black sheep of Little Italy; while the other Italian eateries further west on India Street prospered, it limped along as if waiting for someone to put it out of its misery.

The man who approached Spirito about buying the restaurant looked familiar. The hair was a little grayer, and he had dropped the nickname once his business interests became legitimate. Frank Boncompagni. Lou's bread and butter.

"Good to see you, my friend. My cars miss your brother." There was an embarrassed pause, and Frank's voice became gentler. "And so do I."

Spirito acknowledged the remark with grace. "Thank you. We miss him too, every day."

"I would like to buy your establishment. The location is excellent, right across from the Pickwick."

That's what I thought too, in the beginning, Spirito wanted to say. He saw no need to tell a prospective buyer that location wasn't everything. "What are you thinking of doing with it? Another restaurant? I can let you have the equipment at cost."

"Some of it, certainly," Frank assured him. "I am thinking of opening a drinking establishment that serves food, instead of the other way around. Open patio upstairs, private rooms for parties, entertainment for our maritime crowd."

Spirito was silent. He realized immediately the appeal of such a concept. Why hadn't he thought of that? Jealousy rose up like bile, but he fought it down. He had a sale to make. He had received two offers in six months—one for three hundred dollars and the other for one hundred fifty. "One thousand dollars, and I'll throw in everything."

It was an outrageous offer, and they both knew it. But there was a soft spot in Frank Boncompagni's heart, even if the newspapers said otherwise.

"Done," he said.

The handshake was firm, the smile in place, but when Spirito looked in Frank's eyes he saw pity mixed with something else. That something else looked surprisingly like compassion.

The one bright spot in Spirito's life was his daughter. Just watching her grow into a confident, accomplished woman was a joy. Her passion for language, art, and history made his head spin, and there seemed to be no end to the lectures and club gatherings she was invited to. The only thing missing in her life, as he saw it, was a man. She was so focused on her career that she didn't even notice the young men in the neighborhood. Spirito knew that some of them admired her. Like George Hawley.

"Hey Frank, I saw your daughter at Mass last Sunday. Is she married yet?"

"Not yet. Interested?'

George was sweeping the sidewalk in front of his half-timber on the corner of Hawthorn and Albatross. He stopped and looked at Spirito. "Like she'd be interested in me. I'm nothing more than a shop owner."

"Don't underestimate yourself," Spirito countered. "San Diego Hardware is creating a name for itself here in town."

George had opened his doors on Fifth Avenue at the same time Spirito signed a lease on the *Buon Appetito*. It had grown from a one-room hole-in-the-wall to a full-service hardware store selling anything from crowbars to clawfoot tubs. His focus on high-end fixtures for the fancy homes up on Bankers Hill had put him on the map.

"Virginia's going to State College now, right? I knew she was going to be a scholar . . . always studying."

"Why don't you ask her out?" Spirito volunteered.

"She wouldn't be happy selling toilets." George smiled sadly. "Besides, I need a wife who knows tools and can work a cash register.

That doesn't sound like Virginia."

Spirito had to agree.

On the morning of June twenty-second, the graduating class of 1936 gathered on the field of San Diego State's Aztec Stadium to receive their diplomas. Spirito and Marianna were among the three thousand friends and family sitting in the stands shielding their eyes from the bright summer sun. Through the endless introductions of faculty and the long speeches of administrators, everyone waited to hear that one special name called out and the roar of applause that would follow. Each graduate had a family that had struggled and sacrificed to give them the opportunity for higher education and a better life. Many, like Virginia's parents, hoped their child's degree would translate to a well-paying job and financial security.

The graduates knew they were entering an uncertain future—a continuing Depression and a war on the horizon. Optimism and youth are good companions, however, and as the caps flew in the air, there was a universal feeling that their generation had the potential for greatness.

After the ceremony, Virginia searched for her parents amid the crowds entering the gymnasium where tables of refreshments had been set up for the graduates and their families. When she caught sight of them, she groaned. Dad was sweating profusely in his old wool suit. She knew it was the only one he owned, but *wool*? *It must be eighty degrees in the shade today.* Why couldn't he have bought a new suit for his daughter's big day? *The first thing I'm going to do with my new paycheck this fall is take him to a tailor*, she promised herself. Mom looked presentable as always, but her eyes skittered self-consciously around the room as if she didn't know how to behave. No matter, Virginia reminded herself. These were her parents, and she was not going to be ashamed of them. Academic blue bloods be damned.

"Papa, Mama!" Virginia waved and made her way toward them.

Marianna breathed a sigh of relief and hugged her daughter fiercely. Spirito was struggling to control his emotions.

"We are so proud of you," her parents said in unison, and they all laughed.

"Come, I want you to meet my professors."

They walked through the crowd, Virginia introducing them to students and faculty before stopping at the table reserved for heads of departments and the president.

"Madame and Señor Browning, these are my parents, Spirito . . . uh . . . Frank and Marianna Urbino."

Dr. Browning took in Spirito's sweat-drenched face and Marianna's anxious eyes. She sniffed and extended two fingers. "A pleasure, I'm sure." Her husband barely nodded.

"Virginia, are these your parents?" An elderly man with white hair and rimless spectacles strode forward to meet them. He held out his hand to Spirito and shook it vigorously.

"Papa, Mama, this is Dr. Edward Hardy, our President Emeritus," Virginia said proudly.

"A pleasure to meet you," Dr. Hardy continued. "The essay Virginia wrote in her application was about both of you. It impressed me greatly. The values you have upheld and the sacrifices you have made produced a fine young lady. You should be proud of her."

"We are, Dr. Hardy." Marianna was beaming. The Urbinos were all wiping away tears now. Emotion had taken precedence over propriety, and no one was objecting.

When Eliza Browning addressed the president, her manner was decidedly warmer. "Virginia will be with us another year as a fellow at the college's language department. She will be teaching some classes and finishing up her tutoring assignments. After that, we will let her go out into the real world."

"I hope it will be ready for her," Dr. Hardy remarked with a smile.

Chapter 19

Reunions

COFFEE AND the newspaper were two things Spirito looked forward to even if the rest of the day was a washout; a man without a job has a lot of time on his hands. A headline on page two caught his eye.

"Pan Am Dixie Clipper Makes Maiden Voyage Across Atlantic." There was a picture of two passengers boarding the plane from the harbor at Marseilles. Spirito looked closer at the woman being escorted by a man in his thirties. They both looked familiar. The caption underneath read:

"Agatha Altarocca and son, Santo Urbino, board the Yankee Clipper for return flight to New York. Story on pg. 4."

Grabbing his reading glasses, Spirito flipped to the society section where there was another photo, this time a headshot of a woman nearing fifty.

Images, like flashbacks of a dream, surfaced—a blood-red sunset and a room seared with the last rays of a dying sun, two bodies spent with passion like embers after a blazing fire. If he lived to be a hundred, he would never forget. Spirito read the article beneath the photo:

On June 22, 1939, The Yankee Clipper, carrying 22 passengers, returns to New York via Marseilles, France. Aboard the transatlantic flight are European Tastemaker Agatha Altarocca and her son, Santo Urbino. Santo heads the international branch of the Urbino Tartufo

Foundation, and it is rumored he will soon open a headquarters in Manhattan. His mother, Agatha, has created a name for herself, designing the reception rooms for all the Urbino Offices in Europe. She is planning to do the interiors of the flagship showroom in New York where she will be working with Moriano Fortuny of the famed Fortuny Fabric Company. Miss Altarocca will be in Manhattan for three weeks and will be staying at the Plaza Hotel. When asked why she decided to fly in one of the first airplanes to cross the Atlantic, Miss Altarocca replied: "I have never been in an airplane, and I have never been to America. I am looking forward to doing both!"

Spirito felt the old adrenaline race through his body. Why couldn't he go to New York to see her? Even if it was just a glimpse from afar. No doubt her schedule was busy and her movements closely monitored, but at least he could try. There would be no more trips to Italy for him. At sixty, he was sure of that. This would be his last chance to see her again. He looked at today's date. June twenty-third. Agatha was returning to Italy on July sixth. If he was going to do this, he had to move quickly.

That same day, Spirito notified Marianna and Virginia about his plans to connect with his sister, Ginerva, who lived in Pennsylvania. It had been ten years since he had last seen her, he reminded them. It was time for a visit.

"I will come too," Marianna spoke up. "I haven't seen my sister, Delia or her husband for nearly fifteen years. They have three teenage children now. Since they will never come here, I will go to them. We're not getting any younger, and this could be the last time we see each other."

Spirito had not expected this. Marianna was becoming so set in her ways now that Virginia was teaching full time, he never imagined she would want to come with him. He felt a twinge of guilt. He hadn't even thought to invite her. It would make getting away more difficult, but he could not deny his wife the opportunity to visit her relatives.

"Of course you should go. We will be leaving at the end of this week. It will be a short stay, only two weeks, three weeks including the trip by train. Beyond that, we cannot impose on the hospitality of our families."

The following day, Spirito walked downtown to Marston's Department Store and was fitted for a new suit. He also bought three new shirts, two pairs of pants, and underwear. That evening he dragged out the rusty pair of dumbbells from the basement and started working out.

Marianna watched the transformation with skepticism until the hard liquor bottles were emptied one by one into the sink. Whatever was motivating her husband to get healthy, she was not about to question it.

A few days before the departure date, Marianna began organizing her suitcase. It was already packed to the brim with no place for the little gifts she had planned to bring to Delia's children. *Spirito will have room*, she thought. But looking around, she realized his suitcase wasn't even out yet. A pile of his things was accumulating on the dresser, and she shoved it all aside to make room for the gifts. A bit of newspaper, neatly folded, escaped from the pile and fluttered to the floor. Bending to pick it up, she saw a picture of a woman in her fifties and a younger man boarding a plane. The picture was grainy, but there was no mistaking the fact that the man in the photo looked exactly like her husband. A separate article was included with a picture of the woman and her biography. Agatha Altarocca from Umbria. Her son, thirty-two, was named Santo Urbino.

Suddenly Marianna made the connection. *Spirito Santo*. Holy Spirit in Italian. The man in the photo had to be her husband's child conceived before Marianna had met him in 1912.

She had heard pieces of the story of why Spirito had to leave Italy.

Spirito himself had alluded to a previous relationship during their courtship, and she knew he had left Scheggino under a cloud. There had been rumors about a duel over a girl, a murder, and a quick escape. The existence of a bastard child was never mentioned, but the proof was in the clipping she held in her hand. And now, Agatha and Santo were in New York, the same exact time Spirito was planning a trip there. The abrupt change in his lifestyle made sense now, Marianna thought. He wanted to look his best for a reunion with the Italian family he had left behind.

Carefully, she refolded the articles and placed them under the pile on the dresser. The trip would go on as planned, Marianna decided. Spirito could keep his little secret.

By the time Marianna and Spirito arrived from the train station to her sister's house in Trenton, it was early evening. Delia and Emilio Ricci and their three children lived on Swan Street, in the Chambersburg neighborhood of Trenton, New Jersey. The three-bedroom red brick walk-up was near the wire factory where Emilio worked as an inspector. All the adjoining townhomes, along with most residences, were occupied by Italian immigrants.

As they walked through the neighborhood, the sound of voices carried across the warm summer night. Children rode bikes and played on the narrow strip of sidewalk in front of their houses while parents and grandparents sat on porches watching them. Neighbors called out to one another in snatches of broken English and Italian.

"Marco, dinner time. Dove stai?" A woman's voice rang out.

A young boy answered. "Can Marco eat at our house? He says our marinara has more meat in it than yours."

The woman snorted. "That so? Tell him we pick him up *after* we go for ice cream."

Laughter.

A wave of nostalgia passed over Marianna as she remembered her early years in Trenton and the community that had welcomed her family so warmly. Then she remembered the stifling heat and the freezing winters.

"*Carissima!*" Delia opened the door and held out her arms. "Finally, you are here. Come in and let me look at you."

A boy of about sixteen stood just inside the open door. He had his mother's eyes and his father's build. He pulled himself up like an adult and held out his hand. "I am Primo. Pleased to meet you."

Emilio stole up from behind him and engulfed Marianna in a giant bear hug. Two other faces hung shyly in the background.

"This is Emilia. She is fourteen." A slim, timid girl slipped out from behind her father. She smiled and did a small curtsey.

"And our youngest, Amedeo, will be eleven this year."

The boy stepped forward. "I like to be called by my middle name, John."

"He's ashamed of his Italian heritage. Wants to be an American," his father explained, irritably. "Amedeo was my mother's family name. Means nothing to these kids."

The boy gave his father a scathing look but kept silent.

"John it is, my man," Spirito assured the boy. "In San Diego, they call me Frank." Their eyes met in mutual understanding.

"Let me show you to your rooms." Emilio gestured to the stairs. "You will be staying in Primo's room. It has a view of the backyard."

When Marianna started to protest, Delia winked at her. "Primo prefers the basement bedroom. He has more privacy—to smoke his cigarettes."

Their oldest son's face turned red.

"He thinks we don't know," Delia whispered in her sister's ear.

Delia looked in good health, Marianna thought, and content. The day the two sisters had embraced at the dock in Philadelphia came back to her. Delia had been a frightened but determined little thing, anxious to make a new life for herself. The arranged marriage to an immigrant from Scheggino—who was a little on the short side—had worked out well.

The next morning, Marianna announced to Spirito, "Delia and I are going to Holy Sepulchre Cemetery today to put flowers on Anna's grave. Will you be coming with us?" She stared at him defiantly, daring him to refuse.

"I need to go into Manhattan today to take care of some things. You and Delia go. Spend the day together and catch up. I will be home for dinner."

Spirito's answer did not surprise her, but Marianna hoped he felt at least an ounce of shame for choosing to visit an old lover instead of his daughter's grave.

Spirito's heart ached at the thought of seeing the little granite gravestone again. It had been almost twenty years since the accident. He felt torn in two directions as he always did when it came to his other life.

Over coffee that morning, Spirito had scanned the society page of the *New York Times* looking for news of Agatha. The clipping he had brought mentioned she and Santo would be staying at the Plaza Hotel in Manhattan, but short of walking up to the front desk and asking to see her, he had no plan.

He looked up at the eighteen-story building, mustering up the courage to go in. The Plaza Hotel was magnificent. Set back from Fifth Avenue and Central Park South, its white brick and marble façade dominated the Grand Army Plaza like a monarch surveying her subjects. There were plenty of fancy hotels in Manhattan, but, through the years, The Plaza had maintained her sovereignty and reputation for good taste and sophistication. He couldn't help but be reminded of how high a servant girl from Umbria with similar attributes had risen. Straightening his shoulders and brushing off his new suit, Spirito strode into the lobby.

The man behind the front desk seemed to blend in perfectly with his surroundings. His skin color matched the oak panels, and his gaze was as inscrutable as the safe deposit boxes behind him.

"May I help you, sir?"

Spirito produced an envelope with the name "Agatha Altarocca" written on it. "Will you please give this to the lady when she comes in."

The man behind the desk made no effort to touch the envelope, regarding it as if it might contaminate him.

"Miss Altarocca, I presume you mean?" A long emphasis on the *Miss*.

"Yes. Be sure that she gets it." Spirito looked the oak-colored man in the eye before he turned and walked out of the hotel.

The note inside the envelope was brief:

Cara Agatha,

I am at the Café Negrito across the street from your hotel. I would like to see you.

Your Spirito

He left no last name. He knew there was a chance she would not return for hours, and even then, she may not want to see him. He had to take that chance.

Spirito sat at a table in view of the hotel and ordered lunch. The prices were outrageous, but he had to spend money to keep the table. An hour went by. He ordered a coffee. Another hour, another coffee. The waiter was eyeing him critically now, most likely wondering how long this was going to go on. By three in the afternoon, it was obvious Spirito would have to leave. He was contemplating moving to a park bench when a taxi pulled up to the hotel and a woman got out. She wore a peach linen suit and stiletto heels to match. A veiled pill box hat shielded her face from the crowds on the street, but Spirito recognized her in an instant. As she walked into the hotel, he held his breath and waited.

The desk clerk, nearing the end of his shift, pushed an envelope toward the elegant lady waiting for her key.

"Someone left this for you earlier today."

"Who was it?"

"*A gentleman*." An eyebrow lifted, and the clerk continued. "He didn't give his name. He looked like he didn't belong here, if you catch my drift." The clerk sniffed and smiled knowingly.

"No, I don't believe I *catch your drift*, as you put it." The elegant lady reached for the envelope and walked toward the elevators.

Thirty minutes had passed since Spirito saw Agatha enter the hotel. Too long, he whispered to himself. She was not coming. He dropped his head and covered his face with his hands.

"How long have you been waiting?" A gentle voice spoke to him in Italian. Spirito's head jerked up before he could wipe his tear-streaked face.

He rose quickly and reached for her hands. "I lost count after three hours."

Agatha scanned the bar and the nearby crowds. "Let us walk." Abruptly she turned and headed east. Spirito paid the bill and followed her.

Together they crossed Fifth Avenue and passed into the leafy green anonymity of Central Park. Silently, she slipped her hand into his.

"Let's go toward Gapstow Bridge and the bird sanctuary. It is quiet there."

Hand in hand, they strolled under the branches of giant magnolia trees and breathed in the fragrance of lavender lining the walkways. They talked about her work and her growing commitment to the Urbino Empire. It had all become so grand, so important.

Working with designer Elsie McNeill, who had introduced Fortuny Fabrics to America, had been the pinnacle of Agatha's career. But for the Urbinos, it was only the beginning. Agatha was getting tired of the constant pressure to create something new.

"What about Santo? Is he happy with his life?" Spirito looked at her hopefully.

"His marriage to Lidia is a good one. There is a son, but Santo is gone from home too much to be a good father. He is an important man now. I think you would be proud of him."

"Does he resent me—the father that was never part of his life?"

"The life he knows is not the one you and I would have had, Spirito. Claudio and Olivia are his family—and the Foundation. I sometimes think he is too obsessed with success, but that is the Urbino way."

"What kind of life would we have had, Agatha?"

They were sitting on a bench overlooking the Promontory with the bridge and the outline of Midtown Manhattan in the distance. Agatha laid her head on his shoulder and closed her eyes. "I think about that more often than I care to admit. Our relationship has been like a fantasy. The day-to-day struggle is not so glamorous, I'm guessing."

Spirito was silent. She was right, of course. If he had married her and brought her to America, would she have been happy working in a diner? "Not so glamorous," he murmured.

They sat quietly for a while, the birds and the distant sounds of the city a soothing backdrop for their thoughts.

"Agatha, that day in Spello . . . I want to tell you how much that meant to me . . . how it changed my life." She tried to withdraw her hand, but he held on tight. "It made me realize that you still loved me, that you never stopped. It gave my life some meaning . . . that I had made a difference for someone. Do you understand?"

Agatha nodded. "That day changed my life too."

"How?"

She laughed softly.

Agatha glanced at her watch. He could tell that the subject was closed.

He walked her to the edge of the park where they had first entered. They held each other for a long time without speaking, mentally tucking the memory in a safe place where they could relive it again and again in the years ahead. Spirito breathed in the scent of her, the warmth of her body next to his. He felt the familiar ache. No matter how many years separated them, he would never be free of it.

Agatha was the first to break free. She started to walk away, then stopped and turned to face him.

Fingering a cameo locket that hung around her neck, she reached up and unclasped the gold chain. The locket fell into her palm. Looking into her lover's eyes, she closed his hands over it with her own.

"I want you to have this . . . to remember me by."

Spirito looked down at the fragile cameo. It was an ivory profile of a beautiful woman. "Open it."

Inside, a tiny photograph of a young man stared back at him. Spirito looked at her questioningly.

"Your son."

Spirito closed the locket and brought it to his lips. "I will treasure it always."

Agatha sighed. The sound carried a lifetime of sadness in it. "Your wife is a lucky woman."

She turned and walked out of the park and into the fading twilight.

As he watched her slim, elegant figure cross Fifth Avenue and enter the hotel, he knew it would be for the last time.

Chapter 20

Loose Ends

MARIANNA placed the bouquet of flowers on the grave of her youngest daughter. Long-stemmed roses would have been better, but all she could find was a pathetic bunch of half-dead daisies. The plot at the southern end of Holy Sepulchre Cemetery was covered with weeds. Compared to the other infant graves nearby, it looked abandoned. Was it really nineteen years ago? The memories were dimming, and the face of her little girl was no longer clear. Anna Urbino would have been twenty-four now, and Marianna couldn't help wondering how their lives would have been different had she lived. Would Virginia and Anna have been close? Even at five and six, their personalities had been polar opposite.

Maybe they would have drifted apart like Spirito and his brother, Urbano. You never knew with siblings.

Marianna watched Delia pulling weeds and tidying up the little gravesite. She wished her sister had settled closer to San Diego so they could see each other more often. She needed a confidante.

"Spirito is seeing his old lover today in Manhattan," Marianna said suddenly. She had wanted to tell Delia all day but had been too humiliated. Now it was out.

Delia stopped pulling weeds and looked up. "*Per cari da*, for the love of God, what are you saying?"

"The woman he wanted to marry before he met me is in New York. She is famous now. It was in the paper. That's how he found out."

"This sounds better than the romance novel I'm reading," Delia said as she led Marianna out of the cemetery. Let's find a place to sit, I need to hear this from the beginning."

They sat at a Woolworth's lunch counter in Hamilton and ordered two chocolate shakes. Marianna told Delia everything.

"Are you sure her son is Spirito's? A newspaper photo is not concrete proof."

"They look identical, Delia. And the name . . . he goes by Urbino, not his mother's maiden name, Altarocca."

"Do you know what happened before Spirito left for America the first time? You mentioned a murder. He killed someone in a duel over her?"

"I'm afraid that's all I know. I didn't ask too many questions when we were getting married. I suppose I should have, but everything was so rushed."

"I wonder why." Delia gave her sister a knowing look. "He owes you an explanation, if you ask me. See that you get it. Secrets between married couples can have deadly consequences. Not that Spirito is a serial killer or anything." Delia's eyes had a wicked look.

"I promise I will get the whole story," Marianna assured her. "But don't be surprised if Spirito sleeps in the basement tonight with Primo."

Both sisters smiled over their shakes and ordered two more.

Marianna stood with her back to the window of Primo's bedroom. Spirito sat on the bed facing her. "I know about Agatha Altarocca, so don't bother making up a story."

In a way, Spirito was relieved. He had been dreading coming back from Manhattan and facing his wife's scrutiny. Now he could tell her the truth.

"How do you know?"

"I found the newspaper clippings by accident and put it together. Why didn't you tell me you had a son?"

"I was afraid you would refuse to marry me."

Marianna's resolve weakened. She crossed the room and sat on the bed next to him. "Just tell me what happened."

Reliving it all again, Spirito realized how impetuous he had been, risking his life and his family's reputation by murdering his rival. Then he remembered seeing Agatha's bruised body huddled on the bed like a wounded animal. Armando had brutally raped her and deserved to be punished. Spirito was certain that, had he not intervened, Armando would have gotten away with his crime. He hoped Marianna would see it that way.

Listening to Spirito's explanation, Marianna was forming her own opinions. It was obvious her husband had acted in an outburst of passionate rage when he had shot his rival. He wanted revenge for the assault on his lover. The arrangement he had agreed to with Pietro to leave Italy was a lucky break for him. If he had stayed, Armando's family would have sought vengeance as well.

"When you went back in 1912, did you look for Agatha? She should have been your first choice for a bride."

Spirito hesitated before answering. Truthfully, he should have said yes, but he didn't want Marianna to feel like she was second best.

"I made some inquiries, but she had disappeared. Besides, that part of my life was over." He gathered Marianna in his arms. "I met you, and I saw the woman who would complement the life I was planning in America. Your loyalty, your strength of character, your willingness to follow me into the unknown. You became my first choice in my new life."

These were powerful words, but Marianna wasn't finished. "You have a son."

"Santo does not know me," Spirito answered.

His wife had not asked for details about his trip back in 1923, for the reading of Ferdinando's will, and Spirito had not offered any. He was a firm believer that discretionary confessions were the secret to lasting marriages.

They held each other, her head resting in the hollow of his neck and his face nestled in her gray-streaked hair.

"What was it like seeing her again?"

"I realized what a lucky man I am to have you."

Marianna sighed and held on tighter.

The Riccis stood on the tiny porch waving goodbye. They made promises to visit San Diego, but everyone knew it would never happen. There were too many miles in between, and Delia and her family were not adventurous. The snapshots Spirito had taken would be the last tangible memory of the people and the community they had once called home.

Marianna and Spirito boarded the train bound for Bethlehem, Pennsylvania, and the current residence of Ginerva Urbino Gowenlock. Ginny had moved around a lot since coming to America in 1911. San Diego, Sacramento, and now Pennsylvania. She had three grown children from her first marriage and a new husband no one knew much about. Her youngest son, Albert, was reported to have a learning disability and still lived at home.

The neighborhood where the Gowenlocks lived was decidedly working class—dilapidated houses and neglected yards sandwiched in between bars and seedy businesses. Ginny's two-bedroom bungalow did not stand out.

A young man of about twenty answered the doorbell.

"Ma, those people are here," the boy hollered into the dark interior, never taking his eyes off the visitors. He stared at them suspiciously, without a glimmer of recognition.

"Well, let them in," a woman's voice answered impatiently. "I'm coming." Holding onto a cane for balance, an older woman limped toward them. "Spirito, Marianna. Welcome."

Spirito scarcely recognized his sister. Ginny had always been the beauty in the family—lustrous auburn hair, clear skin, and a figure that turned heads. What he saw now was a woman bowed down with the burden of hard times and broken dreams. She was forty-seven, three years younger than Agatha, but looked twice her age. Not everyone had the benefit of a pampered life, he realized, but the years had been more than cruel to his youngest sister.

"Bet you didn't recognize me." Ginny laughed bitterly. "I've changed some, haven't I?" Sunken eyes glared at her brother as if challenging him to say otherwise.

Embracing her warmly, Spirito whispered into her ear, "We all have, *cara*."

"You probably don't recognize Bertie, either. He was a baby when you last saw him." Albert seemed confused, as if he hadn't made the family connection.

"Bertie is slow. He has trouble figuring things out. Takes a while for it to get through his thick skull." As if for emphasis, she rapped his head with her free hand. The boy ducked and laughed her off. Ginny's eyes turned soft, and she grabbed him in a quick hug. "He's a good boy, though."

Marianna was horrified. The boy was being treated as if he were incapable of rational thought or emotion. Certainly, Ginny couldn't be that insensitive. Spirito chose not to comment on his sister's behavior.

"Where are your manners, Gin. Bring your guests in here," a surly voice called out from the adjacent room where a radio could be heard blasting.

"Guess it's time to meet The Boss," Ginny said rolling her eyes.

The Boss was sprawled out on a well-used sofa with a beer in one hand and two empties scattered nearby. It wasn't even noon yet. Spirito and Marianna glanced at each other, grateful they were catching a train in a few hours.

"Sorry, I got started a little early." Rick raised his beer and saluted them. "It's Saturday . . . don't have to work today."

"Or yesterday," muttered Ginny.

Rick shrugged.

"Between jobs at the moment. Have a seat. Get a load off. Gin! Get the guests some chairs and a couple more beers."

It was clear Rick's chosen profession was giving orders to his wife and son while racking up plenty of overtime on the couch. Chairs and beers were brought, and everyone sat down to await further instructions.

"Cheers!" Rick raised his bottle. "Here's to the mess in Europe. Let's hope we stay out of it." The radio had been turned down, but the ominous voice of a newscaster with an English accent was audible.

"Do you think England will go to war?" Spirito asked, anxious to find some common ground with his host.

"Not unless the Germans do something drastic like invade Poland. My family's Irish. They don't trust what's happening in Germany. That country's got a racist dictator that wants to rule the world. No one is safe."

Rick may be a world-class slacker, Spirito thought, *but his views on politics are right on the money*.

Ginny spoke up. "Hitler and Mussolini are cut from the same cloth. Scheggino has become a fascist stronghold."

"How do you know that?"

"Assunta sends me letters." Ginny looked at Spirito. "Our sister's daughter is married to a Dr. Sabatini. He says Germany and Italy are allies, and it's only a matter of time before Mussolini makes it official."

"Alessandro Sabatini?" Spirito's face paled. He was remembering a room in the Villa Urbino and a man telling him Agatha was with child. "I know him. The Urbino clan's private physician. He must be ninety years old by now."

Ginny laughed. "You're talking about Al Jr.'s father. Teresina is married to his son. Al Jr. became a doctor also, but he is different. He treats everyone equally, no matter what their politics are or how much money they have."

Spirito couldn't believe it. His sister's daughter—married to a Sabatini. He wondered if the son knew the story of a pregnant servant girl and a murder.

Three and a half hours later, Marianna and Spirito said their goodbyes and made it out the door of the Gowenlock home. As Marianna steered a staggering Spirito toward the train station, she sincerely hoped his tumble off the sobriety wagon wasn't permanent.

On the voyage home the next day, Marianna reflected on the Gowenlocks' situation.

"It can't be easy raising a child with special needs," she told Spirito. "Ginny has had a hard life, and it isn't going to get any easier. We were lucky with Virginia."

Spirito nodded. He couldn't wait to see his daughter and catch up on the latest news and her busy social schedule.

Lulled by the soothing motion of the train, they watched the landscape change as they headed west. Smokestacks gave way to wheat fields and farmland and finally to the palm trees of their beloved San Diego. Both were glad to be home and grateful for the many turns in the road that had led them here. The sleepy navy town with the sun-kissed climate was still the best kept secret on the West Coast.

PART IV

Chapter 21

Collateral Damage

DIARY OF Virginia Urbino:

Thursday, January 4th, 1942.

My first entry in the diary I was given for Christmas. I have promised to write faithfully in it . . . for 1 year . . . no matter how busy I am . . . only my innermost thoughts. The things I don't dare say out loud.

Friday, January 5th.

Board meeting for the San Diego Teacher's Association tonight. Two hours of motions, seconds, and ayes can be DULL, DULL, DULL! My fellow legislators make me feel so green, like they know so much more than me about Association business! Good experience . . . I keep saying to myself . . . and a lesson in humility.

Saturday, January 6th.

The weekend is finally here. Mom and I went to Our Lady of the Rosary to celebrate the feast of the Epiphany. The rectory was all decorated and Father Matteo sat at our table. Lots of families but hardly any young men. I think Mom is worried I will not find a husband in the Italian Catholic community as all the eligible bachelors have enlisted.

The war is being felt even in San Diego but when I talk of joining the Waves, Mom and Dad won't hear of it. Two old people abandoned by the only person they can depend on, they say. I am determined to do my part. My hostess work at the Service Men's League at Union Depot starts tomorrow. It is the only USO in San Diego that serves free drinks.

Should be interesting!

Sunday, January 7th.

I met the most amazing man last night! Corporal Lenard Katz. Tall, dark and handsome . . . and loves Opera! We met at the punch table and hit it off quicker than you can say Giuseppe Verdi. He speaks French, passably, and I didn't correct him on his bad grammar for fear of offending him. I gave him my number so we shall see . . .

Wednesday, January 10th.

Len Katz called tonight and invited me to a concert. Jan Pierce, the Jewish tenor from the Metropolitan in New York, is singing at the Russ Auditorium next Saturday. Ahhhh . . . I have nothing to wear!

"What did you think of the concert?" Corporal Lenard Katz flashed Virginia a brilliant smile as they sat over brandies at the bar on the top of the El Cortez Hotel. The Sky Room, with its views of downtown and the waterfront, was the place to go after an evening at the Russ.

"The second part was the best." Virginia was quick to offer an opinion. "The love songs from the Operas. Donizetti's *The Elixir of Love is* my favorite. Mr. Pierce sings with so much emotion in his voice. There was another song . . . the last one . . . so beautiful. 'Gadol Elohai,' wasn't it?"

"I'm impressed you remembered. It means 'How Great Is Our God.' It is an anthem to the Jewish religion and a source of strength to its people."

Len is so knowledgeable, Virginia thought to herself, *and so romantic*. They talked of music, art, languages, and the war.

"The French Idealist, Paul Pericord says it best." Len was serious now. "'We must sacrifice as much to win as the people are to put us in servitude.' Victory over evil is not easily won, Virginia, and we must not give up the fight."

Virginia nodded gravely. "Paul Pericord is a wise man."

Lenard brightened. "He also says, 'Fifty percent of the French want the British to win and fifty percent want the *damned* British to win.' Let's drink to that!" They laughed and raised their glasses.

When Virginia went home that night, she had stars in her eyes—and they had nothing to do with the view from the Sky Room. For the first time, Virginia made space in her busy schedule for a man. In the months that followed, there were lectures, concerts, and phone calls that lasted well into the evening. Virginia was falling head over heels for the corporal who loved opera and his country.

They had been dating for three months, and Virginia had not heard Len talk much about his family. "Your mother is French, and your father is Greek. How did they meet?"

Corporal Katz fell silent, staring off into the distance. When he looked back at Virginia, his carefree manner was gone.

"My father was born in Athens but stationed in Paris at the end of the first world war. He marched down the Champs Elysees in the victory parade. He met my mom soon afterward. I was five years old when we came to the States."

"That explains your French proficiency," Virginia remarked. "Why did they leave France?"

"The same reason as everyone else. Religious freedom and a shot at prosperity—something increasingly difficult to obtain for certain groups in Europe. Upon entering Ellis Island, my father changed his name along with his allegiance."

"His name?"

"My father's family name was Khatzis. He shortened it to Katz to avoid any possible Greek or Jewish association. He believed it would prejudice people against him here. He wanted a fresh start for him and his family."

"Your father is Jewish?" Virginia was shocked.

"My mother and father, actually. By 1920, they were already feeling the wave of antisemitism that would eventually bring the Germans back to power and fuel their success." Lenard's eyes had turned cold. "Our people have suffered so much already. You know what is going on now in Poland, at the internment camps?"

Virginia looked away. She had heard the rumors, the motivation behind Hitler's "work" camps. It was too horrible to contemplate. For her, it was easier to pretend it wasn't real.

Lenard's disclosure of his family's past was a major concern for Virginia. She had hoped for a proposal of marriage from him, but now that seemed in jeopardy. She was a Roman Catholic, and her parents' commitment to the church was strong. They had always assumed she would marry someone of the same faith, and so had she. Did she love Len any less knowing he was Jewish? Of course not. It didn't matter, really. In her mind, all religions were based on similar core beliefs: A benevolent higher being who guides us toward the path of goodness and enlightenment. The differences were in the details.

Unfortunately, it was because of those details that wars were fought and people were killed. Justifying bloodshed in the name of God, whatever God you worshiped, was the worst kind of atrocity. And what about his family? Would they accept a Catholic woman as their son's choice for a bride? Clearly, there were conversations on both sides that had to happen. She would start with her own family.

Marianna listened silently as Virginia explained the situation.

"Has he proposed marriage?"

"Not yet. I guess I am thinking ahead . . . to be ready with an answer when he does."

"*If* he does." Marianna's voice had a finality about it. She saw the look on her daughter's face and tried to be gentle. "Jewish families are even more strict about marrying outside their faith than Catholics. As much as you care for each other, he may have no intention of marrying you. You need to discuss this with him before you become more deeply involved."

The opportunity arose after Virginia and Lenard had gone to see the movie *Sergeant York*. The theme was a patriot's duty to his country and the dirty job that must be done to stop the forces of evil. It couldn't have been more timely. They were back at their favorite spot, the Sky Room, when Virginia decided to take the leap. It was now or never.

"What do you see in your future . . . after the war, I mean? Do you want to settle here in San Diego?"

Corporal Katz considered this. "It's possible. My parents live in San Francisco, but with the war on and the prospect of being shipped out at any moment, I haven't thought too far ahead. Why do you ask?"

Virginia felt like she was free falling with no safety net. If she hit bottom, it would hurt like hell. "If you married a woman outside your faith, how would you raise your children?"

Virginia's words seemed to hit Len like a blast of gunfire. "Whoa there. Where did this come from?"

"We've been dating three months now. I am fond of you, but having a plan for the future is important to me. If we are going to be together, these are important questions."

Len looked at the earnest face of the woman seated across from him and realized he had made a serious mistake. The operas, the intellectual conversations over cocktails, the lectures on European culture, had all been a welcome diversion from army routine. For Virginia, it had meant much more. She was an amazing woman—intelligent, ambitious, and fun to be with—but at twenty-two, he was nowhere near ready to settle down. After the war, provided he lived through it, he wanted to travel and see the world. Then there were his parents. There had never been any question he would marry a Jewish girl. Len knew there would be no wedding bells in his immediate future, and he needed to make sure Virginia understood that.

At eight o'clock, Marianna heard the key in the front door. Virginia was home early. A moment later, the front bedroom door slammed. Something had happened on her date with Corporal Katz, and Marianna could guess what it was.

"*Cara*, are you all right?" Marianna stood outside Virginia's room. No answer.

Marianna tried again. "Tell me what happened." Again, silence. Marianna turned the knob and walked in. Her daughter was curled up on the bed, her body heaving with silent tears. Marianna sat on the edge of the bed and waited.

"You were right, Mama. He never had any intention of proposing. I was nothing but a diversion. How could I have got it so wrong?" The voice coming from the tangled mound of covers sounded hurt and vulnerable.

"Sometimes we see only what we want to see," Marianna began. "You wanted to believe he was in love with you because you were ready. He is young, seven years younger than you. Did he know that?"

Virginia sat up and looked at her mother. "I never told him my age. Why would that have made a difference?"

"He might have understood your needs better . . . that you might want a family before long."

Virginia looked down, embarrassed.

"He was not the one, *cara*. It hurts, but you will meet a man who is ready to share a life with you. I have no doubt."

Marianna took her fiercely independent, grown-up daughter in her arms and rocked her like a little child.

May 10th, 1943.

Corporal Katz has been shipped off to France. There is a big push coming from the Allied Forces. That is all he would tell me. I just hope he comes back alive. We are now good friends and even though my heart still flutters when he says hello, it doesn't hurt anymore. Every girl has her heart broken at least once, Mama says.

On a brighter note, I have been fitted with braces to correct the overbite that has plagued me all my life. The orthodontist says I will look like a movie star when they come off next year. I will be happy with a whistle or two from the boys at the USO! In April, I submitted a request for a year's sabbatical to earn my master's degree at UC Berkeley, in San Francisco. Today I found out I have been accepted into the fall term.

Virginia stood looking at herself in the full-length mirror in her dressing room.

Marianna sat on a chair nearby. A critical assessment of Virginia's "new look" was in progress. Sophisticated but approachable was what they were going for. Her hair was styled in the latest fashion—cut above the shoulders and swept back in curly waves. She wore trousers cinched at the waist and a tailored white blouse. The jacket was short and of a contrasting color, periwinkle blue to match her eyes. Marianna nodded her approval.

Virginia turned sideways looking at her profile. "My nose is too big, and I have a square face."

"You have classic Latin features," Marianna countered.

"So did Michelangelo, but no one ever said he was handsome."

"He had other gifts." Marianna's meaning was not lost on her daughter. "Let me put it this way, you have the determination of your father, the wisdom of your mother, and the ambition to succeed that neither of us ever had. Those are qualities that many men would find attractive—that go beyond good looks." Marianna smiled and held out her hands. "And every time I look at you, I see the most beautiful girl in the world."

"Oh, Mama!" Virginia flew into her mother's arms and covered her with kisses.

The sojourn to Berkeley, and the degree that would follow, guaranteed prestige and a higher salary for Virginia. But, like so many women of her generation, there was an ulterior motive. Master's degrees were rare among women in 1943, and even with a war on, a university with a three-to-one ratio of men to women was a great place to find a husband.

Chapter 22

Walter

LIEUTENANT George W. Wilson and his family stood on the deck of the SS *Monterey* as it steamed into the port of Honolulu, Hawaii. On Shore, the Aloha Tower stood out proudly against the green hills of Oahu, a guiding beacon for vessels and passengers alike. After six days at sea, it was a sight for sore eyes.

Navy personnel, their wives, and a score of islanders rushed to meet the Wilsons as they stepped off the gangway onto dry land. An island girl with long, ebony hair and violet eyes held out a lei, and young Walter bent his head to receive it.

"Aloha," she said, smiling. "Welcome to Paradise."

In early February of 1939, Lieutenant Wilson had received orders from the Department of Naval Operations in Washington, DC, to accept a command post on the battleship USS *Oglala* in Pearl Harbor. His wife, Marie, and son, Walter, would join him. It would be a new adventure for the Wilsons and a departure from their old life on the mainland. Walter, at sixteen, was looking forward to it.

From the moment they stepped on shore, the Wilson family embraced island life and its customs without holding back. They rented a cottage in the residential section of Waikiki, located ten miles from the naval base and George's ship. Many of their neighbors were Hawaiian families who worked for the Navy and had lived on the island for generations. Warm, unpretentious, and generous to a fault, they welcomed the newcomers with open arms.

Wally entered Roosevelt High School in Waikiki as a junior. He was used to joining new schools mid-term whenever his father was shipped out, but being the new kid never got any easier. Subjected constantly to the brutal scrutiny of classmates he had not grown up with, Walter developed an attitude of aloofness to protect himself. Although meant to mask his inherent shyness, it was perceived as snobbery by the other students and only served to alienate those who might have wanted to get to know him better.

The playground, instead of being a source of joy, became a place he feared, never knowing who would try to ridicule or bully him.

It was on the first day of school, as Walter anxiously scanned the groups of young people during recess, that he got his first glimpse of how Western culture had infiltrated Hawaiian society. A class system had developed within the school that mirrored the island as a whole. Many white kids, or *haoles* as the natives called them, did not mix with students of Hawaiian or Asian descent. Children of high-ranking officers, in particular, only socialized within their elite group and were taught from an early age to feel superior. His mother, anxious for her son to make the right connections and improve his social skills, encouraged him to join a young people's club on the base. After only one evening of listening to entitled Navy brats lording it over everyone else, he found himself hanging out with the locals. The Island boys either ignored or chose not to notice Walter's awkwardness and began to include him in their get-togethers on the beach. Because they did not judge him, Wally could relax and be himself. Playing guitar at sunset while girls danced the hula was much closer to Walter's idea of paradise.

There was one girl who had already caught his eye. Roselani Nahalepuna, at sixteen, had the slender build from her mother's Japanese ancestry and the large eyes and brown skin of her Hawaiian father. Her family lived a few doors down on the beach side of Ala Wai

Canal. The Nahalepunas' property was a true Hawaiian homestead built by Roselani's father's family in the early 1920s. Surrounded by flowering plants and trees, the brown shingled bungalow sat well back from the street in an attitude of quiet dignity. Just around the corner, modern trackless trolleys passed back and forth to the center of town.

Wally spent a lot of time at the Nahalepunas' during the first two years on the Islands—carefree summer days listening to the sound of the sea from the shady confines of their lanai. A world away from the life he had known on the mainland, Wally found himself falling in love with Hawaii.

In December of 1941, Wally got up the courage to ask Roselani to a dance for the officers' families at the base. The year was almost over and Christmas was just around the corner. Roselani looked at him, puzzled. "I am not a *haole*. I would not be welcome there."

Wally frowned. "What do I care what they think? You are my date."

"It could hurt your father's reputation if you were seen with me. There will be gossip."

A muscle tightened in Wally's jaw. If there was one thing he hated, it was racial intolerance.

"I have a better idea," she said. "Come with me and my friends to a luau at Kahala Beach this Saturday. It will be much more fun."

The tension in Wally's face disappeared, and his eyes grew warm again. "Sounds like a much better idea. You're on!"

December sixth, the day of the luau, families started gathering at Kahala Beach at sunrise. The pig, already dressed and wrapped in banana leaves, was put in the underground oven, and a slow fire built under it. In a few hours, it would be dug out, fragrant and tender. Tables of food were set up—several kinds of poi, baked fish in crusted sea salt, and dishes of cut papaya, mango, and pineapple. Children ran freely on the long strip of beach while their mothers tended to the preparations. Sunlight danced on the water, and a cool breeze cut through the mid-morning heat. By the time Wally and Roselani arrived, the luau was in full swing.

Wally was glad he had come. He understood and appreciated the simplicity of the islanders' way of life. Family, friends, and respect for the traditions of their forefathers were priorities. Success was measured in terms more precious than material wealth, and it was a generous and open heart that singled men out for greatness.

Day quickly turned into evening, and the festivities showed no signs of slowing down. The waves were calmer now, breaking gently against the shore and rushing to meet the golden sand halfway. A group of boys Wally's age had gathered at the water's edge, talking, smoking cigarettes, and passing around a flask or two. Wally glanced at Rose.

"They're just blowing off steam," she assured him. "They are good boys. Many Hawaiians believe it is better to give teenagers a little rope . . . small falls hurt less than big ones. Don't worry, their parents are nearby pretending not to watch."

It was almost nine when Roselani tapped Wally on the shoulder. "My parents and yours expect us back sometime tonight. We should get going."

At Roselani's door, Wally lingered. "You know, I will be eighteen in a few months. I . . . we . . . Oh hang it, Rose, I want you to be my girl."

Even with only the light of the porch, Rose could see Wally's face was red. "I'm not eighteen 'til April. My parents don't let me go out with boys yet . . . except you." She laughed softly. "They think of you as my big brother."

"I'm not your brother," Wally responded hotly. "Do you think of me that way?"

"Not at all." Rose's eyes danced, and she touched his cheek lightly. "It will be our secret."

Wally bent and kissed her lips. They tasted like the nectar of a thousand orange blossoms. Gently, Rose pulled away and put her finger to his lips as if to stop him. "We have time, Walter George," she whispered. "We have all the time in the world."

At 7:55 on the morning of December seventh, Wally woke with a jolt. The house was shaking, and there was an explosion of gunfire in the distance. He threw on some clothes and ran out into the street. Neighbors were coming out of their houses and looking east toward ʻEwa and the naval base. Black smoke billowed in the eastern sky, and airplanes droned like angry flies overhead. Looking up, Wally could make out a rising sun on their wingtips.

"Pearl Harbor!" someone cried. "They're bombing Pearl Harbor!"

Wally had a sick feeling in the pit of his stomach. He had to get to Rose's house. Another rumble shook the earth beneath him, and he fell. As if in a dream, he looked down and saw blood running from his knees.

Suddenly Rose was there helping him to his feet. "Your father is leaving. Look." She pointed toward Wally's house.

Lieutenant George Wilson slammed his car in reverse and started to back out of the garage. He halted for a minute and called to his son. "The dirty beggars are after our hides. They may try to attack the coast. I've got to get to my ship. I don't know when I'll be back. Take care of your mother. You're in charge now." The Lieutenant's face was grim as he roared down the road heading east.

Looking for her daughter, Kim Moon Nahalepuna, gathered up her youngest child and walked over to the Wilson home. Through the window she saw Rose, Wally, and Marie huddled by the radio. A voice repeated over and over the same message:

We repeat . . . this is not a radio play . . . we are in dread earnest. At 7:55 this morning, Pearl Harbor was attacked by Japanese airplanes. All military and Navy personnel are ordered to report to their posts immediately. All leaves, liberties, and furloughs have been canceled. Those of you who are not military personnel, please stay off the streets. Keep all roads clear for military personnel traffic. We repeat: We are under enemy attack. Martial law has been proclaimed throughout Hawaii.

The sky had turned dark with smoke; gunfire and an occasional bomb punctuated the eerie stillness. Kim was worried. Her parents were Japanese and so was she. She had met Bill Nahalepuna while on a family holiday to the Islands twenty years ago. After she had returned to Japan, they corresponded for a year, and he proposed. Her life was here now, but with her ties to Japan, what would happen to her and her family? There were many Japanese living in Hawaii. Why would they attack their own kin? It all seemed so senseless.

Lieutenant Wilson drove as far into the naval base as he dared. The outline of battered hulls and ships' magazines were barely visible through the smoke. As he stared out into the vast expanse of Pearl Harbor, his worst fears were realized. His ship, the USS *Oglala*, had been hit hard. The flames on deck were still burning as it lay half submerged at the end of the Ten-Ten Dock. The once powerful cruiser was keeling over and sinking into the burning, oily waste. The Lieutenant watched, helpless, as his ship slowly disappeared beneath the water's surface.

America had been caught off guard that Sunday morning. Most of the island Navy personnel were either on a pass or on liberty, and there had been no one to man the ships and return fire. Those who tried perished with the three thousand others who valiantly fought to save the fleet. In a few hours, eight battleships and twenty American vessels were either destroyed or lying in a watery grave at the bottom of the Pacific Ocean.

At Hickam Field and Wheeler Air Force Base, nearly every plane was caught on the ground. Only a few pilots were able to man their planes and meet the enemy. Launching fields were littered with wreckage and burning aircraft. There was nothing left to fight back with. Hawaii lay vulnerable, a political and literal battleground for a world at war.

Wally's father did not return home that night. Families all over Hawaii sat in darkness waiting for daylight and news of the devastation. At dawn on the second day, the bombing stopped, and the sound of the planes overhead diminished. Marine and Army sentries patrolling the streets relaxed their all-night vigil and grabbed some sleep in jeeps along the side of the road. The enemy did not return. The attack had been swift and sure, and they had retreated to prepare for the inevitable retaliation.

On the morning of the third day, there was a knock on the Wilsons' front door.

Marie's heart was pounding as she opened it a crack and looked out. Three uniformed men stood on the threshold, their faces grim.

"We are looking for Kim Moon Nahalepuna and her two daughters. We have been to her home, but no one answers. A neighbor said they saw them come here yesterday morning. Are they here?"

"Yes, we are here." Kim and Roselani pushed past Marie and faced the men. "My husband, William Nahalepuna, works as an engineer at the shipyards in Kauai. Have you any news about him?"

"We have him in custody. He is unharmed," one of the men answered. "You three must come with us."

"The Nahalepuna family? Why?" Marie wanted to know.

"For questioning." The man's expression was unreadable.

Wally stepped forward. "For what? The Nahalepunas are American citizens. Bill's ancestors have lived here for generations. How can you . . ."

Marie turned toward her son, her face registering surprise. Questioning authority was not something her son had been taught to do. She put her hand on his shoulder as a warning.

"Orders from the War Department," one of the men said, ignoring Walter's entreaty. "The Nahalepunas need to come with us now."

Rose's little sister was crying as the men escorted them to army jeeps waiting at the curb.

"We will get to the bottom of this," Marie whispered to Kim. "Be brave."

Lieutenant Wilson returned the night of December ninth. His car had a bullet hole in the passenger door and two more near the exhaust. Marie was shocked at her husband's changed appearance. Dark circles ringed his bloodshot eyes, and he looked like he hadn't shaved in days.

"My ship's gone," he said to his wife. "Most of my men made it out alive, thank God. Everyone at the base is lying low, waiting for a second attack. I was allowed back for sleep and a change of clothes, but I must return in the morning."

"What about the Nahalepunas?" Marie asked. "Did you know they are all in custody?"

The Lieutenant's eyes blazed. "I heard they are rounding up anyone of Japanese descent, but because Bill is Hawaiian, I didn't think . . . Kim is Japanese, and worse, Bill spent time on the continent studying engineering. The US may be concerned that they are spies."

"Can you help them?" Wally's eyes were pleading. "It is so unfair."

"It is unfair, but in wartime, espionage cannot be ruled out. I will see what I can do."

In the morning, when Wally awoke, his father was already gone. Marie and her son could only hope the Lieutenant's intercession on behalf of the Nahalepunas would allow them to return home.

Two more days passed without word, but on the afternoon of

December eleventh, the Lieutenant's car pulled up in front of the house. Bill and Kim Nahalepuna and their two daughters were with him.

Wally and Marie were out the door running to meet them. "Thank God you are safe. We were so worried!"

"The Lieutenant got us out," Bill said. "He talked to Admiral Kimmel himself. Even Kimmel said the Army had no cause to detain us." He grabbed his friend's hand, and his eyes were filled with gratitude. "We will never forget what you did for our family, sir."

For the first time in a week, Lieutenant Wilson managed a smile. "I couldn't come home without Roselani. Wally would never forgive me."

In the weeks and months that followed the attack, Hawaii continued to be on high alert, and all residents were subject to close military surveillance. Martial law remained in effect, and *Kibei* citizens—those who had ties to the US and Japan—were deported to the mainland and placed in internment camps. The Nahalepuna family was spared, but civilian life had changed. Anyone of Japanese descent was treated with suspicion and eventually ostracized from the communities in which they had once been welcome.

When Wally saw the "For Sale" sign on the Nahalepunas' front lawn, he was over there in a flash.

"Where will you go?" he asked Rose.

"We are moving to my father's ancestral estate in Maui, in the hills near Haleakalā. They have two thousand acres. Father feels we will be safer there."

"It is far from here, Rose. I will never see you."

Wally and Rose knew instinctively that their romance was over before it had begun. The war had destroyed their dreams along with the peace and serenity of Hawaii. "Our future is uncertain," Rose began bravely, "but whatever happens, no one can take away what we shared."

Wally reached out for Roselani's hand and held it. "My father has been transferred to the mainland. We are leaving Hawaii at the end of the year."

Rose's face fell. This was not good news, but she wasn't ready to give up. "Maybe one day you will come visit me again."

Wally felt like he had lived all his eighteen years in the last few months.

"Don't wait for me, Roselani. Marry a nice Hawaiian man, and have lots of babies."

Roselani nodded, her eyes filling with tears. She felt a pain in her chest as if a dagger had pierced her heart.

The Navy ocean liner eased away from the port in Honolulu on its way to San Francisco Bay. Wally scanned the faces on the dock hoping to see Roselani's, but she was not there. That part of his life was over, he realized, and a new one was just beginning.

From the deck of the ship, he saw the hills of his beloved Hawaii turn from purple to black and finally disappear into the horizon.

The following year, in the fall of 1943, Walter George Wilson enrolled as a freshman at the University of California at Berkeley. He was nineteen years old.

Chapter 23

The Bell Curve

VIRGINIA'S sabbatical at UC Berkeley was almost over. It was May 1944, and by June, she would be returning to San Diego. She glanced up at the iconic Campanile towering over the campus like a benevolent benefactor and was reminded how lucky she was to be here. UC Berkeley was one of the most venerated learning institutions on the West Coast.

As part of her sabbatical, Virginia had requested a dorm room at International House. Built in 1928, with a donation from John D. Rockefeller Jr., it was the first co-ed residence on campus where students of all nations were welcome. I-House, as everyone called it, encouraged camaraderie among its multi-cultural residents, and a cacophony of different languages echoed through the foyer at all hours. The belief that "brotherhood under all people shall prevail" was heartily endorsed by everyone who walked through its halls.

Virginia's intention at the beginning of the fall term was to acquire her MA in Languages and also to revisit the rich experience of college life. The privilege of being among some of the greatest minds in the country and obtaining her master's degree had been everything she had hoped for. Finding a life partner, however, had proved more elusive.

Shortly after the New Year, Virginia received a letter from Len Katz. They had stayed in touch, as friends, during the last few years while Len had been stationed in France. He had been sidelined with a bullet through the leg in Vichy but would survive. During recovery, he had met a French woman whose family had been killed in the Holocaust. They would be married in the fall. Somehow, Virginia was not surprised.

Tonight was the last Special Supper Dance of the school year sponsored by the Newman Hall Club, the on-campus Catholic Social/Intellectual Society. Virginia had joined up as soon as she arrived last fall and had quickly been enlisted by Cathy Meade, its chairman, to help organize events.

"I'm here, Cath," Virginia called to the frazzled brunette giving orders to a knot of girls hovering over the buffet table.

"Oh, Virginia, good. Can you get these good-for-nothings to arrange the centerpieces on the tables? All they want to do is stand around and gossip." Cathy cast a withering glance in the direction of the buffet.

"No problem. Come on, girls, the guests are due to arrive any minute. If we get the centerpieces done, we will have time to rearrange place cards to our liking. Boy, girl, boy, girl . . . you know . . ." Virginia winked at the girls, and suddenly everyone was moving.

Cathy was at her elbow. "God, I wish you weren't leaving. You have been a miracle this year. There is such a difference with students coming back from the workforce to get their MAs and PhDs. They've been out there; they don't have to be spoon fed."

The guests were beginning to trickle in, looking for their names on the decorated tables.

"See that boy with the navy blazer?" Cathy pointed. "New recruit for the Newman Club. Shy as can be. Took him a whole year to make it in here. Walter Wilson. His father's ship went down at Pearl Harbor, but, thankfully, he wasn't on it. Tough on a teenage boy to go through that." Without missing a beat, Cathy added, "He's definitely your type."

"How old is he?"

"A sophomore this year."

"Oh, he's too young for me."

"Says who?" Cathy countered. "Women live longer than men, so when you're eighty, he'll be taking care of you instead of the other way around. Not to mention, if you want kids, those little minnows of his swim faster upstream at twenty than they do at thirty."

When Cathy's meaning sunk in, Virginia's eyes grew wide, and she clapped her hand over her mouth. "Cathy, I can't believe you said that!"

"I'm being practical. Your odds of getting pregnant are better if you marry a younger man."

Virginia thought for a moment, then looked at her friend. "Maybe you could introduce us?"

"I've done better than that. He's sitting next to you at table ten."

Walter was shy, no doubt about it, but Cathy was right—he was definitely her type. Five feet, eight inches, built like a reed, with a full head of wavy brown hair and eyes that looked kind behind thick, horn-rimmed glasses.

"Couldn't pass the eye test to enlist," he said shortly. Virginia struggled to find common ground with the young man who seemed so socially awkward.

"Cathy tells me your father is a Navy man, that you were in Honolulu when Pearl Harbor was attacked. It must have been difficult for you."

Walter's face changed, and his eyes took on a faraway look. "It was." The silence that followed made it clear the subject was still a raw one. Heedless of the risk, Virginia pushed on.

"Tell me about the Islands."

The eyes behind the glasses grew suddenly warm and alive, and the shyness disappeared. Walter spoke about the lush landscape of

Hawaii—its traditions and the warmth of its people. He became at once passionate, eloquent, and imbued with a sensitivity that appealed to Virginia. These were qualities she admired greatly, especially in a man.

She tried another topic. "They speak French in Polynesia, don't they?"

"*Mais oui, presque tous parle Français*," he answered confidently. "Almost all Islanders speak French."

Virginia smiled. Bingo.

This was not the stars in your eyes, heart-fluttering crush she had experienced with Len Katz. This was more like a methodical assessment of possible marriage material.

Virginia was older, now. At thirty-one, if she was going to have children, there was no time to waste. Walter checked all the boxes: Catholic, didn't smoke or drink, well-educated, and trainable. Short of listening to his heart with a stethoscope, she guessed he was healthy. The fact that he was probably a virgin like herself didn't bother her either. At least he had no one to compare her to, and they could figure it out together.

Walter, on the other hand, was enchanted. He had never met a woman with so much energy. She seemed so sure of herself and what she wanted out of life. Like a swig of good whiskey, the rush of being around her was exhilarating.

On the Saturday before Virginia was to go back to San Diego, Walter invited her to San Mateo to meet his parents. Lieutenant and Marie Wilson lived on the San Francisco Peninsula in a modest Spanish Revival home nestled among stately mansions in the residential suburb of San Carlos.

Walter seemed nervous driving west across the Golden Gate Bridge from Berkeley, the glow of the city retreating as they climbed into the hills of San Carlos.

Virginia had her own worries. After all, Walter's father was practically a war hero, and his mother . . . well, Walter had her on a pedestal so high it made Virginia's head swim. As far as knowing how to make a good impression with prospective in-laws, Virginia was in uncharted territory. Talk about pressure to perform! Entrance exams at the Sorbonne seemed less daunting.

Marie Wilson met them at the door. She was wearing a starched, cotton sundress and high heels. "Wonderful to meet you," she said, patting her perfect hair with long manicured fingers. Virginia couldn't help observing; Marie was a prim officer's wife to a tee. Marie led them into the living room where her husband was seated. Lieutenant Wilson half rose to greet the young couple but after a few minutes, he sank wearily back into his chair.

He looked worn out, hardly the brave war veteran Virginia had expected. After one heart attack less than a year ago, he seemed already a spectator on the sidelines of life.

"The war's about over, Dad. Hitler's caved, and Japan is next." Wally spoke awkwardly, as if trying to encourage conversation among strangers.

The Lieutenant nodded. "The Japs are finished, expecting surrender any day now." He sighed and continued, "I'm glad to be out of it. Seen too much needless destruction. I'm leaving it to your generation to clean up the mess." Focusing his attention on Virginia, his eyes brightened. "Wally tells me you are a language professor. Marie's family comes from Arles, in France. You two should get along fine."

Eager to impress, Virginia turned to Marie and rattled off a complicated phrase in French. Marie stood there with a puzzled look on her face. It was obvious she hadn't understood a word of it.

Virginia turned bright red. *Good move*, she told herself, *you just sucker-punched your future mother-in-law right in the kisser*. "Don't mind me," she added quickly. "I have a tendency to act like a know-it-all. Professor's Neurosis they call it."

Everyone smiled, but the damage had been done. Marie looked like a prize fighter knocked out in the first round. Virginia could hear her mother telling her, *Sometimes you have to let your opponent think they are ahead if you want to win the fight.*

The next day, Wally paid another visit to his parents' home. "Well, what did you think of her?"

Marie's face was grim, but Wally's father was ready to talk. "She's full of piss and vinegar, son. Do you think you can handle her?"

"That's what I like about her, Dad. She doesn't sit around waiting for life to come to her. She goes out and grabs it with both hands."

Marie spoke up. "Do you know her age? She is probably a good deal older than you, already teaching in the school system before getting her MA at Berkeley. She is obviously looking to get married and raise a family. Are you ready for that at twenty-one?"

Wally had been expecting some resistance, but his parents' remarks seemed unduly harsh. It was time to let them know how serious he was.

"I intend to graduate and have a job before we marry—two more years. But there's no doubt I have chosen my bride." Wally looked at both his parents and added, "Sometimes a situation presents itself where you have to get ready quicker than you thought."

"Well said." Lieutenant Wilson nodded his approval. He knew exactly what his son was talking about.

Particles of light like gold dust cut across the foyer of Saint Joseph's Cathedral as the morning marine layer surrendered to the coming day. Virginia turned slowly, the seed pearls of her snow-white gown catching the first rays of the sun.

Marianna examined the dress critically. Not bad for a fifty-nine-year-old woman half-blind with cataracts, she admitted. Three months of sewing and working with the fragile lace Virginia had brought back from Mexico had all been worth it. Her daughter looked radiant. The crown of orange blossoms and the simple veil cascading down the back had been a last-minute touch.

Virginia stood inside the vestibule watching the guests begin to file in. On the bride's side, her SDSU mentors, Elizabeth and Lee Browning, were already seated. Her college French Club, members of the Hoover High School staff, and friends from the neighborhood were quickly filling the pews and spilling over into the nearly empty groom's section.

Dr. Bonaventura had found a seat toward the rear in case he had to leave for an emergency.

Urbano was seated alone at the end of the first pew. Annie Mary had passed away unexpectedly six months ago from pancreatic cancer. Virginia had been devastated. The beautiful lady with the warm green eyes had been like a second mother helping her cope during those months when Marianna's depression had kept her in Trenton. Her upbeat personality and open heart had given Virginia the nurturing presence she had so desperately needed.

Just like Uncle Toni, the deadly disease had chosen another victim, at random and without mercy.

A frail but determined Celia Lallo was marching up the aisle with the help of her daughter, Mary, and grandsons, Jack and Lou Jr. At seventy-one, she was still reminding everyone who was in charge.

There had been only one time during her engagement when warning bells had gone off in Virginia's head. They were in the final stages of planning the wedding, and Virginia needed the name of her groom's best man. Wally could not come up with one person to fill that role.

"He has no friends?" She posed the question to Marianna. "How can that be? I know he lived in Hawaii as a boy, but he's been here five years. He must have made *some* close friends."

Marianna was silent. It was not a good sign, but Virginia would find out sooner or later what her husband was really like. Living together day after day was different than a long-distance courtship, and if Virginia expected perfection, she was going to be sorely disappointed.

"Ask Lou Zamboni," Marianna suggested. "He and Mary are like family. Celia would love seeing her son-in-law stand up for Wally. Toni would have too."

If Lou wondered why he had been chosen to be best man to someone he had never met, he kept it to himself. "I would be honored," was all he had said.

Marianna drew her daughter's veil back carefully and released it. The shimmering cloud of white chiffon floated away from her and settled gently on the ground. The gesture felt symbolic, like a rite of passage.

"I must let you go. You belong to your husband now."

Virginia turned to look at her mother. "You have not lost me, Mama. I am right here." She held out her arms, and Marianna rushed into them. "I will always be right here."

"You have found a man who appreciates you and loves you for who you are. That is the best start a marriage can ever have. Remember that when the going gets rough."

"I will, Mama. Just keep reminding me."

As the first chords of Mendelssohn's "Wedding March" echoed through the church, Spirito turned to his daughter. "Are you ready?"

"Ready," Virginia answered.

Linking arms, they walked slowly down the aisle to where Wally and Lou were waiting.

Chapter 24

Closure

AT THAT hour of the morning, the only sounds were birds calling to each other from the rows of cypress trees. Rolling hills stretched for miles in undiluted serenity, the distant mountains forming a jagged line between earth and sky. In the foreground, granite markers stood at attention along the green expanse of lawn. An occasional bouquet of flowers reminded those who slumbered there that someone still remembered.

A man was walking through the graves. He strode purposefully, his eyes looking neither left nor right, as if he had walked there many times before. On reaching his destination, he stopped and rested his hand on the curve of the stone. His touch was tender, almost loving, as if it rested on the shoulder of someone he knew well.

"Annie, there is something I need to tell you." The tone was emotional but resolved. It was clear his decision had not been an easy one. "I cannot live like this any longer. It has been three years since you left me. At times, I feel so lonely I could shoot myself. I am going to look for a wife. I hope you understand."

The words were met with silence, giving him the assurance that they had been well received. He patted the marker, wiped away a tear, and walked back the way he had come.

"Spirito, I have made up my mind. I am going to Scheggino to look for a wife."

"Are you crazy, Urbano? You are sixty-six years old. The trip alone could kill you."

The two Urbino brothers were seated underneath the tangerine tree in the backyard at Albatross Street. The day was waning, and a half carafe of homemade wine rested on a table between them.

"It has been almost fifty years since I have seen our hometown. Our papa is gone. I no longer want to hate that part of my past. I have always blamed him for our mother's death, but she took her own life because she couldn't control what was happening to it. I have felt that same despair, especially since Annie's death."

"A wife doesn't magically solve your problems or guarantee you will never be lonely," Spirito reminded his brother. "Besides, what woman would be interested in an old man like you?"

"A younger one," Urbano responded candidly. "One that wants to start a new life in America."

Spirito shook his head and studied his brother with a critical eye. Urbano's once-abundant hair was thinning, and from the back, his bald spot was hard to miss. Too many rib eyes and martinis had thickened his once-trim waistline. "What have you got to offer a younger woman? It's not like you are rolling in dough."

"My magnetic personality?" Urbano flashed his still-white teeth in a winning smile. "Why don't you come with me?"

Spirito considered the suggestion. The thought of seeing Agatha again, maybe trying to develop a relationship with his son, Santo, was tempting. For a moment, the years slipped away, and Spirito felt young again. He remembered the treks through the mountains with his brothers when they were boys. The future was still ahead of them then, and it was easy to dream big. He looked around at the few straggly grapevines he still tended, and reality came rushing back. At seventy-two, he knew it was too late for him but if Urbano was set on going, Spirito had a favor to ask.

Spirito looked at his brother, wondering how much he should tell him about his past.

Urbano knew what had happened to Agatha, and he knew about the murder and his brother's banishment to America. He did not know that Spirito had seen her in Spello when he went back for the reading of the will or about their encounter in Central Park twelve years ago. Better to leave it that way.

Spirito stood up and addressed his brother. "There is something I want you to give a dear friend."

Withdrawing into the shed for a minute, he returned with a photo and an envelope. The photo was of a white-haired man, in a navy blue wool suit, holding the arm of a radiant bride.

Turning the photo over, Spirito began writing. The tears were forming, and one escaped and rolled down his cheek as he sealed the envelope and handed it to Urbano.

"Find the Signora Altarocca and give this to her."

Urbano leaned over the railing of the SS *Cretic* and watched the ship's prow slice purposely through the water, its course an unquestioned absolute. His own life, by comparison, seemed to be drifting aimlessly between an unresolved past and an uncertain future.

The thought of seeing Scheggino again made his stomach tighten. For more than half his life, he had carried a grudge against a village because it reminded him of his father's infidelity and his mother's suicide. It would be hard, but he knew he had to confront the bitterness he had been carrying around all these years. The rest of his life depended on it.

He had written his sister, Assunta, telling her of his upcoming arrival. She had seemed pleased to hear from him and suggested he stay with her, her daughter, Teresina, and Dr. Sabatini. The invitation signaled a willingness to bring together the family so long torn apart by grief.

It was late afternoon by the time Urbano walked up the steps to Assunta's palazzo. The sun had already started its descent and was heading west toward the mountains.

Urbano's heart was full. The little village of Scheggino seemed frozen in time; almost nothing had changed in the years he had been away. There were cars instead of horse-drawn wagons, neon signs instead of painted wood ones, but the castle stood strong, lit in golden splendor by the setting sun. Urbano took a deep breath and knocked.

Almost as if someone were waiting, the door opened, and a young woman was staring at him.

"*Zio* Urbano?"

"*Sì, sono* Urbano. You are—?"

"I am Pepina. Teresina's daughter. Well, step-daughter. I have a different mother."

Pepina Sabatini looked to be about twenty-five. She had classic Roman features, a head of thick wavy hair, and eyes that were both penetrating and intelligent. There was a restless energy about her, suggesting a keen intellect and a taste for adventure.

Pepina wasted no time with pleasantries. "Come in and meet the family."

As Urbano entered, he saw a staircase going up to a second level immediately in front of him and a doorway to a dining room opening to the right. On the left, an archway led to a large room dominated by a huge stone fireplace. There was a marble-topped farm table heaped with garden vegetables on one side and open shelves stacked with plates, cups, and jars of canned goods against the wall. It looked like a restaurant kitchen. An old woman stirred a steaming caldron near the flames. When Urbano entered, she turned to look at him. With a start, Urbano realized it was his sister, Assunta. She had been a young woman the last time he had seen her. The once-bright eyes had faded, folds of wrinkled flesh had replaced the smooth skin of youth, and her brown hair had turned to gray. She moved slowly, but as she walked toward him, her arms were wide open.

"Urbano, *fratello*. You are here."

Suddenly everyone was in the kitchen—Teresina and her husband, Dr. Sabatini, and Pepina. "I will get you all sorted out, eventually," Urbano promised. He was touched. After so many years and so much grief, he was back in the bosom of his family. He felt the knot in his stomach begin to loosen.

Seated at the dining room table, waiting for the first course, Dr. Sabatini addressed Urbano. "Did you know Assunta operated a restaurant here in the twenties and thirties?"

The smell of roasting meat and homemade bread coming from the kitchen seemed to punctuate the revelation. "Shepherds from Castelluccio brought their flocks through this village on their way to Monteluco. The cars and the new roads have stopped all that. Too many sheep killed. In her day, Assunta's *osso buco* and lamb stew drew quite a crowd."

"I can believe it," Urbano replied.

Assunta beamed. She looked so much like their mother, Urbano thought. The square face and sturdy peasant body, the capable hands rolling pasta and pastry into magical creations . . . Urbano had missed some great meals in the last fifty years. Of that, he had no doubt.

"Why are you here?" Pepina spoke up, her eyes zeroing in on him like a telescope.

No sense in lying to that one, Urbano thought to himself. She would see through it in a heartbeat. He leaned back in his chair and surveyed the group. "I'm here to find a wife and bring her back to America."

Everyone's forks froze in mid-air, and conversation halted. "I'd like to go to America," Pepina volunteered.

Teresa snorted. "Child, don't even think about it. He's old enough to be your father—and then some."

Urbano held up a hand as if the discussion were over. "Don't worry, not even *I* have the energy for that!"

They all laughed, but Urbano caught Pepina's eye and winked.

After dinner, Dr. Sabatini and Urbano sat on the front steps of the palazzo. Built in the days when proximity to the road was considered an asset, it was steps away from the busy highway. At all hours, trucks passed through town on their way to the industrial center of Terni.

"How did Scheggino fare after the war?" Urbano asked his companion. "I heard it was a fascist stronghold."

Dr Sabatini was unapologetic. "I never hid the fact that I admired Mussolini. He did a lot of good—building roads, infrastructure, putting people to work. It was the alliance with Hitler that did him in. Power corrupts . . ."

"And absolute power corrupts absolutely," Urbano added. "An old American saying. We should know. We've watched the rest of the world succumb for centuries."

"America is still a young country, and abuse of power is not governed by geography," Dr. Sabatini reminded him. "Your time is coming."

Alessandro Sabatini Jr. was well thought of in Scheggino and Spoleto. He had clinics in both towns, and his patients included villagers from neighboring communities. Unlike his father, who had worked only for the Urbino truffle clan, Alessandro had a well-known reputation as a healer among the peasants. The waiting rooms often reeked like a barnyard, villagers holding baskets of eggs, chickens, and even baby lambs in exchange for services. Dr. Sabatini never turned anyone away.

"Almost lost my life one night," the doctor said quietly. "I was asleep in my bed, here, when a local boy pounded on the door. 'The partisans are coming for you, doctor,' he told me. 'They mean to kill you. Get out now, and hide in Spoleto.'" Alessandro sighed and shook his head. "That was a close one. I ran out the back door while they were coming in the front."

The two men were quiet, listening to the sounds of the countryside. In the fields, the cicadas sang, their voices an anthem to the warm summer night. Ghostly clouds hung in the valley like giant puffs of smoke, and as the sky grew darker, the green hills lost their color and disappeared into the mountains.

Urbano turned to his companion. "Did your father ever tell you about Spirito's troubles here? He was Pietro Sr.'s personal physician."

"Yes, I know what happened."

"Then you understand why I ask this. Where is the Signora Altarocca? I have something to give her."

Dr. Sabatini paused. "First, you need to visit your father's grave in the cemetery—for closure. It will do you good. When you return, we will talk."

The next day, Urbano climbed the old Roman road leading to the cemetery at the top of the hill. Families from Scheggino and neighboring villages had been burying their dead there for centuries. Within its stone walls, tiny mausoleums like miniature houses enclosed the remains of rich and poor alike. Some resembled intricately carved villas while others were a single block of marble. Francesco Urbino's grave was one of those. There was a small oval photograph next to the name, taken at the end of his life. A frail old man with a scraggly white beard and battered hat. To Urbano, the image looked no different than others he had seen at gravesites. Ordinary men who had lived their lives vulnerable to life's temptations, sometimes lacking the strength or the will to deny them. Urbano remembered how much he had idolized his father as a young boy. What man could live up to that?

He laid his hand on the marble face, running his fingers through the grooves in his father's name. "I forgive you, Papa," he whispered.

Turning back toward the entry gate, Urbano looked up at the three ornate buildings where the truffle clan were buried. The Urbino name in large, carved letters was emblazoned across the front of each. *Pride of ownership*, Urbano thought. It extended even to the final resting places of the dead. Too bad it was only the living who benefited.

A man in his mid-forties was standing outside the third structure as Urbano passed by. His head was bowed, and his neatly manicured hands were folded in prayer. Something about him looked familiar, but Urbano couldn't place it until the man looked up and met his gaze. Urbano caught his breath. The man standing before him looked exactly like a younger version of his brother, Spirito. This must be Santo, he realized, the son Spirito had left behind.

The two men eyed each other in awkward silence. Urbano was the first to speak.

"I am Urbano Urbino. Spirito's younger brother. I am here visiting my family. You are Santo, Agatha Altarocca's son, yes?"

The impeccably dressed man nodded. He wavered, as if weighing how much he owed this man, if anything. He seemed to come to a decision and stepped forward, extending his hand.

"I am Santo Urbino." He began to close the mausoleum door, then considered something. "So, you know, then."

"Know what?"

Santo reopened the tiny door that led to the crypts and gestured for Urbano to enter.

The patriarch, Pietro Urbino, was on the left, his wife underneath him. On the right, a shower of fading flowers covered a new addition. There was a framed photograph of a beautiful woman wearing a peach suit and a pill box hat resting on the top of the block of marble. By the style of her clothing, Urbano guessed the photo had been taken some years earlier. Her golden hair was pulled back in an elegant chignon, and she wore an ivory cameo on a gold chain around her neck. The words engraved on the stone read, *Agatha Altarocca. Born 1889. Died June 15th, 1951. Beloved by all who knew her.*

Urbano turned back to look at Santo. "One month ago. She was only sixty-two years old. What happened?"

"Breast cancer. By the time they found it, it was too late." Santo's eyes were full of pain. He turned away quickly, as if to protect the intensity of his grief.

Urbano spoke with care. "This is not the best time, but there may not be another. I have something my brother wanted her to have. May I give it to you?"

Santo hesitated, then gave a slight nod. Urbano reached inside his coat pocket and handed over the envelope with Agatha's name on it.

"This belongs to you, now."

Urbano walked back to the entrance of the cemetery and let himself out. Still focused on his encounter with Santo, he barely noticed the young man in the red Ferrari convertible parked nearby.

Dr. Sabatini was waiting when Urbano got back to the palazzo. "You saw Agatha's grave?"

Urbano nodded. "Santo and his son were paying their respects."

"His son?"

"The young man who was with him."

Alessandro Sabatini paused. "That would be SJ."

Urbano looked at him questioningly. "SJ?"

"A nickname."

SJ. Santo Jr. It made sense, Urbano thought. "I gave Santo a photograph of Spirito and his daughter, Virginia, on her wedding day. It is all he will ever have of his father. For Agatha's sake, I hope he treasures it."

"I'm sure he will." There was a pause. "And your father?"

"I have forgiven him, Alessandro. I want to be free of the hate so

I can heal. It is time to put the past behind me and focus on the good memories of my childhood . . . and Scheggino. Look at Assunta. Her open heart, her generosity. She took care of our father despite what he had done. She has shown me that love of family . . . "He paused and smiled. "And a good bowl of lamb stew—transcends life's difficulties and gets you through the hard times."

"Amen to that!" Alessandro put his arm around Urbano, and together they walked into the kitchen to join the others.

"Did you see her?"

Urbano put a hand on Spirito's shoulder. His face was grim.

Marianna watched the two men from the laundry room window. She saw her husband put a hand over his mouth and slump forward. She was out the door and running toward him when Urbano put up a hand to stop her. A few more words passed between them, and Urbano walked to the house.

"What is it? What has happened?"

"It is a personal matter . . . someone we knew it Italy."

"It's about Agatha Altarocca, isn't it?"

Urbano looked surprised. "You know?"

"Spirito told me everything. I know about Santo too."

Urbano spoke softly. "Agatha's dead. Cancer. A few months ago."

Marianna blanched. "You saw her grave?"

Urbano nodded. "I also saw Santo."

"You spoke to him?"

"I came across them in the cemetery."

"Them?"

"Santo has a son. I presume from the woman he married."

"Olivia and Claudio's daughter," Marianna murmured half to herself. "Spirito never told me Santo had a son."

"Let it rest, Marianna." Urbano's voice was firm. "That part of

Spirito's life is over. It was obvious when I met him that Santo wants nothing to do with us. Agatha was our last link to that family, and she is gone."

"Santo is blood. It is not done." The look in Marianna's eye made it clear this was not the end of the story.

PART V

Chapter 25

Breaking New Ground

"WE'VE BEEN married almost four years now, Dr. B. I can't seem to get pregnant, even with vitamins and prayer."

"I hope you're doing more than praying."

Virginia blushed. "That is not the problem, I can assure you."

Dr. Bonaventura had been the Urbinos' family physician since Virginia was a teenager. He had seen Uncle Toni through his terminal illness and had been there for more than one emergency at the Albatross house. His bedside manner had always been unorthodox; he cut right to the chase and never used more words than were necessary.

"Sometimes, ambitious, high-strung women such as yourself have trouble relaxing. This tenseness inhibits the process of conception. I have examined both you and Wally and have found no reason why you can't conceive. I have come up with a treatment that includes specific supplements: folic acid, vitamins E and D, and magnesium to calm your nerves. There are also techniques to relax the mind and body that you can do when you are most fertile. You know when those times are, right?"

"Yes, I know."

"Good. We will begin immediately." Dr. B rose and escorted Virginia to the door. "I know your powers of concentration are formidable. Start concentrating on making your husband happy, and the rest will follow."

Virginia was frowning as she drove home to Mission Beach. She kept thinking about what Dr. B had said. High-strung. Ambitious. What remained unsaid was that she was not devoting enough time to the art of love making. It's true, sometimes sex felt like a job, a means to an end, and that was the problem. If she wanted results, she was going to have to learn to enjoy it.

From the moment Wally and Virginia had returned from their honeymoon, the pace had been nonstop. Purchasing the lot on Venice Court, one block from the ocean and buying the house kit from Sears Homart had been a brave step. They had hired a contractor and built the 900-square-foot bungalow a year later.

In the first year of their marriage, Wally had found it difficult to hold a job. One engineering firm had called it a "personality conflict with other employees," while another had cited "an inability to work well with others." Wally had skills. He just had trouble controlling his emotions. An unexpected disruption or a sudden change of plan would set him off. His fists would ball up and his whole body would shake while he tried to get himself under control. When Virginia saw it coming, she would grab his hands and murmur soothing words until he relaxed. The first time he put his fist into the wall and damaged his hand, she suggested he seek help.

"Honey, why don't you talk to someone about your behavioral problems?"

"Behavioral problems? You make me sound like a raving lunatic! I just get angry when things don't go as planned . . . usually some idiot fouling up."

"A psychiatrist could help." When Virginia saw Wally's lip tremble and the hurt in his eyes, she backed off. If her husband couldn't accept that he had a problem, there was no way he would be receptive to treatment.

That didn't mean she had to stick her head in the sand too. She made an appointment to see Dr. B.

"He has these episodes whenever something unexpected happens," Virginia said. "Which is all the time. Let's face it, life is unpredictable."

The physician sat back and tented his fingers, thinking. Virginia knew what was coming: One of Dr. B's not-so-clinical diagnoses. "Classic symptoms of Obsessive-Compulsive Disorder. OCD. It is a new clinical term. They used to call it Anxiety Disorder. A reaction based on the fear of not being in control."

"Is there a treatment for it?"

"Some drugs seem to be working. Iproniazid, for one, but it has side effects. Cognitive ones. It could affect his performance at work and . . ." The doctor cleared his throat. "In the bedroom. I know you want kids."

"Three of them, to be exact," Virginia said.

"I am not a believer that medication solves all problems," Dr B continued. "I recommend an environment that is peaceful and stress free."

Virginia sighed. "A house full of screaming children doesn't exactly fit that description."

"You didn't notice this behavior before you were married?" Dr. B asked gently.

"We barely spent any time together before the wedding. Wally was in San Francisco getting his degree, and I was teaching in San Diego." *Love letters written in French by a besotted young man do not tell the whole story*. "I knew he was in love with me, and I was in a hurry to get married and raise a family. Was I wrong?"

Dr B's eyes were kind. "I understand how it might have influenced your judgment. It wouldn't be the first time a young lady with an agenda made a decision like that."

"There's another consideration," Virginia volunteered. "I am a Catholic. I can't get a divorce, and it's too late for an annulment."

Dr B nodded. "My advice to you is to make the best of it. Miracles can be achieved with patience and love. I know you have those in abundance."

Love, yes. Virginia thought. *Patience* she wasn't so sure of.

Mission Beach, with its casual lifestyle and friendly vibe, reminded Wally of Hawaii. By 1951, the jetties and the bridges linking Mission Beach to downtown were completed and the Channel was open. In the evenings, the bayfront became the perfect place for Virginia and Wally to walk and unwind. Wally had been hired by the State Highway Department to help design the new I-5 freeway. It was going on two years, now, and he still had a job. Virginia had her fingers crossed.

A couple of months after Dr. B's pep talk, Virginia missed her period. This had happened before, so she tried hard not to get her hopes up. After two months went by, Virginia paid her physician another visit.

"Congratulations. You are two and a half months pregnant." The older man's eyes twinkled. "I guess you took my advice."

The picnic on the beach had been Marianna's idea. "Invite the French Club ladies," she had suggested to her daughter. "I will make risotto, a fruit salad, and my orange-frosted sugar cookies."

"What if I go into labor at the party? My due date is next week."

"The due date is an approximation," Marianna assured her. "There is only one person who determines when the due date is, and that person is right here." She patted Virginia's stomach with an air of authority.

The beach party was scheduled for early April, a week before Easter. So far, the weather had co-operated. At the coast, the morning mist had burned off, revealing a warm sun and a bright blue sky. Ruth Covac and Lois Chambers were lounging in their swimsuits, their beach chairs pulled up to the picnic lunch. Cathy and Beth were down by the shore making sandcastles with their kids. Virginia could see Madame Browning waist-deep in in the bay with Mimi Brill, the oldest member of the French Club. They were laughing and splashing each other like sisters. No, not like sisters, Virginia thought. Like best friends. Madame seemed so different outside of the classroom—happy, youthful . . . free.

Virginia was propped up against a pile of pillows, her legs spread out in the sand. She felt enormous, like an overblown balloon ready to pop.

"Where's Wally?" Lois was eating grapes from the salad bowl and looking around.

"Watching TV in the house. I think he's afraid of all these women."

Lois nodded. "I guess the men had a ballgame to watch today."

Virginia lay back against the cushions letting the sun beat down on her. Maybe a little nap . . .

"Ahhh . . ." A jolt of pain made her sit upright. She felt moisture between her legs and saw a dark stain of wet sand beneath her. *Someone* had decided today was going to be the due date. "Mama! Get Wally!"

Marianna was on her feet in seconds, and everyone ran toward her. Eliza and Mimi lifted her gently and walked her to the house.

"Call a cab," she called out. "This baby is on its way."

Wally came rushing out of the house. He was hysterical. "Where's the suitcase? I can't find it!"

Marianna stared at him calmly. "I've got it."

"Whaa . . . whaaat do we do now?" Wally's lip trembled.

"I'm taking Virginia to the hospital. You are staying with the guests." The cab pulled up, and Marianna helped Virginia in.

"What do I do with the guests?"

"For God's sake, Wally, figure it out." Marianna sounded exasperated. "Think of something. Entertain them." She got into the taxi and slammed the door. "Mercy Hospital," she barked to the driver. "And make it quick!"

Virginia sank back into the seat as the car sped off. "Poor Wally. I hope he'll be all right."

"You hope *he'll* be all right. You're the one having the baby!"

"Congratulations, Mrs. Wilson. You have a six-pound baby boy." The nurse was smiling, but her arms were empty.

Virginia corrected her. "The baby's name is Anthony. Tino for short. Can I see him?"

The nurse kept smiling. "Tino is still in intensive care. A little trouble with his lungs."

"Lungs? What's wrong with them?"

"He's having a little trouble breathing. We have him on a ventilator."

Virginia's face turned white. *A ventilator, Oh God*. "Can you get Dr. Bonaventura in here? I need to see him."

Dr. B was standing at the foot of the bed when Virginia opened her eyes. "Tino is going to be fine. He just needed a little help getting started."

Virginia breathed a sigh of relief. "It's hereditary, isn't it? I had weak lungs as a child. It's why our family ended up in San Diego. Trenton winters can be deadly."

Dr. B nodded. "Many children outgrow asthma after a few years. In the meantime, it wouldn't hurt to do a little of that praying you're always talking about."

While little Tino improved, Wally struggled with the challenges of fatherhood—especially when it came to changing diapers. He would hold the baby at arm's-length and call out, "Mommy! Someone needs changing!"

Virginia hated when he called her that. Maybe it was a term of endearment when he was growing up, but it made her cringe. She was not his mommy. It also reminded her how immature her husband could be when it came to certain things. Like fatherhood. Virginia was disappointed but undeterred. She was going to have a few more babies even if she had to raise them all by herself.

The Mission Beach bungalow had only one bedroom, and with Tino's bassinet in one corner, no one got any sleep. Virginia began looking at real estate in the Mission Hills area where Eliza and Lee Browning lived. After attending a French Club gathering, she always made it a point to check out what was for sale.

"It would be lovely to have you up here," Madame Browning gushed enthusiastically. "Instead of that cesspool where you live now. Such an unsavory element living down there. Beach bums and surfers. I don't know how you stand it."

Virginia ignored the pointed snobbery and tried to get the subject back to Mission Hills. "If you notice anything interesting, even an empty lot, let me know, won't you?"

After lunch, the six ladies, all San Diego State University graduates, got up and moved to the garden for coffee. Virginia was helping to clean up and heading for the kitchen when she heard voices coming from the pantry.

It was Eliza and Mimi Brill. They laughed and spoke in subdued voices. Virginia poked her head in to ask where to put the plates and saw Eliza put her arm around Mimi's waist and draw her close. The embrace was reciprocated, and a second later, they were kissing. Virginia withdrew quickly, hoping no one had seen her.

In the garden, Lois Chambers whispered in her ear. "Are you alright? You look like you've seen a ghost."

Virginia did not like gossip, especially if it involved people she worked with, but she had to know. "I saw Madame and Mimi . . . uh . . . together." Virginia's face was bright red. "Are they . . . ?"

"Lovers?" Lois finished the sentence for her. "You didn't know?"

Lois laughed. "Oh, Virginia, you are so naive. Madame Browning is a lesbian."

"What about her husband? Does he know?"

"Lee's known for years she prefers women. They have an understanding. At his age, he's probably glad she doesn't want sex with him anymore."

"So, she is bisexual?"

"Men are not her cup of tea. She married Lee for appearances and because they are a great team, professionally. I think I can safely say the bedroom is one place they do not collaborate."

Virginia was stunned. She was not so sheltered that she didn't know that homosexuality existed among women, especially in the academic world. She just had not known anyone like that. At least, she didn't think so. She thought back to her professors and colleagues. Maybe there were women, like Eliza, who chose to hide their sexual preference for the sake of their careers. Virginia knew that Catholics forbade such practices. They called it a sin. But Virginia did not always agree with her religion on matters of morality. What was sinful about feeling love and affection, even if it was for someone of the same sex? Sins were things that hurt people and caused destruction.

Virginia had to admit she felt a little strange now that the secret of her mentor's love life was exposed. It would take a little getting used to, but she was not going to allow it to affect their friendship.

Eliza came out of the house and joined Virginia in the garden. "Mimi knows about a piece of property over on Arden Way that's for sale. Canyon lot. Cheap." She rested her hand on Virginia's shoulder.

Virginia jumped and stepped back before she could catch herself.

No time like the present to prove friendship was thicker than doctrine. She turned to Madame and smiled. "I will go look at it on my way home. Thank you."

"Mimi knows the owners. I imagine if you ask her, she can put in a good word for you." Eliza's eyes were warm, and she linked her arm through Virginia's as they walked back into the house to talk to Mimi.

The lot on Arden Way looked like a challenge. It was listed at ten thousand dollars, but Mimi said the owners would take less. Eyeing the narrow strip of level land that bordered the sidewalk then plunged headlong into the canyon, Virginia knew why. Putting even a two-bedroom house on this lot was bound to be costly. Still, in this neighborhood, it could double in value in a few years even if she never built on it. That evening, she put in a call to the agent with a cash offer of eight thousand dollars. It was accepted within an hour.

Marianna and Virginia drove out to the site the next day.

"Have you spoken with a contractor yet?" Marianna asked, looking over the steep cliff and the tangled mess of vegetation running down the canyon.

Virginia had little Tino in one arm and the deed to the lot in the other.

"Not yet. Wally has surveyed the square footage and knows someone at work who can give us some numbers. We'll see what he says."

Wally's contact had bad news. "Building on this site will set you back way more than what you paid for the lot. The pylons alone will cost you twenty thousand dollars. You could be looking at forty grand to put a 2,000-square-foot house here."

Virginia's face fell. Forty thousand dollars on top of the eight thousand was too much money to invest so early in their marriage. There were going to be expenses coming up. Raising a family cost money, and Virginia was just getting started.

"Cheer up," Marianna said, putting an arm around her daughter.

"There are plenty of other properties to be found in this neighborhood, and some of them even have houses on them."

In the exam room the next day, Dr. B said, "How many bedrooms does that beach cottage have?" He pressed his stethoscope against Virginia's tummy and listened intently.

"One."

"Well—" The doctor smiled broadly now. "You'd better start looking for a bigger house. In seven months, you are going to need another bedroom."

Chapter 26

A Question of Timing

VIRGINIA often said that Tino was an angel compared to her second child, who was self-centered, tantrum-prone, and a class-A pain in the ass. Many years later, my grandmother, Marianna, told me Mom had demonstrated similar characteristics as a child. Having a great respect for her, I hoped that, despite my shortcomings—or perhaps because of them, I might grow up to be just like her.

Virginia discovered the two-story house on Sunset Boulevard in Mission Hills by accident. A family who lived back east owned it, and it was obvious, because of its condition, that no one was living there. The crumbling stucco was painted a sickly green, the windows were practically hanging off their frames, and the eyebrow around the top was collapsing. Its thirty-five-thousand-dollar price tag encouraged Virginia to look beyond the surface and focus on the four bedrooms, two-car garage, and big backyard.

"Make an offer, any offer," the realtor had said.

Twenty five thousand dollars," Virginia countered, without batting an eye. They settled at thirty thousand.

Mom was ten months pregnant with my younger sister Terry, Tino was three, and I was barely a year old when the Wilson family moved in. After a slow start in the baby-making department, Virginia was on a roll.

How Mom did it all, I will never know. She was now teaching at Crawford High School full time, raising four children, if you counted

Walter, and buying up real estate bargains whenever she found them. There were the duplex near the Roller Coaster in Mission Beach, two rental properties on Georgia Street, and a three-unit complex in North Park. Virginia had a formula. The properties she bought had to be free and clear, income producing, and located in relatively good areas. She always paid cash and never sold anything. As soon as she accumulated enough revenue from the rents, she bought another one. Instead of baking bread and cleaning house, Virginia found herself scouring neighborhoods for tear-downs that nobody wanted.

Virginia's hobby did not always sit well with her family. Wally admired his wife's enthusiasm—it was what had drawn him to her in the beginning—but he did not approve of her sinking every dollar earned into rental property. He wanted to take a vacation once in a while or go out to dinner. The only time we went to a restaurant was when the sum of our "misbehaving money" swelled. Every time the kids were bad, we had to pay Mom a dollar from our allowance, and the booty was carefully kept in the top drawer of her dresser. When the coffer was full, we went to Jimmy Wong's Golden Dragon for dinner.

The mall was something we only fantasized about. Our clothes were bought at thrift stores and church rummage sales, and steak was never on the menu at mealtime. If my dresses were not the latest style or my shoes were a little scuffed, I figured Mom was saving her paycheck for something more important, something called her family's future.

In April of 1962, Mom hit the mother lode.

It was a Sunday morning, and all three kids were in the car. We had picked up Marianna on our way to nine o'clock Mass at Saint Joseph's Cathedral when Mom spied a For Sale sign on a property at the corner of Cedar and Front Streets. It was a large lot with three dilapidated bungalows on it and corn stalks growing shoulder high in the front yard. The sagging roof lines and peeling paint advertised the fact that the property had seen better days. To Virginia, it looked like manna from heaven.

Downtown was going through a change. Retail shops and commercial businesses were moving to Mission Valley, and once thriving office buildings were abandoned in the exodus. Virginia saw an opportunity to purchase prime downtown real estate at a time when its value was underappreciated.

After Mass, remembering that realtors worked on Sundays, Mom called the number on the For Sale sign. A sleepy voice answered on the fourth ring.

Virginia cut right to the chase. "Front and Cedar. What's the price?"

The agent on the other end of the line was offended. Who was this brash female calling on a Sunday afternoon at naptime? *People were so rude.*

The agent's voice was smooth but firm. "The owner will not consider anything under twenty five thousand dollars. It is a prime location and a large lot."

"Is there a loan against it?"

"I don't believe so."

"Who is the owner?"

This was too much. Rudeness had its limits. "I'm afraid I can't answer that question."

"If I'm going to make a cash offer," the woman's voice fired back, "I'd like to know who I will have the pleasure of working with."

There was silence at the other end. The agent was reconsidering. "It is owned by the Boncompagni Estate," he finally said.

Frank Boncompagni. Lou Zamboni's best customer. Virginia remembered the shady businessman who had bought her father's restaurant twenty years ago. He had turned the *Buon Appetito* into a thriving night club and started the trend toward eateries that served cocktails, food, and entertainment. He must have fallen on hard times to be selling property with so much potential. *Papa would know.*

The next day, when she went to Albatross Street to pick up the kids, Virginia headed for the shed.

"Papa?"

Spirito's shed was pitch black inside, but, after a minute, she made out a hunched figure warming his hands over an old wood-burning stove. When she crossed the threshold, her father looked up. The eyes were vacant at first, then a glimmer of recognition came into them. "*Cara figlia*." He smiled weakly and held out his hands.

Virginia was shocked. Her father had become an old man. Often, in her haste to pick up the kids and get home, she didn't even go back to the shed to visit. A wave of guilt washed over her. No matter how busy she was, she must never abandon the father who had always supported and encouraged her.

"Papa, I need your advice."

Spirito laughed and shook his head. "I cannot possibly guess how I can be of help."

"Frank Boncompagni. You remember him. He is selling a nice piece of downtown property a few blocks from here. Is he in financial trouble?"

Spirito seemed to sit up a little straighter, and his eyes lost their vacant stare. "I think I saw something in the paper. Money laundering scandal . . . or . . .?"

"Tax evasion, to be exact," Marianna interrupted. She was standing in the entrance to the shed with a newspaper in her hand. "Listen to this: *'Frank Boncompagni, longtime businessman in San Diego, has been indicted on two counts of tax evasion stemming from his extensive real estate holdings. Mr. Boncompagni has long been suspected of having ties to the underworld but has turned legitimate in recent years. His questionable business practices continue to haunt him . . .'*"

Marianna looked up. "Maybe this would be a good time to make an offer."

"Lowball the son of a bitch," Spirito growled, his face lighting up in a mischievous grin.

"I intend to," Virginia assured him.

In the end, it came down to a simple matter of timing. Virginia had the money, and Frank needed it, fast. She made a cash offer of twenty thousand dollars with a three-day escrow.

Within hours, it was accepted. In the end, the high-flying gangster, who once had downtown in his pocket, surrendered to a spunky little lady from the old neighborhood.

The day escrow closed, Virginia, Spirito, and Marianna drove down Cedar Street and stopped in front of the newly purchased trio of bungalows. Part of the deal had been that the property was as-is, and the tenants could stay. Virginia tried not to look too closely at the falling-down porch or the rotting siding as they walked the lot in silence.

"Remember the location," Spirito told his daughter. "Someday, this will be worth a fortune."

"It will. I just couldn't wait that long." The voice behind him sounded familiar. Spirito turned to see who it was.

An old man stood nearby, his big, meaty hands leaning heavily on a cane. The smile was still there, a little less cocky than Spirito remembered—and the eyes no longer looked like they could take on the world. Frank Boncompagni reached out and shook his old rival's hand. "I still remember that brother of yours. Good man. What a way with cars he had. Never seen anything like it."

The Urbinos nodded in agreement.

"You have quite a daughter, there, Spirito. Congratulations."

Spirito ducked his head in embarrassment. "Sorry she couldn't give you the great deal you gave me. It's all business with this one."

"As it should be." The cocky grin returned to Frank's face. "I would have expected nothing less."

Virginia was flushed with excitement when she got home. Wally was poking around the kitchen, opening cabinets and eyeing the cold stove.

"Oh, honey, Papa, Mama, and I just came from the Front Street property, and guess who we saw there?"

"I'm hungry. Where's dinner?" Wally's eyes were cold.

Virginia hadn't thought about dinner, and eating out was not an option. Too expensive. Mentally she visualized the contents of the refrigerator. "We have leftover meatloaf, and I can boil some potatoes."

Wally's jaw clenched. He looked like he had made up his mind about something, and this was the last straw. "I want to take a trip to Hawaii. You are welcome to come, or not, but I'm going."

Virginia paused with the leftovers halfway to the counter. "When did you decide this?"

"While you were *busy*."

Suddenly Virginia understood. Wally felt left out in all this. He was never going to share her passion for real estate. It bored him.

"What will you do there?"

"Relax, swim, enjoy myself. What *normal* people do when they are on vacation." The sarcasm again. "And see an old friend."

Virginia was curious. "A friend? You've never mentioned him before."

"Her. My friend is a woman."

Virginia's face turned red. "What woman? An old sweetheart?"

"You could say that."

Virginia couldn't believe it. Her husband was admitting he was going to Hawaii to see an old flame. She burst into tears and sat down.

"Relax." Wally put a hand on her shoulder. "We were just friends. I knew Roselani when we were teenagers. Her family lived next door to us in Oahu. When Pearl Harbor was attacked, my father saved them from the internment camps on the mainland. She probably has five kids and walks around barefoot wearing a muumuu now."

I'll bet, Virginia thought silently. It took her about one minute to realize the future of her marriage was at stake. "I can leave as soon as school's out. The kids can stay with Mama. It's about time I saw the Islands."

Chapter 27

Letting Go

WALLY AND Virginia were on the train headed for LA International Airport.

"This is going to be an adventure. I had planned this itinerary with only me in mind. Do you want me to change it . . . make it easier?" Wally glanced at his wife. He looked like he didn't want her to say yes.

Virginia saw the faraway look in his eyes. The look he had the night they met at the Supper Dance, when she had asked him about Hawaii. "Don't change a thing. I invited myself, remember?"

Wally shot her a look of gratitude and admiration.

"Can you give me an idea of the itinerary?" Virginia asked timidly. She wasn't as brave as he thought she was.

"Let's just say it will involve a bit of island-hopping."

"Sounds expensive."

"I knew that was coming!" Wally fired back. "Look, if this is going to work, there is to be no nickel and diming. I am paying for it."

He saw the hurt look on Virginia's face and tried to backtrack. "Sometimes you have to allow yourself to let go a little, especially when you're on vacation. Let me be in charge for once. Who knows, you might enjoy it." His lips twitched. "I have a few surprises in store."

I hate surprises, Virginia thought.

Virginia had never flown before. When the plane started down the runway, she had a vision of being trapped inside, consumed by flames from an undetected malfunction. She had read about them.

She white knuckled the arm rests and held on. In the next moment, they were airborne and floating above the clouds. This letting go was going to be hard.

"A cocktail, ma'am?"

Virginia looked up. A flight attendant was bending over her with a tray of drinks. Her Pan Am insignia glinted on the lapel of her teal blue jacket. Virginia noticed the short skirt hiking up shapely legs. *I bet those skimpy little outfits keep the male customers happy*, she couldn't help thinking. Wally was sure getting an eyeful.

"How about a martini?" the attendant said.

"How much . . .?" Virginia caught her husband's eye, and her voice trailed off.

"It's all free. No charge." The attendant smiled and winked. "It helps with first-time flying jitters."

Virginia tried to laugh. "Is it that obvious?"

"Let's just say I've seen it before. Drink up!"

Six hours and three martinis later, Virginia and Wally landed at Honolulu Airport on the island of Oahu. This is where Wally's father's ship went down during the attack on Pearl Harbor, she realized.

"My old stomping grounds. Before I met you," Wally said as if reading her thoughts.

He looked at the new parking garage across from the airport entrance. "A lot has changed in twenty years."

Driving down Kalakaua Avenue, Virginia saw high rise hotels lined up shoulder to shoulder on both sides of the street. The little grass shacks she had envisioned were nowhere to be seen. The taxi turned into a circular driveway and stopped under a gigantic porte cochère. Behind it rose three stories of impressive Hawaiian Gothic architecture. As soon as the taxi doors opened, a smiling dark-skinned man, impeccably dressed in white ducks and a colorful shirt, helped Virginia out and placed a lei over her head.

At the front desk, a young woman greeted her. "Aloha. First time in Hawaii?"

Virginia nodded. "Is everyone always so nice here?"

"Don't worry," the woman answered. "You'll get used to it."

The Moana Hotel, as Virginia soon found out, was the oldest hotel on the Island and the most prestigious. Traditional elegance meets the modern world. There were wrap-around verandas with teak rocking chairs, a bikini bar facing the ocean, and air-conditioning in every room.

Virginia tried not to think about what it cost to stay there.

"Take a nap before dinner," Wally suggested. "We have reservations at Duke's for dinner. Don Ho is singing tonight."

"What are you going to do?"

"Take a walk. See if my old house is still there."

At Duke's, the choices were endless. Scallops wrapped in bacon. Poi in fried banana leaves. Steak Diane. When the dessert cart came by, Virginia closed her eyes and pointed. Waikiki's very own celebrity, Duke Kahanamoku, stopped by every table to welcome his guests. "How is the beautiful lady doing tonight?" A standard line, no doubt, but his warm brown eyes made Virginia feel like she was the only woman in the room.

He had been a surfer, an Olympic swimmer, and a Hollywood actor in his day, and even at seventy-two, he still knew how to lay on the charm. His band, The Hawaiian Boys, warmed up the stage with a few old chestnuts before The Ali'is took over. The young man headlining the group opened with "I'll Remember You." By the time he launched into "Tiny Bubbles," Don Ho had the crowd in his pocket.

Wally was happy, Virginia noticed. He was a different person here among the Islanders. He was nothing like the tense, irritable husband back in San Diego holed up in his bedroom trying not to listen to the kids screaming downstairs.

"Big day tomorrow," he whispered in Virginia's ear.

"Can you give me a hint? A girl has to know what to wear."

"Dress conservatively. No bikini."

At nine the next morning, Virginia and Wally's taxi stopped in front of a low-slung military building. Behind it lay a body of water and ships tied to the dock. A sign read, "Pearl Harbor Memorial."

"We have a reservation for Mr. and Mrs. Walter George Wilson," Wally told the uniformed man behind the desk.

The man searched his records. "For the USS *Arizona*, right?" He handed them two tickets. "The ferry leaves in fifteen minutes."

"My father's ship, the USS *Oglala*, went down at Ten Ten dock. Can you tell me where that is?"

The man's face changed. It was no longer impersonal. "I remember. The mine carrier. It was made of wood, so it caught fire from a nearby explosion. Didn't have a chance. Your father?"

"He was not on board that morning, but he saw it go down."

The man nodded. "Relatives of those lost on the *Arizona* have been coming in droves ever since the museum opened. Your father still alive?"

Wally shook his head. "I am here *for* him."

As they approached by ferry, the USS *Arizona* Memorial rose out of the middle of the bay like a ghostly replica of what lay beneath its surface. The pure white walls had openings, like the holes of a burned-out ship, showing glimpses of blue water and sunlight from every angle. Wally and Virginia were drawn to the back where a wall of names in black letters filled the space—the names of the 1,102 men who perished when the ship went down.

"Are they all still inside the ship?" Virginia asked.

"All of them. Submerged in forty feet of water."

Wally was deeply moved. For the first time Virginia could

remember, he talked about that day. The Day of Infamy.

"I lost friends . . . boys who were caught on their way to the beach to go surfing that Sunday morning. Blasted with gunfire from the planes overhead. My father aged twenty years in twenty-four hours. His health was never the same after that. You can imagine what it must have been like to see your ship go down in flames and not be able to do anything." Wally reached for her suddenly, and Virginia held him. He was shaking. She understood now why he never talked to her about the trauma he had experienced, why he could never talk about it with his father . . . or mother. It would have made him look weak. She knew why he wanted to come back. For closure.

A burden seemed to lift from Wally's shoulders as they left the harbor and headed back to the hotel. He had left a dark piece of his past behind him. The rest of the day was spent enjoying the amenities the hotel had to offer: swimming at the private beach, afternoon tea, and cocktails at the Bikini Bar.

"Ready for part two of our adventure?" Wally teased over dinner at Duke's that night.

"Ready," Virginia answered. "Bathing suit or evening gown?"

"How about bomber jacket and khakis? Be ready by six A.M. sharp."

Virginia's stomach lurched. Now she remembered why she hated surprises.

Part two came in the form of a twenty-one passenger DC-3 plane headed for the island of Maui. As soon as she was strapped in, Virginia flagged down the stewardess with the drink cart. This time she didn't even ask if the martinis were free.

Bump . . . sip . . . *bump* . . . sip . . . sip . . . *bump* . . . This had been going on for an hour. Only one more hour to go. Wally was droning on and on about the merits of the aircraft now tumbling through space—air currents, wind velocity . . . It was all making her head spin.

The martinis didn't help. Suddenly she felt sick.

"Barf bag!" Wally yelled.

The stewardess made a valiant effort, but at least half of what looked like Duke's beef medallions ended up on one pant leg. The sight of it sent Virginia off on another round. This time, she missed the bag entirely, and tomato aspic ended up in her lap.

Virginia glanced at Wally. His shoulders were shaking, and a hand covered his mouth. He was laughing at her.

"What do I do now? My clothes are all in my suitcase at the bottom of the plane."

"Relax," Wally managed to get out. "Roselani will know what to do."

"Roselani?"

"Didn't I tell you? She's meeting us when we get off the plane. We're going to her family's estate in Haleakalā."

Virginia rushed into the tiny bathroom and slammed the door. She took quick stock of herself in the mirror. Mascara was careening down her blotched cheeks, there was vomit in her hair, and she smelled like a distillery. *I'm going to kill him. He knew we were going to meet his old girlfriend, and he let me have all those martinis.* Emergency measures were needed. She cleaned herself up and washed off the smelly pants, trying not to focus on the red spot on her crotch. The tomato aspic was not going to come out.

After deplaning, Virginia heard a voice call out, "Walter George? Is that you?"

A stunning looking woman with light brown skin and a flying mane of dark hair stood on the edge of the tarmac. The muumuu she was wearing had slipped off one shoulder, and the wind had wrapped it around her generous curves like a caress. Her smile was dazzling.

"Roselani!" Wally called out as she ran to meet him. They hugged, double kissed Hawaiian style, and stood staring at each other. Virginia waited patiently to be introduced. After a few minutes, Roselani's eyes flicked over at Virginia and back at Wally.

"Where are my manners." Wally turned and looked at his wife. He was taking in her splotched appearance as if for the first time. "My wife . . . uh . . . she had a little accident. Martinis and small planes don't agree with her."

Roselani smiled uncertainly.

Virginia rolled her eyes. *Oh great. Now she thinks I'm a lush* and *a fashion nightmare*. "Hi. I'm Virginia." *The woman he married instead of you*, she almost added.

"Wonderful to meet you." Roselani smiled that brilliant smile again. "Lovely. Shall we go?" She gestured to the dusty four-by-four pickup. "Mom and Dad are so anxious to see you."

Virginia sat on the far end of the front seat. She felt safer closer to the open window. As they climbed into the hills of Haleakalā, she felt her stomach doing somersaults with each hairpin turn.

"Dad still works Keanuwai Farms, but he has help now," Roselani told Wally. "Mom stays busy keeping the critters out of the house. A constant battle. The flying cockroaches are the worst."

Virginia rolled up the window.

"What about you?" Wally asked. "Where is your husband?"

There was an embarrassed laugh. "It didn't happen for me. One daughter has to stay home and take care of the parents. It is the Hawaiian way."

"Your sister?"

"On the big island. Married to a Dole exec."

Roselani turned a corner and stopped in front of a wooden gate. "Here we are."

A large, brown, shingled house stood back from the road, partially concealed by tropical plants growing thickly on either side. The branches of an enormous sandalwood tree hung over the wraparound lanai.

"Come in. My parents are waiting for you."

Crossing the threshold was like stepping back into another age. Vintage bamboo furniture covered in native island prints clustered near the hearth, and white linen curtains billowed at windows flung open to the warm breeze. There was a timeless quality to the way the rooms were furnished—simple and comfortable, not meant for entertaining or showing off to strangers.

Bill and Kim rose to meet their visitors. "Walter George, you do us a great honor." Bill's broad Hawaiian face was filled with emotion. "Without you and your family, we would have been sent to the camps on the mainland. Who knows what would have become of us. You will always be welcome in our home."

Wally embraced the couple and turned to include Virginia. "This is my wife. Her first time in the Islands."

"*Ho'ohanohano au.*" Virginia spoke the words carefully. "I am honored." Bill and Kim Nahalepuna nodded in appreciation. They were impressed.

Wally beamed with pride as he put his arm around his wife. "Virginia teaches French and Spanish back in the States. Languages are her passion."

"You must be exhausted," Roselani broke in quickly. "Let me show you to your rooms." She led them outside and down a short path to a tiny cottage. It was a miniature version of the big house—wood shingles with white trim and a front porch with two rocking chairs.

"This is where guests and family stay when they come visit. We call it the 'Honeymoon Cottage.' My father built it. I think he was hoping one of his daughters would raise a family here." Roselani looked at Wally. He colored and looked away.

Virginia caught the exchange. So that was it. This was to be their

"Honeymoon Cottage." Who knows what would have gone on here if she hadn't decided to tag along.

"I'm taking a nap," Virginia announced walking into the bedroom. The bed was already made up in fresh white sheets. Before climbing in, she remembered what Roselani had said about critters on the way up. With a quick movement, she threw back the covers—in case someone had left a little present for her.

The sun had moved west by the time Virginia roused herself. She was alone. She took a quick look at herself in the mirror. Ugh. Bloodshot eyes and blotched skin. No comparison to the exotic beauty of her hostess. Carefully, she washed, applied some make up and put on the new muumuu Wally had bought her in Waikiki. Somehow it had looked better in the store.

Virginia walked down a lava path that led away from the cottage. Pink and white geraniums with gray leaves lined either side, and here and there giant silverswords grew, their slender spears reaching for the sky. Birds chattered as they flitted from flower to flower, gathering pollen. Up ahead, the terrain opened to reveal a hollow where a frothy stream cascaded into a pool of dark green water. At the opposite end, she could make out two figures under the flat space behind the lip of the waterfall. The female was swaying, as if in a trance, and the man sat cross-legged on the ground, watching. He was bare chested and wearing a pareo. With a start, Virginia realized it was Wally and Roselani. She was dancing the hula for him.

Hidden by foliage, Virginia watched them. Roselani's hips swayed close to him and moved away. She was laughing... taunting. He reached for her...

Virginia didn't want to see any more. She turned away and ran back the way she had come. When she reached the cottage, she collapsed in one of the rocking chairs and covered her face with her hands.

Wally came running up. "Honey, I saw you and waved for you to join us, but you left."

"You . . . you were . . . She . . . she was dancing for you. I know what that means."

Wally laughed. "Oh, it wasn't like that at all. The hula is a dance of courtship, it's true, but Hawaiian girls dance it also as an expression of femininity."

"She is still in love with you."

Wally did not deny it. "I think Roselani has a fantasy of what might have happened between us if the war had not gotten in the way. The truth is, she was just a young boy's first crush." Wally lifted Virginia's chin and looked at her. "I am a man now. A man in love with his wife."

"Bill built that cottage for the both of you hoping you would come back. She never married. Don't you see?"

"I see, now, that Bill and Kim would have expected me to follow in their footsteps if I married their daughter. Can you picture me as a farmer? And Roselani . . . she would never have joined me in the States. Her life is here."

"Not such a bad life."

"It is peaceful and wonderful. Don't get me wrong. For a vacation. Not the rest of my life." Wally gathered Virginia in his arms. "I know in the last few years I haven't told you that I love you as often, and there have been times when I felt that our lives were going in opposite directions and that we wanted different things. But being here with you, and having you by my side, makes me realize what a wonderful, special woman I married. I know I made the right decision." Wally looked into his wife's eyes and smiled. "Even one minute with you is more exciting than a lifetime in paradise with Roselani."

Virginia settled into her seat and stared out at the hills beyond Honolulu International Airport.

"Cocktail, miss?"

Virginia eyed the martini shaker and shook her head. "I think I'll pass, thanks."

Wally chuckled. "So, did you enjoy yourself? Tell me the truth."

"I did. Surprises and all. I learned something. After all, isn't that what travel is all about? Learning something new?"

"Absolutely. What did you learn?"

"That letting go can help you grow . . . as a person. For me, that means learning to enjoy special moments without constantly worrying about what it costs."

"I'm glad to hear you say that." Wally took a sip of his martini and turned to face his wife. "I have a proposal to make. I will put up with your real estate obsession"—he put a finger to Virginia's lips when he saw her eyes narrow—"if you will agree to take one . . . no, two vacations every year. Just the two of us."

"Who pays?"

"We alternate. That way I can count on at least one decent hotel a year."

"Agreed." Virginia reached out and slipped her arm through her husband's. "And one more thing . . . the minute we get back to San Diego, I'm buying one of those off the shoulder muumuus and signing up for hula lessons."

Chapter 28

Precious Heirlooms

SPIRITO woke with a start. The dream had seemed so real this time, like he could step inside it and be carried away. The lamp on the nightstand cast an eerie glow against the half light of the dying day. For a minute, he couldn't remember where he was.

"Papa, are you awake?"

As if sensing her presence, his lids flickered open, and his eyes rested on the woman bending over him.

"*Figlia*." His cracked lips mouthed the words and a hand reached out.

"I am here, Papa. What do you need?"

"A scotch and a thick juicy steak," Spirito croaked. A raspy laugh followed.

They sat in silence in the darkening twilight, father and daughter, already feeling the pain of separation and the gratitude of a lifetime of memories.

After Spirito's second fall, Virginia decided she needed to have her parents closer. She bought a two-bedroom bungalow one block from the Sunset Boulevard house in Mission Hills. It was either that or a rest home.

After forty-five years of living at Albatross Street, Spirito found the adjustment difficult.

"Why did we have to move?" He would say to Marianna when he couldn't remember where the bathroom was.

"Albatross was too far away. I need help taking care of you now."

"I don't need help. You and Virginia are worrywarts. I know exactly what I'm doing."

"Is that why we found you at the bus stop, heading for downtown?"

"Just trying to get back home," Spirito replied matter-of-factly.

There were good days when Urbano would drop by unexpectedly, bringing a bottle of Chianti from Di Filippi's Pizzeria in Little Italy. The two brothers would take their glasses of wine and head for the garage. Rummaging through the stuff from the Albatross house was like wading through piles of gray matter: an old all-in-one pewter cheese grater from the twenties, a ragged butcher knife blackened with age, an old wooden sign with the words "*Buon Appetito*" painted on it. It stirred up their brains and helped them remember.

"What's this?" Spirito lifted up a metal contraption with two flaps that hinged together.

"A tamale mold," Urbano replied. "My brilliant idea to replace the corn husk. Got a patent and everything. No one bought it."

"What's wrong with a corn husk?"

"Nothing, obviously."

"The French fryer!" Spirito hauled out a rusted metal basket with handles. "One of the first they made. Cost me a fortune."

"The beginning of the end," Urbano muttered.

"The end of what?"

"Real cooking. I still say my gnocchi were the best thing that ever happened to San Diego—until the French fry came along."

Spirito nodded. "I remember. That's why we took it off the menu. Everyone wanted the fries instead."

"Not everyone. When Vinnie DePhilippis got tired of making his American version of pizza, he'd come by my restaurant and order *gnocchi con spinaci*. Stood over me as I made it and ate every last one. 'You gotta gimme that recipe,' he always said."

"Did you give it to him?"

"Never did. I think I was afraid he would use it in his restaurant and make a fortune."

"Too bad you didn't patent *that* recipe."

Urbano cleared his throat and looked around furtively. "I wanted to tell you and Marianna something. I'm getting married."

Spirito slapped his knee and laughed. "That's a good one. Who is it? Sophia Loren?"

Urbano looked hurt. "No, really. Her name's Myrna. She's fifteen years younger than me. Tits out to here." He held his hands a foot away from his chest and winked.

Spirito's eyes widened. "Hold on to your bank account," he warned.

Urbano waved his hand. "You're just jealous. She makes me feel young again. You wouldn't believe the things she does to my pecker. She can—"

"Spare me," Spirito interrupted. "I can't even remember where that body part is, much less how to use it."

"Maybe I'm making a mistake, but I feel good. Better than I have in a long time. What's wrong with that?"

Spirito shrugged his shoulders. "Enjoy it while it lasts." He patted his brother's knee. "And keep separate bank accounts."

There were the not-so-good days too. Spirito would stride out into the backyard looking for his shed. "Where are my vines? The fruit trees are gone." He would stand in the yard, puzzled. The fire in him would begin to die, and he would slowly walk back into the house and sit in his chair.

Then there were the bad days when Spirito lay in bed refusing to get up, even to relieve himself.

The cold gnarled hand squeezed Virginia's warm one. "*Figlia*, I need you to do something for me." Spirito raised himself from the bed, his eyes anxious.

"Yes, Papa."

"Look in the closet . . . upper shelf, far corner . . . metal box." He was gasping the words.

Virginia searched through the jumbled mess and found a safe deposit box hidden in the back. It was locked.

"Key taped to the bottom, open it."

Virginia turned the key and lifted the lid. A single item, carefully wrapped in velvet cloth, lay at the bottom. It was an ivory cameo locket on a gold chain. She lifted it up, and the chain caught the last rays of the sun. It flashed like fire for a moment before the light faded and darkness claimed the sky.

"It is a locket, isn't it?' Virginia asked gently. "Shall I open it?"

Spirito nodded, his eyes intent.

As the clasp sprung open, Virginia saw a tiny likeness of a familiar face staring back at her. The young man had a square jaw and intense blue eyes.

"Is this you, Papa? As a young man?"

Spirito looked at his daughter as if trying to remember. "No . . . yes . . ." A sigh escaped his lips. "I don't know," he finally said.

Virginia tried again. "Is this your mother's locket? Did this belong to her?"

Spirito made an effort to raise himself, and his hand opened. "Let me hold it."

Virginia laid it gently in his palm, and his fingers closed around it. Spirito closed his eyes. He was remembering a beautiful woman, a bench in Central Park, and a peach dress.

"It belonged to someone I loved very much." A tear rolled down his cheek as he handed the locked back to Virginia. "It belongs to you now. Keep it safe. Don't tell your mother about it. She has been through enough."

"Rest, Papa. We can talk tomorrow."

He waved her hand away. "No. Let me say it." He seemed to find strength from somewhere inside him. His eyes were clear, and he looked straight at his daughter. "The end is coming. I can feel it. Take care of my Marianna. She needs you now more than ever."

Spirito sank back into the pillows, drained, as if a burden had been lifted from him. Marianna would be cared for, and the locket was safe. It would be up to his daughter now to keep the memory alive. Someday she would put all the pieces together.

He felt the pull of the dream again. He let it envelop him like a warm embrace.

The light was fading, and he could barely make out a girl by an iron gate. There were graves all around her. She was dressed like a servant, golden hair loose about her shoulders and an apron tied around her slim waist. Her profile reminded him of a Botticelli painting. Suddenly, he knew.

"Agatha," he cried out. The girl turned to look at him and smiled. Now she was running toward him, hair flying and arms outstretched. The blood red sunset at her back covered the sky. He reached out to touch her, and she fell into his arms.

We buried my grandfather next to Antonio at Holy Cross Cemetery. It was a bright winter morning, the cold crisp air contrasting sharply with the brilliant blue of the sky. Next to the gravesite, Marianna was flanked by Virginia and Wally on one side, and Urbano, the last surviving Urbino brother, on the other.

Urbano had brought his new wife with him. I had heard he'd married again, but he never brought Myrna by the house to visit. Maybe he wanted it that way. At the grave, against the serene backdrop of Holy Cross, Myrna stuck out like a sore thumb. Too much cleavage, too much make up, and too young. Her manicured fingers were grabbing Urbano's arm possessively, and her eyes were darting back and forth to see who was looking at her. Urbano seemed restless and unsettled, avoiding eye contact instead of welcoming it.

In between the priest's prayers for the departed, I heard snatches of conversation several rows behind me, from a pair of old ladies too deaf to know how loud they were.

"Never seen her at church . . . she's young enough to be his daughter," one whispered.

"Annie Mary must be turning in her grave."

"No fool like an old fool," the other one responded.

Urbano did not turn around.

I stood one row behind my parents between my brother, Tino, and my sister, Terry. Tino stirred restlessly, his features composed in a mask of polite grief. He had never been close to his grandfather, and at fifteen, he was probably thinking of a million places he'd rather be.

I glanced to my left. My sister's eyes were anxious and her mouth was set in a thin line. The last year of Spirito's life, we had both kept our distance, staying away from the house on Fort Stockton Street. When we were eleven and twelve, we were too young to fully understand why our grandfather had changed from the man we knew growing up. When we did go to visit, he often didn't remember who we were.

I could see my grandmother's face one row ahead. I watched her staring at the coffin being lowered into the ground, and I imagined what it must be like to lose someone you have lived with most of your life. Like having your leg cut off. A big empty place where part of you used to be. I reached out, grabbed her hand, and squeezed it. Virginia caught my eye and nodded her approval. We both knew Marianna would need companionship and love in the years ahead, and I was determined to help my mother give it to her.

Without taking her eyes off her husband's coffin, Marianna squeezed back.

Chapter 29

Something to Live For

I LET MYSELF in through the back door and listened for the sound of the TV.

I was coming every day after school now. The bus from Roosevelt Junior High School stopped at Fort Stockton and West Lewis, and I walked down Stephens Street to my grandmother's house. There would be tea and homemade biscotti waiting, and the TV would be tuned to Nonna's favorite soap opera, *General Hospital.*

Terry, at thirteen, had begun hanging out with friends whose families lived in the best part of Mission Hills. I think she preferred their posh homes to ours, maid service not being in the Wilsons' household budget. She had discovered that people had dishwashers, barbequed steaks on weekends, and shopped at the mall. A whole new world was opening up for her, and she was embracing it.

Tino, a junior at San Diego High School, was obsessed with cars. He usually had his head under the hood of a beat-up jalopy as soon as he got home.

Crossing through the laundry room into the kitchen, I heard voices. One of them sounded like Uncle Urbano. I stood outside the swinging door that led to the dining room and listened.

"She fleeced me, Marianna. Cleared out my bank account. Now she wants half the house. I will be broke."

"I warned you not to marry that floozy. Nothing but a gold digger. What were you thinking?"

Urbano was silent.

"Never mind. I can guess." More gently, she added, "A new wife can only mask the pain for so long."

Urbano nodded. "You're right. No fool like an old fool, and now I'm a broke old fool."

"You need to find some joy of your own, Urbano. That's what I did after Anna was killed. I took some time for myself. It helped me grow so I could come back to my family."

"I'm eighty-five. What's left to enjoy? My body hurts, my mind wanders. Sometimes I wonder what there is to live for."

"There is always something to live for," Marianna reminded him. "Life is a gift, and only God can decide when to take it away."

I waited in the kitchen until Urbano had left. The conversation felt too personal for me to intrude.

"Was that Uncle Urbano? Is he in trouble?"

"Heartbroken and lonely, more like." After a moment, Marianna added, "It comes with the territory."

"What territory?"

"Old age. Hard for someone like you to understand."

"Are you lonely, Nonna?"

"Of course not." Marianna smiled. "I have you. Now where are those biscotti?" We caught the tail end of *General Hospital* and sipped our tea. Marianna reached for her knitting, and I settled into a chair opposite her.

"Tell me about when you were a girl back in Italy. About your father's castle."

Whenever Marianna spoke of her father, Ettore Brandi Orsolini, a quiet reverence would come over her. "I was nine when he was murdered, but I can still picture his face. He was handsome and elegant, with the polished manners of the upper class. His parents had been rich, with a beautiful estate in Loreto near the Adriatic coast. But the family had a secret. Ettore was a *bastard child*." Marianna whispered the words as if they were forbidden. "His father had slept with a servant girl, and she had given birth. La Signora Brandi Orsolini raised the boy, but as soon as he came of age, she kicked him out of the house. A stipend arrived every month for us to live on. Hush money. In return, he was to keep his mouth shut and not bring scandal to the family."

My eyes grew large and intense as I listened. I loved these stories. "Nonna, don't you have a picture of him? I know I've seen it."

"We have paintings of both my parents and Spirito's. Fausto Tasca painted them. They were hanging at the Albatross House."

"Where are they now?"

"When we moved, we brought them here. I think they're still in the garage."

"Why haven't you hung them?"

"It was always something we were going to get around to, but then Spirito started to have problems and . . ." Marianna shrugged her shoulders.

"Let's get them out."

Marianna started to protest. "Wait until your mother gets here. They are too heavy for you."

"No, I can do it myself. I'll be right back."

The garage was in shambles. No one had made an effort to sort the good stuff from the junk. I saw things I remembered from my childhood at Albatross Street—a bronze statue on a pedestal, Spirito's old wrought iron bed with Victorian posts, rusted-out dumbbells. I picked my way through cardboard boxes filled with empty five-gallon jugs rimmed with purple residue and piles of restaurant-grade kitchen supplies. Off to one side, away from the junk, I saw a box labeled "Family Records." I bent down, undid the twine, and opened the dusty flaps. Inside, I found carefully stacked letters in Italian, all of them addressed to "Ninina."

Nonna's voice called from the back porch, "Have you found the paintings yet?"

"Not yet, I'm still looking," I called back.

There were important-looking papers alongside the letters. And pictures. There was a photo of a birthday party in a park and two little girls dressed alike, and a grave with the name Urbino on it. "*Holy Sepulchre Cemetery, New Jersey*," it said on the back. Digging deeper, I spied a document in heavy parchment with "*Ricordo delle Campagne D'Africa*," written in large black letters. There was a medal attached on the right side and a seal of the Republic of Italy, dated 1894. Antonio Urbino's name was inscribed by the Ministry of War. Uncle Toni's medal from Africa. Did Nonna know this was here?

Quickly, I closed the box, making a mental note so I could find it again later. I needed to stay focused on the task at hand. On top of a rusted spring mattress, I saw a thick, rectangular bundle wrapped in blankets. I knew I had found the paintings. One by one, I carried them into the house, maneuvering the double one of Ettore and Teresa with a small dolly I found. Marianna helped me bring it up the steps and into the house.

We spread them out in the living room. I remembered the paintings, strangers from a forgotten time, staring down at me when I was a little girl at Albatross Street. Now, they looked different. Nonna Marianna's stories had brought them to life. I could see the naïve look on Ettore's face, shielded from a brutal world by a wealthy family until it was too late. Teresa, next to him, looked like the strong one. I noticed a gold necklace nestled against the turned-up collar of her velvet jacket.

"What is that around her neck?"

"An amulet."

"Amulet," I repeated.

"An amulet is like a locket. Ladies of that era wore them as remembrances. Inside was usually a likeness of a son or daughter or other family member."

I glanced over at the two paintings of Spirito's parents. "Grandpa's mother, Virginia—she's the one that killed herself, right? Why?"

"When someone is not strong enough to climb out of the darkness, it can seem like the only way out." Marianna pointed to the portrait of Francesco. "Her husband couldn't keep his hands off the servants. Typical Italian male, liked a mistress or two on the side."

"Good thing Nonno Spirito wasn't like that," I said.

Marianna looked at me and said nothing.

Gently, I pulled out the painting of my Uncle Toni. His medal was displayed proudly on his right jacket lapel. "His eyes are so sad, Nonna."

"Your great-uncle saw terrible things in Africa. Something he lived with his whole life."

"I don't think I've seen any terrible things."

"You are lucky, but you are still young." Marianna put down her knitting and looked at me intently. "Every life has many things in it—joy, sorrow, regret. If you live long enough, you experience all of them."

"What do you mean by regret?" I asked.

"The feeling when you know you could have done something different than you did."

"Can't you just undo it and make it right?"

"Some things can't be undone." Marianna said simply.

"I found a box of letters in the garage addressed to Ninina. That's you, isn't it? Who wrote them?"

"My mother Teresa, the beautiful lady in the portrait. They are letters she wrote me after I left for America."

Marianna's eyes filled. That was a subject for another time, I decided. I already had a project lined up for today. "As soon as Mom gets here, we will hang the painting of your parents in your bedroom.

And tomorrow, we will get that box out and bring it in here. I want to know everything your mother had to say in those letters."

"You have given me something to look forward to," Marianna said. As if to remind herself, she added, "And something to live for."

Marianna's stomach pains started two years after Spirito's death. I knew something was wrong when I arrived after school and she was in bed. Tea and biscotti were not waiting for me, and the TV was dark.

"Nonna, these pains are not normal. You need to see a doctor."

"No doctors. It is just indigestion. I am fine."

I knew she wasn't fine. I had to tell Mom.

The next day, all three of us were in Dr. B's office. At eighty-three, he no longer saw patients, but the Urbinos were family. It didn't take him long to see there was a problem.

"My associate will do some tests. Stay off the sweets and red meat." He pointed a finger at Marianna. Her face fell; sweets were one of her guilty pleasures. Lamb chops in cream sauce was another.

The news was not good. The test results showed a cancer in the colon that had spread.

The pain she experienced was caused by the tumor blocking the colon when a bowel movement occurred.

Dr. B broke it to her gently. "Surgery will be necessary to create a passage to bypass the colon so you can eliminate. The waste will flow into a bag attached to your stomach."

I watched Marianna's face grow white. I could tell she was terrified.

"Can you empty her bag when it is full and insert a new one?" Mom's face was drawn, and she looked exhausted. It was a week after the surgery, and Marianna was home. "Let me show you how to do it."

I looked at the bag and the hole in my grandmother's side and backed out of the room.

When Virginia found me, I was curled up on the sofa sobbing.

"It's okay. I will do it when I get here after teaching. Just stay with her." Virginia paused, then added quietly, "I would be glad to pay you."

I was shocked and angry. "How can you even ask that? Of course, I will stay. I love coming here."

Mom grabbed me in an uncharacteristic show of emotion. "Thank you," she whispered.

Marianna did not get better. Her bouts of pain were more frequent, and she spent most of her time in bed. I still spent time with her, but I was in my sophomore year of high school, and I felt the yearnings of adolescence. The outside world was calling, and I wanted to join it.

There was something else I barely admitted, even to myself.

Marianna was dying.

A part of me knew I was pulling away to save myself from the pain . . . the pain I would feel when she was gone.

"I'm going to put Mama in assisted care," Virginia told the family. "I can't care for her properly anymore."

"No!" I cried out. I knew, if Marianna went to that nursing home, she would never make it out alive.

"She's too sick. She needs special care."

I visited her once at the facility. The smell of urine, the colored mounds that passed for food, and the dead eyes of the orderlies emptying bed pans filled me with dread. In my youthful ignorance, I didn't understand that each bed had a person in it who had lived a meaningful life, had a career, had given birth, had loved someone passionately. All I saw were rooms full of people waiting to die. I remember walking toward someone who looked like my grandmother, but the hollow white face was barely recognizable. She looked dead already. Bile rose in my throat, and my hands trembled.

Suddenly she was grabbing at me and holding on. "Anna, I am

dying," she kept saying over and over. Instead of holding her in my arms, I backed away, horrified at the panic I saw in her eyes.

Virginia looked at her watch. Dinnertime. Wally and the kids would be waiting around for her to come home. Seeing the figure on the bed, so still, barely a breath coming, she knew she couldn't leave. Virginia's grief hovered, threatening to overtake her, but she couldn't even allow herself to acknowledge it. Her mother needed her.

She was thinking back to that day at the train station when Marianna had returned to them. How strong she had looked standing there on the platform, and how happy Papa had been. Through all the challenges they had faced, it was Marianna who had held the family together.

"I love you Mama," she said.

Marianna looked at her daughter. "I am afraid of what is coming. I am not as strong as you. I never have been."

"You are stronger than you think." Virginia gently touched her mother's wasted face and looked into her eyes. "You stood up to the Franzeses and got our money back, remember? You were the one who helped Papa achieve his dream, made it a success, and picked up the pieces when it shattered. When my heart was breaking, you held me in your arms and told me I was worth loving. You taught me to reach for the sky, that there was nothing I couldn't do if I wanted it bad enough. You are the bravest person I know."

Marianna was listening.

"It's time to let go of fear. Where you are going, it doesn't exist. Everyone is waiting for you: Papa, Toni . . . and little Anna. You will see your daughter again, alive and whole."

Marianna smiled. "Yes, my little girl. I will see my Anna again." She turned her eyes to her daughter. "The hardest thing is leaving you behind. I wish you were coming with me."

Virginia struggled to keep her composure. "I will be there soon, Mama. Give them all a kiss for me."

Marianna's hands reached out to find Virginia's, and she felt the fear dissolve. It was time. She held on and let herself go.

I was over at a friend's house when the call came.

"Your grandmother is gone," Virginia's voice broke. "She died last night."

"I'm sorry." My voice was cold and without emotion.

"Don't you care?"

"Of course, I care." My response sounded lame, even to me. I couldn't believe how callous I was acting. I pushed back the shame and hung up the phone.

The phone was ringing . . . again. The sound seemed far away, like a foghorn in the middle of the ocean. Ten rings this time before it stopped. Urbano opened his eyes and looked down at the letter. "*Cara Urbano*," it began. He picked it up, and a laminated card fell out. "*Marianna O. Urbino. B. 7-3-1889. D. 2-9-1972.*" Next to the card was a .38 Colt revolver.

I sat in the front pew of the Goodbody Mortuary Chapel with Tino, Terry, and, my mother and father. In the second row was Luigi and Mary Zamboni, our old friends from Little Italy. "Where is Urbano?" Luigi whispered to Virginia.

"I called him many times," Virginia said. "I sent him a copy of the memorial service announcement at the address I have for him. A trailer park in Hemet. I never heard back." Virginia shook her head. "I don't understand it."

I watched my mother look at her family and gesture to the open casket in the front of the chapel. "It is time for us to say goodbye."

Everyone stood except me. I was starting to shake. They would all see how afraid I was.

"Get up. Go pay your respects to her."

I looked up. My mother was staring at me in quiet fury. I rose and followed my family.

Urbano picked up the gun and fingered the trigger. He knew just where to place it on his temple. He had practiced many times in the last ten years, but he had always put it down. There had always been something to live for, a glimmer of hope, before the darkness descended again. This time it did not lift. He looked at the card. Goodbody Memorial Chapel. February twelfth. Today. He knew he should be there. Virginia needed him, but he felt so weak . . . so tired. They were all gone now—Toni, Spirito, Annie, and now Marianna. Why had he been spared? If cancer had claimed him, there would be no choice to make.

Marianna's features were stark and drawn . . . and lifeless. This was not the warm, loving person I had spent so many happy hours with—talking, laughing, listening to tales from the past that filled my head with wonder. It finally hit me—my grandmother was gone. Because of my selfish fear of being hurt, I had missed out on those last precious moments of her life. Moments I could never get back. *Some things can never be undone*, she had said to me. I turned and ran down the aisle toward the half-open door of the chapel. I stood on the sidewalk and wept for the part of me that was gone forever.

Urbano raised the gun higher and felt the cold steel graze his temple. He knew why his mother couldn't face the future, why she had run toward the river all those years ago. There was only one way to stop the pain. *Mama!* he cried out. He closed his eyes and pulled the trigger.

PART VI

Chapter 30

Back to Our Roots

"SO, WHERE are we going this year? What about Australia?" Wally was at the kitchen table, poring over a map of the Southern Hemisphere. "Will 1995 be the year of the kangaroo?"

Virginia was peeling potatoes in the sink. "The year of the boot, more like. Tino wants to meet us in Italy, says he wants to get back to his *roots.*"

Wally made a face. "We've already been to Italy, twice."

"Well, he hasn't. At least not with us. He's been living in Paris almost three years now, working for that airline company."

"Air*craft* company." Wally corrected her. "Allied Signal Aerospace is an aircraft company."

"Right. Like I was saying, he's been in Paris for three years, and we haven't done any traveling in Europe with him. It's about time."

Virginia remembered the phone call. "Let's meet in Rome," Tino had suggested. "We can look up Emma, Marianna's sister, the one who was always looking for a rich sugar daddy. She has an apartment there, right? She's got to be ninety by now."

"Ninety-nine, actually."

"Ninety-nine? Jesus. I want to meet her before she croaks."

Virginia was curious. "Why are you so interested in the family's relatives all of a sudden? You never cared when your grandparents were alive."

"Being here in Europe, I guess. I am more aware that this was the starting place for a lot of immigrant families that made their way to the States. Like ours. I'm working on a family tree, but I need your help—and Emma's—to fill in the blanks. Oh, and another thing, I'm booking the hotel in Rome. If I leave it up to you, we'll be staying in some fleabag pensione near the train station."

Later that evening, Virginia reached into the top drawer of her dresser and pulled out the safe deposit box. She removed the key taped to the bottom and opened it. The locket was still there, nestled in the velvet cloth. She fingered it lovingly. *Keep it safe.* It was the last thing Papa had said to her. She put the locket around her neck. *I am taking this to Scheggino. Maybe someone there can tell me who it belongs to.*

The taxi stopped in front of 173 Via Emanuele Filiberto. The ten-story modern high-rise looked like it had been dropped from an unseen hand right in the middle of ancient Rome. Not exactly quaint, Virginia noted, but definitely well located. The Colosseum was a couple of streets over, and The Victor Emmanuel Monument could be seen rising over the Forum like a gigantic wedding cake topper.

Wally counted out the change for the taxi driver and looked up. "This is nice." He took in the glass-plated entrance and spacious lobby. "Better than the last place we stayed in Rome. I remember the bathroom was down the hall and we had to share it with two other people. Instant coffee for breakfast and no elevator. Who picked that hotel, I wonder?"

Virginia ignored him. She did remember the rock-hard rolls, though. Almost broke a molar. "Tino's not coming for a few hours. I say we forgo the nap and find Emma's apartment."

Wally looked longingly at the bed in their stylish suite. The digs Tino had picked out were a major improvement on their usual accommodations. A quick nap was tempting, but staying up probably meant they would sleep better later. Even with a number of international trips under his belt, jetlag never got any easier.

Emma's apartment, 57 Castelfidardo, was not far from the train station, centrally located and brimming with life. Prime real estate, Virginia couldn't help noticing. No one answered the intercom, so they tried the next-door neighbor.

"*Sì?*" A woman in slippers and a bathrobe opened the door a crack. One eye looked suspiciously through the sliver of light.

"*Cerco la Signora Brandi Orsolini*," Virginia said in her best Italian. "*Sta qui*? Is she here?"

The woman opened the door and grinned broadly. There were two teeth missing, front and center. She pointed upward. "Fourth floor, but she's out. With her boyfriend." The grin got wider.

"Here is our number at the hotel." Virginia pantomimed dialing a phone. "Tell her to call us."

Virginia and Wally went to bed at nine. At eleven, the phone rang.

"Viergeenia?" a lively voice chirped.

Good God, Virginia thought, *Emma is still up*.

"*Bienvenuti!* I weel see you *domani*, here, *alle nove*. Nine o'clock." *Click*.

Tino, Virginia, and Wally were standing outside Emma's apartment at 9:05 A.M., looking like they could do with double espressos. They buzzed the intercom. It buzzed back.

"Come up!"

Virginia recognized the chirpy voice.

"At least there is an elevator," Wally muttered, as they trudged up the set of stairs that led from the landing to Emma's door.

A bearded, middle-aged man stood holding the door open when they came up. "I am Bruno. *Piacere*." He gestured for them to enter.

"Emma, shee in dere." He pointed to the living room.

"You speak English?" Tino looked surprised.

"A leetle." Bruno tilted his hand back and forth and smiled. He was a good-looking man, Tino observed. Artistic type. Soulful eyes and delicate white hands. Definitely not a bricklayer.

The apartment was old world—and old lady-ish, Tino decided. There were lots of doilies covering armchairs and figurines crowding the tops of antique furniture.

Probably gifts from her paramours. He had heard the stories of Emma's various lovers. According to Mom, they all had one thing in common: They were loaded.

Emma sat near the window, her back to the partially closed velvet curtains. With her carefully made-up face and immaculately coiffed hair, she reminded Virginia of a dowager queen ready to greet her subjects. Even the lighting in the room had been carefully considered to make her look her best.

Emma's eyes flicked over Virginia and Wally briefly, before they rested on Tino. "*Che bello!* How handsome! How old, you?"

"I am forty-two. Uh . . . *quar-anta due*." Tino stumbled over the numbers. Clearly his Italian was not as good as he'd thought it was.

Virginia sat respectfully and waited for Emma to speak. Her mind was doing some quick calculations. Emma had no heirs and a *very* nice apartment in Rome. Maybe something could be worked out. After all, they were blood relatives.

"Theeze eez Bruno. Mio companion. Hee weel get thee appartamento when I die."

Virginia's jaw dropped. Emma was reading her mind. She may be ninety-nine, but she hadn't lost any of her marbles. Virginia looked over at Bruno. Poor guy, he looked like he wanted to crawl under the table. With everything he had to put up with, he probably deserved the house.

"Mom, did you see the portrait?" Tino pointed to a photo over the doorway. "It looks like the painting we have."

Virginia recognized it immediately. The photo was large, at least twenty by twenty-five inches. Ettore and Teresa Brandi Orsolini, Marianna and Emma's parents, were in the exact same pose and wearing the same clothes as the oil painting Fausto Tasca had painted.

Virginia decided to switch to her great aunt's native language. "Emma, that photo, who took it? Ettore died in 1897."

"It was a studio portrait." Emma answered her in Italian. "Very expensive in those days. It turned out to be the only picture the family has of our father. He was murdered shortly after it was taken. Marianna took a copy when she left for America."

Virginia and Tino's eyes met. The "finding our roots" trip was gaining momentum.

Emma rose and spoke as if issuing a proclamation. "Wee are goe-eeeg to Doney's, on dee Via Veneto. *Pranzo delizioso*. Good lunch. Bruno weel drive."

Tino thought it sounded more like an order than a suggestion, and to refuse would have been like insulting royalty. An imperious "Off with their heads!" with Bruno brandishing a sword, did not seem entirely out of the realm of possibility. Besides, the trip was just getting started, and he was sure everyone wanted to make it to Scheggino with all their body parts intact.

The next day, the Wilsons were tucked into a rental car and heading out of Rome. Tino steered the Fiat Panda expertly up the ramp from the parking garage onto the Via Salaria. From there, it was a straight shot through the outskirts of Rome onto Autostrada A1. In two hours, they would be at Teresina Sabatini's palazzo in Spoleto.

"Quite a pistol, that Emma."

"Runs in the family," Wally quipped.

Tino gave his father a rare smile of approval, and they both glanced at Virginia in the back seat.

Virginia beamed. She seldom saw her husband and son getting along. It was a difficult relationship. Wally's unpredictable behavior had embarrassed Tino growing up, and it had diminished the respect he had for his father. It was a shame, really. They had so much in common. Both had graduated from Berkeley with engineering degrees, and both loved to travel. They even looked alike, slightly built, with thick, dark hair that showed barely a hint of gray. Tino had the Urbino eyes, though, blue and intense, and the Urbino smile.

"I guess Bruno will get that fancy apartment," Virginia called up to the front seat. "Too bad. We are the blood relatives, and she has no heirs . . ."

"Nuda Law, Mom. Ever heard of it? Old Italian custom."

"*Nuda?* That means 'naked' in Italian."

"More like 'bare.' It is when an older person with no heirs gives their property to someone before they die. The one who inherits gets to live there, rent free, until they own it outright."

"Maybe we can convince Emma to change her mind."

"Don't even think about it. You don't want Bruno's relatives coming after you. There's another old Italian custom. It's called vengeance."

It was noon when they rolled into Spoleto. Teresina Sabatini's palazzo was in the newer section of town, right outside Piazza Garibaldi. Another intercom, another landing, and another walk up a flight of stairs. No wonder Italians lived so long, Wally thought. They had to exercise just to get home.

The Wilsons heard voices even before they knocked. It sounded like a party was going on inside. As the door opened, five people filled the doorway.

"Holy crap!" Tino blurted out before he could stop himself. Long-lost relatives were coming out of the woodwork.

Teresina Sabatini pushed through and double-kissed all three of them. Six kisses, and that didn't even include the rest of the relatives. Introductions were a blur. The only name Tino could remember was Brunetta, the good looking brunette. A short skirt and cleavage always got his attention.

The Italians didn't know English, and the Americans, except for Mom, weren't faring any better. Fortunately, shoveling in forkfuls of *spaghetti alla milanese* and *cicoria con brodo* required no language skills, and after three liters of wine, no one cared what language they were speaking.

Tino needed some air and a smoke. He motioned to Brunetta, and they excused themselves and headed to an outdoor balcony. "You are Pina's daughter, right? You speak English?" Tino asked hopefully.

"*Sì!* I learn from Amereekan roc songs. And feelms."

"Movies? Name one."

"Deertie Dancee-ng. Onngree Ice." Brunetta looked at him proudly.

"Dirty Dancing." Tino repeated. *Chick flick. Never seen it. Ongree ice? What the hell is that?*

"You know dee song?" Brunetta was looking at him with her big brown eyes.

Tino thought hard. His reputation for impressing hot Italian girls was hanging in the balance. "Ongree . . . Ah! Hungry Eyes!" Tino burst out laughing. "Eric Carmen. Big hit in the eighties."

"*Sì*. Ongree Ice. I not say it right?"

"You said it perfectly," Tino assured her as he slipped an arm around her waist and stared at the cleft between her breasts.

Tino finished his cigarette and he and Brunetta walked back into the dining room. The group around the table looked catatonic, their rosy cheeks and glazed eyes demonstrating proper gastronomic tribute to the meal they had just eaten. Tino and Brunetta stacked plates and empty bottles and headed for the kitchen. No one volunteered to help.

"You know, when Uncle Urbano came in dee feefties, Mama want to go to Amereeka weeth heem. Teresina say noooo." Brunetta waved her finger back and forth while shaking her head. "But me, no one tell me what to do."

Tino's eyes widened. *Oh, no. Not a chance. I've still got plenty of wild oats to sow*. "Reminds me of another great movie," he said out loud. "*If It's Tuesday, This Must Be Belgium.* Seen it?"

"*Sì!* Sowsanne Pleeshette."

"My favorite part is when the Italian relatives try to set the American up with their daughter. He escapes out the bathroom window."

The dining room was getting fuzzy and Virginia felt herself sliding backward in the chair. A nap would feel good about now . . . soft couch . . . twenty minutes max . . . *bang!* Her head hit the table.

"Oh!" She jerked it up and looked around. Teresina was eyeing something on her chest.

"*Che e quello?* What eez that?" Teresina pointed to the locket. "*Amuletto?*"

Her amulet! It had slipped out when her head hit the table.

"Pepina's husband, he know jewelry." Teresina looked at her knowingly. "Gianni, come look."

With an air of authority, Gianni took a small object out of his pocket and studied the necklace.

"Spirito gave it to me right before he died," Virginia explained in Italian. "He could no longer remember who gave it to him. It might have belonged to his mother."

Gianni shook his head. "No. It's too new. It's from the late thirties, early forties. Nice Italian piece. May I open it?"

"Of course. Is it Spirito as a young man?" Virginia asked.

"No, definitely not." Gianni examined the photo carefully. "The picture was made to go in this locket. Doesn't fit the time frame."

Virginia turned to Teresina. "You've been around here the longest. Who is it? Was there another member of the family we don't know about?"

Teresina studied the picture. "It looks like Spirito, but it is not him. The *amuletto* looks familiar. I know I have seen it somewhere before."

"Are we going to the cemetery in Scheggino?" Tino stood in the doorway, keys in hand. "Part two of the *back to our roots* trip, don't forget."

"I show you dee way," Brunetta said, still practicing her English. "Who weel come?"

They ended up in two cars. Tino, Wally, and Virginia in one; Brunetta, Teresina and Pepina in another.

Gianni declined. "I will be there soon enough," he said in Italian, "for good."

Brunetta shot out of the parking garage and through the congested streets of Spoleto at breakneck speed.

"Jesus," Tino muttered. "Give me a break. I don't know this town. Hang on!" he yelled into the back seat. "Brunetta's in training for the Grand Prix!"

They drove up into the hills separating the two towns. Winding along on two-lane roads, they passed stone villas and aqueducts arching over their heads. Tino wished he could stop and take in the views, but Brunetta's Alfa Romeo convertible was always a length ahead. He could see gray hair flying as they whipped around hairpin turns that edged drop-off cliffs and the valley below. Crossing

SS395, they raced up the old Roman road, past the village of Sant'Anatolia and into the clearing at the top of the hill. Scheggino's cemetery was on the right.

"You're sure you're not related to Mario Andretti?" Tino chuckled as they all got out. "You were clocking 128 kilometers back there."

"That's eighty miles an hour," Wally calculated quickly.

"Ees fast for Ameerikans, thees eighty meels?"

"Very fast," Tino and Wally answered together.

Brunetta flashed them a smile. Tino was rethinking those wild oats all of a sudden.

They were standing in front of the family plot. "Alessandro Sabatini. *Beneficiando Sempre Tutti*." The words stood out against the grayish-white marble.

"He worked to help everyone always," Virginia translated.

"*Quatro anni e morto*." Teresina held up four fingers. "Four years he gone. I am ninety-four. Soon, I am with him."

"He was ninety-eight. You are ninety-four, Emma is ninety-nine," Tino cut in. "I'm hoping I got some of those genes. What's your secret?"

"Pasta, fresh air, and amore," Teresina answered him.

Wally reached for Virginia's hand. .

Tino felt everyone's eyes on him. He ran a shaky hand through his hair. "Okay, let's move on to the other names here." He turned to Mom. "Francesco, my great-grandfather died in 1932. His wife is not here because . . .?"

"She took her own life. Suicide was a sin in the Catholic Church in those days. Francesco refused to allow her to be buried here."

Bastard, Tino thought.

"Assunta is also here, opposite Francesco, your great-aunt."

Tino noticed several empty spaces. He didn't need to ask whose names were going there.

While the women tidied up the gravesite, Tino looked around.

The Urbino Truffle Foundation had an impressive chunk of real estate, and that was just *inside* the cemetery.

Three miniature villas, with their last name at the tops, stood to the right of the iron gate. *Same name as ours*, Tino thought. *Might be a story there*. He walked over to the one with "*Claudio*" written on it and tried the door. It was locked.

"Teresina, have you ever been in one of these crypts?"

Teresina nodded. "*Una volta*." She held up one finger. "Claudio's funeral. My huzeband good friend."

"*Andiamo!*" Brunetta called out. "I ongree. You stay for dinner?"

Lunch was barely three hours ago, Tino thought. *I'm still stuffed.*

Wally and Virginia were nodding their heads vigorously. "*Sì. Grazie!*"

"Meet you back at dee ranch," Brunetta tried out the words slowly. "Giovanni Wayne, *Sì?*"

"*Sì*. True Grit. 1969," Tino answered. The quote was actually "meanwhile back at the ranch," and John Wayne probably didn't say it in *any* movie. He was hoping Brunetta wouldn't call him on it.

The gray hairs climbed into the Alfa Romeo, and Brunetta revved up the motor. "You know how to go?" She was looking at Tino.

Those big brown eyes were making him crazy. "Of course, I know. Uh . . . *Piedi . . .*"

"*Piedipaterno* sign. Past Vallo di Nera. *Ciao!*" With a squeal of the tires and a cloud of dust, she was roaring down the road and out of sight.

Tino had just reached the entrance to SS395 when he saw the flashing yellow lights up ahead.

"Looks like an accident," Wally said.

Tino's first thought was Brunetta. He whipped out his flip phone and called her. "Are you all right?"

"*Sì*. Why?"

"There is an accident here on SS395. The road is completely blocked. Must have happened after you passed."

"Take udder road. Troo Terni. You know way?"

Tino looked at his father. Wally nodded his head. "We'll figure it out," he whispered.

"Meet you soon," Tino said and shut the phone.

"SS204 heading south . . . connect at Terni . . . then north on SS675 to Spoleto." Wally had the map out and studied the route.

Tino leaned over, and their heads bent over the map together.

After the guests had left, Teresina sat in her darkened living room. It had been good to see Virginia, she thought, and Walter. So nice for them to have made the trip. And Tino—what a nice young man. Some day he would settle down. Alessandro would have liked him. She felt herself nodding off when something flashed in her head. The amulet! She remembered where she had seen it before. Claudio's funeral. The photo of the woman in the crypt was wearing it.

Chapter 31

Bucket List

"HOW'S THAT book about me coming?" Mom shielded her eyes from the glare and looked at me. We were on the front porch of the Sunset Boulevard house basking in the early morning sun, our usual routine between breakfast and lunch.

I gave her a sly look. "It isn't finished yet."

Mom chuckled. "Waiting for the last chapter maybe?"

I wasn't touching that one.

"Seeing as how I may not live to see this masterpiece, I have a request."

I frowned. "I can't wait to hear this."

"I want you to put in a chapter about how you and Terry become best friends again, like when you were little."

I rolled my eyes. The sibling rivalry between my sister and me had been going on all our adult lives. Not likely to change now.

Mom continued, "You remember that little Anna and I were the same distance apart in age as you and Terry? When you both were born, I couldn't believe how lucky I was. It was like I had been given a second chance." She spoke more softly now. "I could watch you grow up together. A luxury I forfeited when I turned my back on my sister that day."

"Mom, you were so young. You didn't know about the dangers—"

"Or the pain of a lifetime of regret?" She looked at me hopefully. "It's not too late for the both of you."

I knew what she was getting at. Terry and I had been given the gift of growing up with each other. A gift Mom had not fully appreciated until it was no longer there. The sibling rivalry, the competition to be more successful, more worthy, was something she had missed. I had never thought of it that way before.

"Request noted." I smiled and patted her hand.

As if on cue, a white BMW pulled up in front of the house.

I watched Terry stride purposefully up the steps. Everything about her screamed success. Ever since she had gotten her real estate license and taken over the management of Mom's properties, her self-confidence had soared. Terry had brokered the deal for the sale of the Front Street property when a large hotel chain had offered to buy it. Half a million dollars was the price tag. In 1987, that wasn't exactly chump change. When Mom refused to budge, the hotel chain met her price.

I was jealous. I didn't have my sister's brains or her looks, and I had always struggled with the missteps of my impulsive nature. Terry, on the other hand, never stumbled.

Standing there on the porch in her four-inch heels, Terry looked sharp. Her chestnut hair was cut stylishly short, and she wore a hunter-green silk sheath that clung to every curve. She had Mom's expressive blue eyes and her great-grandmother Teresa's pensive mouth, a mouth now settling into a smile she reserved for unavoidable family obligations.

She put her hands on her hips and surveyed the two of us. "You look like a couple of slackers. I wish I had time to laze about all day."

She meant it as a joke, but I felt my hackles rise. I resented the inference that taking care of Mom was a nothing job. I'd like to see her change diapers at five in the morning.

"Are you going to Mass at Saint Vincent's today?" Terry's eyes were on both of us. "I am singing in the choir."

"Uh . . . we were just discussing that." I turned to Mom for support.

"I have another idea." There was a twinkle in Mom's eye. She was definitely up to something. "I want my girls to give me a bath."

Terry looked at her watch. "I'm due at church in two . . . uh, an hour and a half."

"It won't take that long," Mom assured her.

I heard an exasperated sigh. "Let's get going then."

We marched Mom into the tiny downstairs bathroom with the old clawfoot tub, the same one we had used when we were kids. Cast iron and indestructible. Terry removed her silk jacket and kicked off her pumps before we maneuvered Mom into the tub. "First one leg," I told her, holding her shoulders and back while Terry guided her other leg over the rim. Slowly we eased her into the lavender-scented water. I soaped her arms and legs while Terry shampooed her hair. Mom looked happy watching us work together, and I had to admit, Terry and I made a good team.

"I remember bathing you two girls together in this tub."

I heard Terry mutter, "Yeah, probably to save the water."

"It was fun," I countered. "We had our favorite toys. Mine was Rubber Ducky, and yours was a penguin. What was its name?"

"Napoleon," Terry said. She had a sheepish grin on her face.

"Because he was an Emperor Penguin. That was cute. I remember something else." I felt a wicked grin coming on. "I remember you always had to get out of the tub before Mom pulled the plug because you thought you were going to go down the drain."

Terry turned bright red, and I thought she was going to whip me with the washcloth. Instead, she started to giggle. Then I started. Soon, all three of us were cracking up.

As we were drying Mom off, I reached for the baby powder on the counter.

"That reminds me." Terry had a funny look in her eyes. "Mom's fancy face powder in the box with the big powder puff in it. Remember it by any chance?"

I blanched. She wouldn't dare . . . or would she?

"You never knew this, Mom, but we used to douse ourselves with it until we ran out one day. Annie substituted it with Dad's athlete foot powder."

Mom slowly turned to me. "You mean, all that time I was putting foot powder on my face?"

Terry and I both lost it, and I practically fell off the rim of the tub onto the floor.

"Okay, that's enough remembering." I said quickly and poured some baby powder into my palm. I made a move toward Mom.

"Wait a minute." She put her hand up and looked at the two of us. "I think I'll pass on the powder, thank you very much."

By the time we got Mom into bed for her nap, Terry and I had made plans to give her a full beauty treatment the following Sunday.

Nestling into her pillows, Virginia watched her two daughters whispering and laughing as they left the room together. It wasn't exactly a love fest, she admitted, but it was a start. Another one for the bucket list, she noted before drifting off to sleep.

"Mother? Are you awake?"

Virginia's eyes popped open, and she saw a heavily made-up blonde stick her head in the doorway. It was Jinelle, Tino's new wife. They had both come down from Atlanta, Georgia a week ago to "help out." So far, all Jinelle had done was clog up the toilets with tissue and use all the hot water for her twice-daily thirty-minute showers. She had *drama queen* written all over her. *Well, get in line, honey*, she wanted to tell her. *In this family, there are already a few ahead of you.*

"Have you seen my panties? I put them in the dryer, but they're gone. I'm sure someone stole them."

Stole your panties? Seriously? Virginia looked up to heaven. *God strike me dead, but I'm going to have fun with this one.* "I'm sorry, dear, I must have put them on by mistake. I thought they were mine." She paused for effect. "Would you like them back?"

"Bu—But they're thongs."

Virginia nodded. "Yes, I know."

The look on her daughter-in-law's face more than made up for a weeks' worth of exasperation and no hot water. And payback for being called "mother" by someone she barely knew. Come to think of it, Virginia smiled, that bucket list was filling up nicely.

For all her wise-cracking and good humor, Virginia was aware that her time was running out. There were episodes of extreme fatigue when she felt like she couldn't catch her breath.

She hadn't told anyone, but she suspected her children knew. Tino seemed more attentive, even finding time to sit and reminisce until his wife came along and found something better for him to do. Terry hid her concern behind a veneer of blithe correctness as if anxious to avoid a family blow-up. Who could blame her? With three drama queens sharing the same space, the Sunset house was an emotional minefield. One wrong word, and there could be an explosion of epic proportions. As a caregiver, Annie focused on the present, making it through one day at a time. Nobody wanted to talk about the inevitable. Virginia longed to reassure her children that it was a subject she had come to terms with long ago. She wasn't afraid of dying, like Marianna had been—just sad that she wouldn't be a part of her children's future. She believed what lay beyond this world was anybody's guess. No one knew for sure. It was a one-way ticket, and there were no refunds.

Her breath was shallower today, I noticed. The hands on the coverlet were no longer busy. They were quiet now, waiting.

"Annie?" Mom's eyes were open, and she was staring at me. "We have to talk."

My throat tensed up. If this was going to be a conversation about dying, I did not want to have it. I could handle the daily caregiving duties—taking care of Mom had been more pleasure than duty—but preparing a loved one mentally for that final journey was beyond my capability.

"Don't worry." Mom waved her hand as if she were reading my thoughts. "This is not about me kicking the bucket. Let's face it. The game is in overtime, and the bases are loaded. The way I see it, I've had a great life. I'm ready for my home run."

I reached down and kissed her forehead. She had said it better than I ever could have.

"It's something else. I don't know why I never thought about this before, but now I can't get it out of my mind. Our trip to Italy three years ago was one of the highlights of my life. I wanted you to know that. It not only brought you and me closer together, it helped connect us to our relatives and to Scheggino . . . where the story of our family began. We uncovered a whole chunk of my father's past, but there's still a lot we don't know. The servant girl who fathered his child—what was her name?"

"Agatha Altarocca."

Mom drew a deep breath, her eyes intent. "Yes, Agatha. Right before my father died, he entrusted me with a cameo locket. Inside was a picture of him as a young man, or so I thought. He couldn't remember anything at that point. All he said was that it belonged to someone he loved very much. I thought the locket was his mother's, but now I realize it could have been Agatha's. Maybe the photo is not of Spirito but his son, Santo."

"But how did Spirito get it? He left for America before Santo was born."

"The only explanation is that he saw Agatha again . . . maybe when he went back to Scheggino for the reading of his uncle's will."

"Wow. You have done a lot of thinking about this, haven't you?"

Mom laughed sadly. "Not much else to do when you're my age. We have to find that locket. It's in a safe deposit box somewhere around here." Mom stopped to catch her breath. "Try the top drawer of the dresser."

I searched through all sorts of crazy mementos. Mom never threw anything away. I pulled out a coin purse stuffed with one-dollar bills. "Our misbehaving money!" I called out. "By the look of it, we are due for a big night out at Jimmy Wong's. Too bad it's not there anymore."

"Try the closet," her voice was weak but determined. "Concentrate."

I glanced at Mom and realized she was deadly serious and in a hurry. The bedroom closet was a mess. Decades of junk stuffed into corners and boxes piled on top of each other in no particular order. Then I saw it—a small metal safe deposit box shoved against the back wall. I carried it out and set it on her dressing table.

"Key is underneath." Her voice was getting weaker.

I turned the key and the box opened. At the bottom was something wrapped in a velvet cloth. I pulled out a cameo necklace on a gold chain. "This is it," I called to her. "I found it."

"Open the locket."

The tiny likeness looked like Spirito, but there was something wrong. The photo was in color. Color photography wasn't invented until after the turn of the century. The boy in the photo looked to be about fourteen. Mom was right. It *couldn't* be Spirito.

"Dad wanted me to keep the locket a secret, not to tell Marianna." Sighing deeply, Mom shook her head. "So many secrets."

"What do we do now?"

"You . . . it's up to *you* now. Go back to Scheggino and put the pieces together. Finish what we started. The memory of my father's legacy is in your hands."

I held the locket up to the light, watching the gold chain sparkle as it turned. Gently, I covered it in the velvet cloth and closed the lid. "I will, Mom. I promise."

The room was quiet.

Turning back to the bed, I saw Mom's eyes were closed, and there was a peaceful expression on her face. I rushed to the bedside, but even as I searched for her pulse, I knew she was gone.

Chapter 32

Agatha's Secret

I TURNED my red Cinquecento onto the narrow two-lane road that branched off the Autostrada A1. I figured I had another forty-five minutes to go.

"Almost home," I said aloud even though I was the only one in the car. Wait . . . had I really said home? I guess that's how I thought of it now. Scheggino was home.

The mountains of Monteluco rose up on my right, and minutes later, the walls of the castle came into view. I glanced over at the empty seat beside me, remembering the journey I had taken with Mom three years ago. Who knew? Maybe she was somewhere watching and egging me on. The thought comforted me as I pulled into the piazza and found a parking spot.

My first stop was going to be Leonia and Enzo Verrocchio's little apartment. I was hoping the old man was still alive and that they were both well. I couldn't wait to see them again.

Walking through the cobbled labyrinth of the castle was bittersweet. All the memories I had of this place had Mom front and center. I had reached the last tier that led to the Verrocchios' when I noticed a "*Per Vende*" sign tacked to an ancient wooden door. An apartment for sale. It was just a sliver of stone, two stories high, squeezed between two larger residences. As I looked up at the tiny balcony and set of French doors, I wondered what a place like that would cost.

I walked on and passed through a partially covered foyer. This was a different way than I had gone before. I was about to backtrack when I saw the little patio that made up the Verrocchio front yard. I knocked on the door.

"Leonia, Enzo, are you there?"

The door opened a crack, and I saw a mop of red hair and a puzzled face staring back at me.

"*Ti ricordi di me?* Do you remember me? I am Anna. My mom and I met you a few years ago."

The eyebrows shot up, and a huge grin appeared. "*Certo!* Of course! Where is Virginia?"

I looked at her and shook my head. "*Morta.* Four months ago. Enzo?"

Leonia's eyes filled with tears. "*Un anno fa.* Last year."

Instinctively, we grabbed each other and held on tight. Sorrow has no geographical boundaries and doesn't discriminate.

Leonia wiped her eyes. "Come in, please."

"*Caffè? Vino?*"

"Prosecco?" I countered.

Two glasses and a bottle were on the table within seconds. "A toast to Virginia and Enzo," I said as we raised our glasses. I hoped they were watching.

"Are you hungry?" Leonia eyed her pantry for inspiration. "I cook for one now, but there's always enough pasta con tartufo to go around."

"Truffles?" My eyes lit up. "I would be delighted."

Leonia topped off our glasses and set the table.

An hour later, our bellies full, we moved to the two chairs in front of the fire. The sun had already gone behind the mountains.

"Where are you staying?"

"The Ponte Hotel. Right here in town."

Leonia whispered as if someone could hear her: "The best place, but the most expensive. The Ricci family owns it. You could have stayed with me. Enzo's room is empty."

"Next time," I promised her.

Leonia smiled. "I am glad to know there will be a next time. How long will you be staying?"

"As long as it takes to solve the mystery."

"Mystery?"

I pulled the locket out of from underneath my jacket. The cameo profile shone against the light from the flickering logs.

Leonia's face changed, and she reached out to touch it. "I have seen this before. Did you bring it last time you were here?"

"No. It was misplaced for years. I found it right before my mom . . . wait, where have you seen it?"

Leonia's brows furrowed. "Let me think."

"Maybe it will help if we go over what Enzo told us and what I know now." In halting Italian, with accompanying hand gestures, I recounted the locket's journey and how it might have been related to our family.

Halfway through, Leonia let out a cry. "I remember where I've seen it! The photo in the cemetery."

"What photo?"

"Of Agatha. She's wearing it in the photo on her tomb."

"And this?" I opened the locket and showed her the picture inside. "Is this her son Santo?"

Leonia brought the likeness up close and studied it. "Maybe."

"Well, who else could it be?"

Leonia released the locket and let it fall against my chest. "You must talk to the Urbinos. They would know."

"Beniamino's clan, you mean. Not my side of the family."

She nodded. "Tomorrow. Now, you need to go to the hotel and check in. At those prices, you'd better at least spend the night there."

Early the next morning, I drove up the hill toward the Villa Urbino and the adjacent cemetery. The verdant hills of the Valnerina beckoned as if I had never been away. Agostino's villa lay off to the left, and as I panned north, I saw an even more imposing residence. Why hadn't I noticed it the last time I was here? A well-groomed dirt road lined with cypress trees wound directly from it to the cemetery.

The iron gate squeaked open as I entered the burial grounds, the three Urbino tombs on my right. I stepped toward the one with the name "*Claudio*" at the top, grabbed the handle of the door, and pulled. It was locked. I jiggled the handle and pulled harder.

"*Signora?*" There was an old man standing a short distance away. He was eyeing me suspiciously.

I jumped and stepped back. Breaking and entering might be a serious crime in Italy, especially in a graveyard.

"*Cerco una tomba*," I stammered, turning red.

"I speak English," the man replied.

"Oh, what a relief," I said, before realizing how rude that sounded. I hoped I hadn't offended him. Italians are notorious for expecting foreigners to love their language as much as they do. "I am looking for the tomb of Agatha Altarocca. Are you an Urbino?"

His eyes narrowed. "And you are?"

"My name is Anna. My grandfather was born here. Francesco Urbino was my great-grandfather." I gestured to the small monument at the back of the cemetery. "He is buried over there."

The man was alert now. "What was your grandfather's name?"

"Spirito. Spirito Urbino."

The old man's face turned white.

"I'm sorry," I continued. "I don't mean to intrude, but I am trying to solve a mystery, and it may involve the Signora Altarocca. Here—"

I removed the locket from around my neck and held it out to him. "Have you seen this before?"

The man seemed visibly shaken as he held it in his palm and examined it. While his attention was diverted, I took a minute to study him. Late eighties, square face, penetrating blue eyes, and a full head of white hair.

"I don't think I can help you." The man handed the locket back to me. His eyes were cold.

I could not believe what I was hearing. To come this close to finding the missing piece and then be turned away? *Not on your life.* I pulled myself up to my full height of five feet one inches and let him have it. "Listen here, whoever you are, I have come a long way to find the truth about my grandfather's connection to this locket. His last words were, 'Keep it safe. It belonged to someone I loved very much.' If I'm not mistaken, Signora Altarocca gave this locket to him. Throughout his whole life, he never stopped loving her, and I'm not leaving here until I know the whole story."

I must have looked scary, because the man backed off to a safe distance before reaching around to unlock the crypt. "If you are finished . . .?" there was a hint of a smile on his face as he gestured for me to enter.

On the left, the tombs of Claudio and Olivia lay one beneath the other. Photos of them receiving the Capo di Lavori title and numerous other awards rested on the surface of the sarcophagi. On the right, Santo and Lidia Urbino's tombs were stacked above a block of rose marble that looked like it had been there for many years. Etched into the stone was an inscription: "*Agatha Altarocca. N. 1889. M. 1951. Beloved by all who knew her.*" On the top was a photo of a beautiful woman wearing a cameo necklace.

"This picture was taken shortly before her trip to the States in 1939."

"1939," I thought out loud. "My grandparents went back east to visit relatives that year. Agatha must have met Spirito and given the locket to him then." I turned to the man beside me. "You must be Santo's son. Forgive my earlier behavior. Speaking my mind has always been one of my worst qualities. I won't trouble you any further." I turned to leave the crypt when a hand touched my arm.

"My mother loved your grandfather very much."

The words stopped me in my tracks. I whirled around and faced him. "Mother? You mean grandmother, don't you?"

The man shook his head. "Agatha Altarocca was my mother."

I looked puzzled. "I don't understand."

The old man quietly closed the door to the crypt and took my arm. "Come, I can see I have some explaining to do."

As we left the cemetery, I noticed my car was the only one on the hilltop. "How did you get here?"

My companion pointed his cane in the direction of the cypress trees. "I walked."

I looked down the road at the lavish residence I had spotted earlier. "You live there?"

The old man nodded. "Can I have a ride home?"

My mind was racing as we drove past acres of vines loaded with grapes and stopped before a massive stone entryway. I gazed up at the ancient bricks intricately fitted together without mortar. "This looks old. When was it built?"

"About 1941. My mother wanted it to look as old as the castle in town. Everything was constructed with local materials and using ancient techniques. There is no stucco or wall board anywhere on the property."

We stepped through the foyer into an enormous light-filled living room. A stone fireplace dominated one side, and a wall of glass doors opposite the entrance displayed the picturesque valley like a tapestry brought to life. The décor was a mix of mid-century chairs and sofas sprinkled here and there with valuable antiques. Against walls and behind sofas were sideboards made of rough-hewn slabs of marble.

I sighed. "It is absolutely exquisite."

My host made a slight bow. "Thank you. My mother had good taste."

I saw several silver-framed photos placed discreetly around the room. One was of Agatha receiving an award from an important-looking Italian.

"My mother receiving the Tastemaker Award from the Vice President of Italy."

I walked toward another photo, one of a distinguished gentleman in front of a gothic-looking building with a glittering canal in the background.

"Mariano Fortuny in Venice. My mother decorated the interiors of his residence."

"And this?" I picked up a photo of a young man in front of a smart-looking shop.

"My brother, Santo, at the Urbino Tartufo Headquarters in New York."

"Your brother?" I turned to face my host. "Who are you?"

"My name is Spirito Urbino. My friends call me SJ."

"SJ?"

"A nickname adopted by my family to replace 'Junior.'

My eyes widened. "You are my grandfather's son."

"And your great-uncle."

I sat down heavily in a low-slung leather chair. "I think I need a drink."

"It so happens I am trying out a new product. We are calling it *La Grappa del Re*. The King's Grappa. It is a high-end version of the peasant drink so popular in these parts. We are using different grape skins and a new production technique."

"Sure, fine. I just hope it's strong enough to clear the cobwebs from my brain."

"It is, I assure you." SJ poured two glasses of clear liquid from a crystal decanter and handed one to me. "My vines surround the property. You must have noticed them when we drove in."

"My grandfather also made wine in his backyard shed." I gave SJ a sly look and we both laughed. "It was during Prohibition. Afterward, when it became legal, he served it in his diner."

"Diner?"

"A place where the working classes can get a reasonable meal. They are all over the US."

"Amazing."

My host chuckled. "I was a chef. Before I retired, I ran the Urbino culinary demonstrations at the headquarters."

"Quite a chip off the old block, aren't you?" We looked at each other, and I felt an easy camaraderie developing between us. The kind you feel with family.

I downed the grappa in one gulp. "OK, SJ. I'm ready."

"Ready?"

"The story. The story of Spirito and Agatha . . . and you."

My host took a deep breath. I could tell this was not going to be easy for him.

"I assume you know about the relationship between my mother and your grandfather . . . and what happened to her."

I nodded. "Enzo Verrocchio told me when I was here four years ago. What Armando did to your mother was a terrible thing."

"It is a painful subject for our family, and some scars never heal. Within a year after Agatha gave birth, it was obvious that Santo was Spirito's child, not Armando's. The Urbinos kept their part of the bargain and gave my brother a happy childhood. He repaid their generosity many times over with his success."

"So, where do you come in?" I asked gently.

"Do you know about Spirito's visit here in 1923?"

"I think so. The reading of his uncle's will."

"Yes." SJ paused as if searching for the right words. "Spirito found out where my mother was living in Spello and went to see her." Another pause. "I was born nine months later."

I felt another piece of the puzzle fall into place. "Agatha never told Spirito that she was pregnant with his second child?"

"A scenario was concocted that made that difficult. Santo and Lidia were married as soon as Agatha found out she was pregnant. They raised me as if I was theirs. In 1924, there was still a stigma attached to unwed mothers, especially when the identity of the father is kept secret. My brother wanted to shield our mother from all that. As I grew older, it became impossible to reveal the truth without hurting my mother and Santo's reputation in the community and within the Foundation.

"Who else knew?"

"Dr. Sabatini. He delivered me."

My great-aunt Teresina's husband, I thought, remembering what I had heard growing up. The doctor who took care of everyone.

"Alessandro kept the secret his whole life. Not even his wife knew my real identity."

I made a movement to rise but my host stopped me.

"There is more. Spirito's brother, Urbano, came to Scheggino in 1951. Santo ran into him at the cemetery."

"Really? Did he know Santo was Spirito's son?" This was a part of the story I had not heard before.

"He knew."

I sighed. "It looks like my family had secrets too."

SJ rose from his chair. "I have something to show you."

SJ went into one of the other rooms and returned holding a small photograph. Gently, he laid it on the table in front of me.

The photo was of a man in his sixties wearing a navy blue wool suit. His arm was around my mother.

"How did you get this?"

"Urbano gave it to Santo. It was meant for Agatha. She had passed away a month before."

I turned the photo over and read the faded words: "*Cara Agatha. This is me with my daughter, Virginia, on her wedding day. Do not forget me, as I have never forgotten you. Your Spirito.*"

SJ's emotions were finally getting the best of him, and mine were not far behind. "The photo is yours now," he said.

"No." My voice was firm. "You keep it. Spirito wanted your family to have it."

"And you keep the locket." SJ's tone was equally firm. "Agatha gave it to the love of her life."

I opened the locket and looked at the face of the young man. "This is you, isn't it?"

"It is me. It was taken right before my mother left for America. I was fourteen years old."

The last piece of the puzzle clicked into place. I heaved a giant sigh of relief.

"Here's to the Urbinos!" I said, raising my glass to my new friend and relative. "I have one more question."

"Just one?"

"There's something my mom and I could never figure out. Are we related to the Truffle Empire or not?"

"Ah." SJ's hint of a smile was back. "That's another story altogether. How long will you be staying?"

Urbino
Our Family Tree
Brandi Orsolini
servant
?
Teresa
Pasqualini
Ettore
Brandi Orsolini
Virginia
Lorenzetti
Francesco
Ferdinando
Pietro
Delia
Emilio
Ricci
Assunta
Urbano
Ginerva
Teresina
Annie
mary
Francesca
Primo
Emilia
Amedeo
Toni
Spirito
Marianna
Emma
Agatha
Listina
Anna
S.J.
Virginia
Walter
Santo
Lidia
Tino
Anna
Terry

Acknowledgments

A SPECIAL thanks to my brother, Tony Wilcoxson, for his unfailing efforts in researching the family history. And to my sister, Tess Wilcoxson Nelson, for her archival contributions.

A deep gratitude to my editor, Molly Lewis, for her insight and attention to detail, and to the team at Acorn Publishing, in particular, Leslie Ferguson, for helping me navigate uncharted technical territory with patience and good humor.

To my photographer, Washington Nabong, for making me look good.

To Tess Wilcoxson Nelson for believing in the journey . . . and in me.

www.ingramcontent.com/pod-product-compliance
Lightning Source LLC
Chambersburg PA
CBHW030527310726
48979CB00010B/1830/J

* 9 7 8 1 9 5 2 1 1 2 6 4 5 *